Annie is the author of a poetry anthology *Listen to My Heart*. After studying mental health nursing at the University of Southampton, she had to give up after suffering serious illness, including a diagnosis of breast cancer. This led her to spend more time writing as a freelance journalist, and enjoying her family.

This is her first novel.

Annie Watkinson

Faith Under Fire

Olympia Publishers
London

www.olympiapublishers.com
OLYMPIA PAPERBACK EDITION

A CIP catalogue record for this title is
available from the British Library.

ISBN: 978-1-84897-538-5

(Olympia Publishers is part of Ashwell Publishing Ltd)

First Published in 2015

Olympia Publishers
60 Cannon Street
London
EC4N 6NP

Printed in Great Britain

To Michael, Joanna, Ian and Rebecca- For love, joy and inspiration,
I thank you.

Acknowledgement

Thank you, Ian, for your wonderful interpretation of my imaginary village. You have managed to extract the concept right out of my brain cells!

GRAVEYARD
HEALTH CENRTRE
RETIREMENT COMPLEX
TO BASINGSTOKE
VICARAGE
UNDER-TAKER
YEW TREE INN
POST OFFICE
THE HUT
ST JOHN'S CHURCH
YEW TREE
VILLAGE GREEN
HAIR-DRESSER
CHERRY TREE COTTAGE
BUTCHER
GREEN-GROCER
WISTERIA COTTAGE
COUNCIL ESTATE
ASHTON KIRBY

Prologue

The Child

August 1952

Butterflies churned in the Child's stomach at the thought of having to see the pastor on her own. It was bad enough that she had to stand in front of her parents and recite huge chunks of scripture. Her father would glare at her and make her forget where she had got up to. In her mind and on her own, she had no trouble, but when she was being watched, she became nervous and forgetful.

The pastor terrified her, with his hooded eyes, and baggy jowls. He never smiled, and roared hell and damnation at the congregation. The Child was unable to have friends home, as outsiders were said to be unfit to sit at their table. She could not make out why Jesus spoke of loving your neighbour, when the church told them to shun their neighbours. Even if she did make friends with any of the girls at school, she never really had time to see them outside of the playground, for her life was tightly ordered with housework and church activities.

Her mother had told her the stark facts of life when she was thirteen, the day she started her period.

'Men only want one thing from you,' she said to her, 'It is horrid, evil and filthy, but it's your duty to give 'em what they need. Just lie

down, open yer legs and let 'em get on with their fornicating, and keep yerself clean down below.'

After that, she had left her with a packet of sanitary towels, and told her that she would have to buy her own from now on, and she never wanted to see any evidence of her 'monthlies'.

The girls at school often giggled and whispered of love and kisses with the boys, and this left the Child perplexed. But she was not one of the girls. She was isolated from the group, because of her shabby, dowdy clothes, her ragged hair style and her strange way of talking. They laughed at her when she said grace before eating her school dinner, but although she was embarrassed, she was fearful not to, as she knew that her father had his spies everywhere. He told her that all the time.

As she walked away from school that afternoon, her mind was constantly going over the long passage of Isaiah that she was to recite to Pastor Jenkins. But she kept thinking of his moustache, with bits of food caught up in it, and how drops of the communion wine would hang upon its fronds when he passed her the cup. He would stare at her intently, and his eyes would drop down to her chest, where she was now developing a sizeable bust, much to her horror and consternation. Her mother would not entertain buying her a brassiere, and she did not earn enough to buy her own, so she would wear two thick vests at a time to try and hide her changing shape.

She knew that Pastor Jenkins wanted her to go through the rites of baptism and to take up full membership of the church, but the Child was reluctant. She did not seem to feel the presence of God the way the adults all seemed to. She did not faint when the pastor laid hands upon her (which he seemed to do very often nowadays) and she did not sense her redemption. For her it all just felt like lip service, and nothing more. But she could not tell her parents or they would give her another beating. There was no one she could discuss this with, for fear that it would get back to them. Was she so evil that God refused to let himself be known to her?

As she reached the pastor's door she had a mighty desire to turn and run, far, far away. Instead of God's presence, all she sensed here was evil. The house was built of dark grey stone, and had a forbidding black front door. The porch was low and heavy, covered in a thousand cob webs, with a huge brass bell hanging from a dirty, twisted piece of cord. She took hold of the cord, and pulled it, gingerly at first, but it made no noise or echo in the house, so this time, she grasped it firmly and she could hear the clanging bell resonating through the old house. Footsteps sounded on the other side of the door, and the Child began to shake, as the door was opened with a dramatic flourish. Now there was no turning back.

Three Months Later

A packed church building. A frightened child. The organ played a sombre tune as she stepped gingerly into the baptismal pool, the water reaching her shoulders. She stared with terror at the pastor, and trembled as he placed his left hand behind her back. She shuddered at his touch. He stared into her eyes with his crocodile grin, then grabbed her shoulder and pushed her under the water....

Panic tore at her throat as she felt the pressure of the water force its way into her nose and ears. He was holding her down too long. She didn't think she could hold her breath any longer, and she tried in vain to push her weight against his vice-like grip. Then, as suddenly as he had pushed her under, he pulled her forcefully up, the organ now triumphantly playing 'Up from the grave He arose' *at full volume. The Child coughed and spluttered as she tried to catch her breath, pushing at the sodden hair that covered her eyes. She walked clumsily up the stairs: the lead weights sewn into the bottom of her virginal baptismal robes added heaviness to the drenched garment, which wrapped itself viciously around her thin ankles. She did not feel cleansed. She felt small, humiliated. She knew that she was not virginal as the robes suggested, but that she was tainted.*

The child had known no other life than this strict Brethren church. It had broken away from the mainstream churches because it wanted to hold on to its extreme views, and would not embrace change; its views were stifling, violent and oppressive. Her father was an elder of the church, and her mother part of every group there was. She had attended Sunday school, Bible class and was now initiated, through baptism, as a full member. This was not through choice, but compulsion. On top of her school work, she had to learn whole passages of scripture by heart, and recite them. If she stumbled over the difficult words, she felt the sting of her father's belt burn into the back of her legs. She could, and frequently did, recite the books of the Bible in her sleep. Genesis, Exodus, Leviticus, Numbers, Deuteronomy, Joshua, Judges... Matthew, Mark, Luke, John, Acts, Romans... *and of course the horrors of the vision of Revelation.*

She knew only a world of punishment and control. She knew nothing of a loving God, only a terrifying all-seeing presence, from whom there was no escape, and that everyone outside of their fellowship faced eternal hell, fire and brimstone. She was never allowed friends who were not affiliated to the fellowship. School was a misery. Life was unbearable now. She would rather die than face what was going to happen to her once her secret was out.

Chapter 1

You would not have thought that in this day and age someone could die and be buried and then have their life celebrated in great style without any form of motor transport being involved. Well, it did happen and I can bear testimony to the truth of that fact. As you can see from the plan of Ashton Kirby, life revolved around the village green.

The Reverend Arnold Archibald Hillier, or Reverend Archie to his friends, had been retired for just over a year. He had celebrated his seventy-sixth birthday in great style two days before his demise. A grateful member of the congregation had let him have one of the modern retirement flats adjacent to the church for a peppercorn rent when he retired, and had to leave the vicarage. The dear old Reverend, still sprightly in his eighth decade, had been energetically painting the kitchen walls, high up on a stool, when he suffered a massive stroke and dropped dead. It was a dreadful shock to friends and family, but the perfect way to go for the Reverend. And so it was that the doctor was called, and he rushed straight over from the health centre located just behind the retirement complex. He certified the death, and got in touch with the undertaker, next to the pub. Reverend Archie was measured up for his coffin and left to rest in his home. This was a tad unusual, but the retired vicar was well known to Rob Bolton, the undertaker, and he was willing to bend the rules a little for his old friend. The undertaker also prepared the body at home, and the pall-bearers then carried his coffin into St John's church for an amazing celebration of the much loved vicar's life. Afterwards, he was buried in the graveyard, alongside his parents and grandfather. His grandmother, who was of Spanish descent, chose to be buried in her family vault in Spain, much to the disgust of the Hillier clan. But last wishes have to be respected. The Reverend's wife had run off with the organist twenty years previously, and was not welcome in the village. She had been notified of his death by the wife of the errant organist, who had been quite glad to see the back of her wayward husband. The organist had been tone deaf anyway, so the village was well shot of him.

The service was attended by some three hundred plus people, and the church was bulging at the seams. Many had to stand at the back, but they were more than happy to do so in honour of this great legend of a man, whose kindness and generosity of spirit had affected so many. There was not a dry eye in the building, but some of those tears were caused by gentle ripples of laughter, for Archie had not been a sombre man, and was well-known for his jokes and gags, many repeated during the service of remembrance with humour, dignity and great respect.

After the burial, the entire group of mourners headed for the village green, at the front of the church, for the day was beautifully warm and sunny. Under the shade of the yew tree, the mothers of small children congregated, whilst the men went to fetch refreshments from the Yew Tree public house. The publican, Paul Soames, had generously laid on food and drink for the wake. The vicar had been a popular and frequent visitor to their premises over the years, and had regaled them with tales of parishioners past and present. Indeed, he had probably baptized or married most of the men and women gathered there, and given their dearly departed a good old send-off. Yes, he was going to be sorely missed.

As the gentle June day faded into evening, the crowds began to thin, and as parents took the small folk home to be bathed and put to bed, those who had long distances to travel hit the dry tarmac. There was a good handful of parishioners, however, who stayed until one day melted into the early hours of the next, reminiscing on old times, and ruminating on what the future held for Ashton Kirby village church. Changes were happening and, as anyone who has ever been a part of village life knows, change is not always the most welcome visitor.

The new vicar, Reverend Joshua Mercer, known as Josh to his friends and family, was well aware of that fact. He had been in his post for just under a year, and it had all been quite pleasant when he and his family had first arrived. The parishioners had been keen to welcome them to St John's, and what a welcome it had been! The vicarage had been given a new coat of paint, the garden had been spruced up, and a wonderful larder of food was waiting to greet them. Scarcely an hour had passed after their arrival, when they were welcomed by their first visitor. Then the next. And the next... It seemed that every person on the electoral roll was determined to have a good look at the new family, no doubt to pass their opinion on to their friends. Josh and Vikki's children did not take too kindly to being paraded in front of countless strangers and, as would many youngsters of their age, they began to behave very badly indeed. Vikki was feeling humiliated and indignant. She knew this bad behavior was unlike her brood, but she could do nothing about it, as question after question was hurtled in her direction. Distractedly, she half-answered, and half-reprimanded the children, as they raced up and down the long corridor, and pointedly ignored questions from the nosy invaders. *What sort of impression were they giving?* she thought agitatedly. No doubt the word was, even now, going round the village that she could not control her wild children.

Vikki Mercer thought of Josh, and she remembered his first service here as the new vicar. Obviously he was going to be compared with the very popular Reverend Hillier, and this was only to be expected. It was going to take some getting used to though, when they insisted on calling him 'Reverend Mercer', even though he kept reminding them, 'Please call me Josh'. It was nearly a year ago, and it still felt like a battle, with the old school parishioners fighting every change that Josh tried to implement. They had been used to having a vicar without the ties of a young family, but they did not seem to appreciate this, and would think nothing of calling on Josh night and day. Vikki had tried to suggest that he should have a day off during the week, so that they could enjoy some quality family time. That had gone down like a lead balloon!

St John's church was a pretty little village church nestled in the heart of the community. Its Saxon walls had stood firmly against time and weather, and the old timber bell tower graced the side of the grey stone, complementing it perfectly. The churchyard was a glorious riot of colour, whatever the season. A bed of snowdrops and crocuses heralded in the spring, even when the snow fell upon them like a thick duvet. After they had faded, the camellias and azaleas supplied a riot of colour and scent. The roses and dahlias spread among the gravestones throughout the long summer months and continued through the autumn, as the leaves fell from the trees, providing a copper and golden blanket for the children to run through. In the winter, a hush fell among the gravestones, as nature still continued below the soil, where the buds and bulbs were safely guarded from the bitter frosts and winds.

The noticeboard on the lych gate welcomed visitors to the church, announcing details and times of services, the graffitied wood bearing testament to generations of reprobates. As you ambled up the pathway to the entrance of the church, the porch greeted you with yet more information as to the business of the church. On entering the building through the heavy studded wooden door, a visitor would at once sense the centuries of history surrounding them. From the ancient stained glass windows to the modern, brightly coloured banners, the church announced, 'Life!'

This was no quiet, unused relic of a bygone era, but the centre of a vibrant family, a testament to love, faith, hope and spirit. Its battered pews and worn kneelers spoke of troubled prayers and grateful thanks to a God who listened to His people. The altar was a simple affair, with a communion table and single lectern, where the Word was preached faithfully week after week. There was a simple wooden cross, declaring the Love of Christ, and a small chapel beyond; used mainly for intimate services and private prayer.

Kate Hartwood was thirty-five years of age, and spinster of the parish of St John's, Ashton Kirby. She had moved to the village around the same time that Josh and Vikki had arrived. Their meeting, in fact, was rather serendipitous. She had not yet joined the church, but Vikki and Kate kept turning up at the same places, at the same time. The first occasion was at the health centre, when Kate was booked in to see her new GP, and Vikki's youngest child Amy had taken a shine to her, bringing her books to read from the playroom.

'Leave the lady alone,' said Vikki, smiling, but Kate had assured her that she didn't mind in the slightest. Although Kate had never been fortunate enough to have children, that didn't mean that she disliked them. Amy, as she soon found out, was a chatty child, with a beautiful nature. She had fine blond hair cut in a sweet bob, and a lovely giggle. When Kate started to read Goldilocks to her, she laughed and informed her that she was supposed to read *Daddy Bear* in a deep voice, like Mummy did. Vikki was mortified, but Kate soon reassured her that she didn't mind! She started to read the story in her deepest, growly voice, which soon had the whole surgery tittering.

They bumped into each other again in the supermarket, just minutes later, and Amy threw herself at Kate's legs as if she were her long lost friend. It was the start of a beautiful friendship, and they both found their feet in the village together. Obviously, Kate was not around as much as Vikki, due to her long working hours and commuting, but they often spent happy evenings in each other's company, complaining about the natives. The one sour note in their friendship was Vikki's twin brother, Samuel. They had taken an instant dislike to each other, after he had torn Kate off a strip when she had called round to Vikki's house one evening. Kate had not even known Vikki had a brother, and when the door opened, she was met by a scowling male version of her best friend. When Kate asked if she could speak to Vikki, he shouted at her, 'Don't you people ever give them any peace? It's nine o'clock in the evening for God's sake!'

Vikki had come running to the front door, horrified to hear Samuel sounding off at Kate.

'Do you mind, Sam, that's my best friend you're talking to!' she exclaimed, but he had turned away in a huff.

'Nice man,' Kate said sarcastically, 'where did you dig him up from?'

'I am so sorry, Kate,' she said. 'That's my twin brother, and he is a little protective of me, I'm afraid. It all stems from the first time he came to visit, and he found me in floods of tears in the bedroom, after I had been plagued with visitors, and he now tars everyone with the same brush. He's harmless really.'

'Hmmm, I'm not too sure about that,' Kate replied, rather put out to be spoken to so rudely. She decided there and then to avoid Samuel Cornell as best she could, even if he was Vikki's brother. The likeness was quite amazing though. Kate had always been in awe of Vikki's stunning looks and figure. She must have been six foot tall, and had the most fabulous thick, curly, auburn hair, that reached almost to her waist. It was truly sensational, and she was always accosted on the street and complimented on her flowing locks. Sam was tall, too, and it was apparent that he had difficulty containing his thick, golden mane, which curled at his ears and over his collar. Both of them were covered with a thin veil of freckles, which Vikki hated, but Kate thought were rather fetching. It was a bit of a shame that she had taken an instant dislike to Sam, as Vikki obviously adored her brother, but every time his name was mentioned, Kate felt her hackles rise, and so they changed the subject.

Kate, in contrast to Vikki, was petite and pale, with jet black, shiny hair cut into a short, glossy, modern bob. Her eyes were the shade of black onyx, and her skin porcelain white. For some reason, as a child she had always been cast as Snow White, but that was clearly the obvious choice to any onlooker. She was of incredibly slim stature, and this, coupled with her pale complexion, led many to worry about her health. But it never worried Kate, who had the energy of three men, and could eat like a horse without ever putting on an ounce. She had spent nine years working in the city, but commuting had started to wear her down. She was growing tired of getting up at the break of dawn every day; crowded tube carriages and bustling, busy streets, full of impatient people. That was when the tubes were running; when they weren't affected by strikes, storms, leaves, snow or drought. When there were not bomb alerts and train breakdowns or repairs. It had all become quite insufferable. So when her Aunt Valerie had left Kate the little cottage in the quiet village of Ashton Kirby, she had felt that it was a pivotal point in her life. Rather than sell the property, she would move there! It was far enough away from her parents, yet with just forty miles between them, she would be near enough in case of emergencies. But what was she to do about employment? Kate knew that she could neither bear, nor indeed afford to be unemployed. Her aunt's legacy was not large enough for that, anyhow. She also had a great aversion to the unemployed, having watched her younger sister Melanie sponge off her parents and the State for most of her employable life. Her mother and father accepted all her excuses with amazing gullibility, and continued to provide a roof over her head and food in her stomach, all without charge. It simply made Kate's blood boil just to be in the same room as that lazy, lying, alcoholic sister of hers.

Kate came from a zealous church family, but she had never really felt comfortable at the old Truth Brethren church where her parents worshipped. It was a breakaway group that seemed to have no real allegiance to any of the main churches, and they were a tight, repressed bunch. Mum and Dad had forced them to go when they were children, but both Kate and her sister had left in their teens, much to their parent's horror and disgust. Kate had later found much comfort in the mainstream churches, but her sister had rebelled, and never gone back. Melanie had got mixed up with a bad group of teenagers at senior school, and left school at sixteen. Things went from bad to worse, when she was brought home by the police for stealing alcohol from the supermarket. Their parents were horrified, as one of the church members worked there, and the gossip soon went round the Brethren, resulting in them being hauled up before the elders. Alcohol was forbidden except on special occasions, and they both had to endure the humiliation of having to 'repent' in front of the whole church for being bad parents. Kate could never understand why they stayed there; it was as if there were some horrid force that they could not escape. The punishment hadn't done much good, for Melanie still continued in her amoralistic ways.

Kate's poor parents thought things were looking up when Mel told them that she had become involved in the children's group, and was growing some plants for them. That was, until they discovered she was illegally growing cannabis! Melanie never managed to hold down a job, even though she seemed to be able to convince people to employ her easily enough. But drunken nights and laziness meant that she was never able to complete a full week. It was all too easy for her to live on benefits and to sponge off Mum and Dad. Kate frequently had countless arguments with them regarding their attitude towards her sister, but they always had some excuse. Why couldn't they see what a user she was? She was glad to put some distance between them all.

Kate's good fortune came about through the unwelcome changes wrought to the 'old school' parishioners of Ashton Kirby. Since Josh had taken over as shepherd of the flock, the church had experienced both growth and dissension. His appeal to younger families had led to the need for new children's groups and mother and baby groups. He had also introduced house groups, a coffee shop for the villagers, and 'Men's Breakfasts'. Out had gone the old hymn books and in came overhead projectors and even laptops! The dusty, wooden hymnal board now lay derelict in the corner of the old chapel. It was exciting! It was disturbing. It was unsettling. And, unwanted by some.

With so much change, came a lot more paperwork. Weekly newsletters needed collating, notice-boards needed to be created to keep the parish up-to-date with all the latest developments, and the church calendar and the vicar's diary needed a much more careful eye kept on them to avoid any conflict of interest. For the parish now had 'visiting speakers' and other forms of Christian ministry coming. Administration was what was needed. An administrator was required! An advert was placed.

Kate was in the Post Office, situated between the Yew Tree Inn and the Undertakers, when she spotted the postcard. Was she seriously considering taking a job advertised on a *postcard?* she wondered to herself. She was a young, talented, city worker for goodness sake! Well, not so young any more. She was pushing thirty five this year, in fact. Her mother was simply horrified that neither sister had ever received a single proposal of marriage between them. She felt that they should both have been married with two point four children at the age of twenty-two like she and their father had been. But had she ever stopped to consider that was exactly the reason why? They agreed on nothing; not the weather, food, décor or friends. Travelling in a car with them was sheer purgatory. Her father would shout that her mother had read the map wrong. *She* would holler that *he* drove too fast. *He* should have taken *that* road. *She* should just keep her mouth shut! And on and on it went. Being home was no different. *He* left the toilet seat up, *he* was untidy, and *he* left his clothes out. *She* was a fussy old gasbag, and *she* talked throughout his radio programmes. The arguments were never-ending. Kate had escaped as soon as she was able. Melanie stayed put. That was something Kate could never really understand. It was almost as if they were so busy arguing that they never actually noticed Melanie was there; eating their food, drinking their wine, using their electricity, water and gas, and turning into an alcoholic right under their very noses.

Kate took down the details from the postcard. It was a full-time position for an administrator at St John's parish church. The salary was not mentioned, which was a bad sign, but something about the role held her interest. It was a new post, and as such involved setting up the office from scratch. She had fulfilled this role once before, when she was employed in a firm in Leatherhead, to set up a new banking system from scratch. This had been with a large lending concern who wished to set up a bank after new laws had been brought in, affecting the money market. That job was probably the most fun she had experienced since she had been a child playing offices! Kate had a small but flexible budget, and was left to order the computer software and design all the equipment and logos needed for the cheque books and bank cards, and to order all the office equipment that she felt was needed. It was then left to Kate to attract customers, so the advertising campaign was also hers.

It had all ended a year later, when their status as a bank was fulfilled and she went back into 'real' employment. This administrative role looked on the surface to be a similar venture. Kate had started to go to the church after she became friends with Vikki, and found it to be a very friendly community, with plenty of activities for all ages. She felt sure that with her experience in city finance, she would have plenty to offer the role. Although the salary was bound to be a fraction of what she was earning now, she felt that she could exist on much less, and would not be paying out a fortune in commuting up and down to London. Goodness, she could even walk or cycle to work if she was offered the post.

So it was that two weeks later Kate attended the vicarage for an interview with the new vicar, Josh, and three members of the Parochial Church Council. She was one of four candidates who had been short-listed. In actual fact, she found out later that they were the *only* applicants. The other three were all long-standing members of the church. Kate did not realise how much grief this fact was going to cause her until after she was offered the job. She was correct in thinking that the salary was lousy, but hey, if she could convince them of her worth, she might be able to ask for a raise in a few months. How could she have been so naive?

That same evening Kate received a phone call from Josh to tell her that she had been the best candidate by far, and they would like to offer her the position. In a moment of recklessness, she accepted. As she travelled on her long, boring commute to London the following morning she had a real feeling of excitement. Her rose-coloured glasses were firmly on, and she thought how lovely it would be to work in the house of God, with all those nice people. How wrong could a person be? The glasses were soon to be knocked forcefully from Kate's eyes.

She went straight into her boss's office to hand in her notice. To say that Donald, her boss, was shocked was an understatement. He simply did not believe that Kate was going to work in an office consisting of one member of staff. Just her. Believing this to be a sinister ploy to move to one of the firm's rivals, he gave her immediate garden leave, and told her to clear her office and go. She was, however, to be given two months' salary. Ah well, at least his suspicions had done her a favour. Kate could now have that holiday she was in desperate need of, and have time to do some much needed repairs to the house before she started at the church office.

Kate had the insane desire to rush straight into the nearest travel agents and book something there and then, but she was loaded down with all her personal possessions, including her laptop, which surprisingly Donald had let her keep. He had demanded her Blackberry back though, so she was now without a phone, as she did not yet have a landline. She had hardly been home often enough to warrant the installation, and had been quite content with her wireless internet and mobile phone. As Kate travelled on the virtually empty tube, she was listing in her head all the things that she now needed to do. Number one priority was to get a phone. Number two was to buy a bike; she really fancied the prospect of riding around the village. Number three was to break the news to her parents. Kate already knew how they would react. They had been horrified when she had told them that she was moving to Ashton Kirby and had so far refused to visit her there. She knew that her mum and sister had not got on too well, although Kate herself had always loved and admired her aunt and her wonderfully eccentric ways. They were also very proud of the fact that their daughter was 'someone important in the city' as they loved to tell their friends. Kate thought that it made up for the fact that her sister was a useless lay-about, although their pride flew in the face of their church's image of poverty and piety.

Kate picked up her car from the station and drove home. It was only now that she started to worry if she had really done the right thing. Would she live to regret this? If the administrative post failed, would she ever get a chance to go back to a high-flying city job? Would she be able to live on such a meagre salary? Kate now had two whole months to dwell on her somewhat rash decision. She walked slowly up the cracked pavement, hardly noticing the neglected garden and flaking paintwork. She opened the door, threw all her paraphernalia on the floor, and slumped down in the sagging armchair. There she stayed for hours, mulling over this new situation she found herself in.

Chapter 2

Kate had returned from a fortnight in the Caribbean; probably her last decent holiday for a while, judging by the pittance of a wage that the church had offered.

Still, it felt good to relax, and not have to face the horrors of the daily commute any more. She was wandering around Homebase, picking up tins of paint for both the outside and the inside of the cottage. She still had a couple of weeks left before she started her new job, so she had decided to spruce up the place. Tomorrow the guys from the village were coming to replace the soffits, guttering and fascias, and a young lad from the Youth Group was helping her out with the gardening before he went to University later in the year. Kate had to admit, he was very good at the job. The straggling flower beds and overgrown lawn had been transformed into a spectacular country garden, bursting with pots filled with smiling pansies and delicate fuscias in brilliant scarlet and pink. The lawn was now neatly trimmed and a lush emerald green; perfect for sitting and relaxing in her sun-bed, topping up her holiday tan, while she contemplated her new future with a mixture of excitement and foreboding.

'Hello, Kate, I haven't seen you around for a while. How are you?'

'Oh, hi, Bill,' she replied, pleased to see the church treasurer peering myopically round the wallpaper aisle.

'I've only just returned from holiday, just doing a bit of decorating while I've got the time. Do you know, I feel as if the cottage finally belongs to me now? I think it is because I have now spent more than the odd weekend there. When I used to come home from work, I was too tired to do anything more than sit down with a glass of wine and an M&S ready meal, and then go to bed. It was no life really. I am looking forward to starting my work in the parish.'

'Yes, well,' said Bill, slightly hesitantly, 'I hope it is everything you expect it to be, although I must warn you....'

'Bill!' A loud crowing voice came from the end of the wallpaper aisle. 'Just the man I need to see. Will you let me have a cheque for the Ladies' Lunch next week? I need to settle up with the caterers. Drop it round on your way home, there's a good chap. Goodbye.'

It was Mrs Barrow, one of the churchwardens. No one seemed to know her Christian name, for certainly nobody ever used it. She seemed to think she owned the village and the church. Indeed, no one could remember a time when she hadn't been around, and bossing everyone in sight. It was noticeable that Mrs Barrow had not even so much as glanced at Kate, let alone said hello.

I wonder why? she thought to herself, and then enquired, 'What was it you were going to say, Bill?'

'Oh, nothing,' said Bill, 'it can wait. You carry on enjoying your holiday. Don't even think of the job until next Monday morning. You have two whole weeks after you actually start, before the parish office is officially opened, so there's plenty of time for planning then.'

'Okay then,' Kate said, 'I had better get on. I have the telephone people coming round to fix my broadband at midday. Bye for now.'

'Bye-bye, my dear, and take care,' said Bill, as he headed off towards the tills.

He is such a sweet man, she thought, *so kind and helpful.*

Bill had been treasurer for many years, and even though he was in his seventies, his mind was still razor sharp when it came to figures, and he also possessed an amazing memory. He often entertained the younger members of the church with stories of some of the old vicars and curates. And what tales he could tell! But he was not one for gossip, and you always knew that you were safe telling Bill anything. He was a common sight in the village, with his basket hooked over one arm, and his walking stick on the other.

She walked back to her little cottage, a typical 'biscuit box' picture home, with wisteria trailing up the front, and ivy struggling to gain entrance through the window panes. It really was an enchanting place, and once again she thought how lucky she was to own it. There was some mystery in the family that Kate had never got to the bottom of. Her aunt was supposed to have been a bit of a character, a non-conformist in a family with strict Brethren beliefs. There had been a major row of some sort, but Kate didn't really know what it had been about. She only knew that Aunt Valerie never spoke to her grandparents or her parents, and they never spoke of her. Kate didn't really like her grandparents either. They gave her the creeps, and so did the people who always seemed to be hanging out there. Anything Kate and Mel ever did when they were children was wrong. The house they lived in was sparse and foreboding and they had never owned a television set. As children they were made to say grace before every meal, and then sit quietly when they had finished, or read the Bible. Kate's mum seemed terrified of her parents, even as a married woman. There were no photographs or pictures up on the wall; just long framed Bible passages. It was all somehow unnatural, and creepy. Very, very creepy.

Vikki often stopped and wondered what had possessed her to marry a man with a dog collar round his neck. There had to be strings attached, and those strings of course, were the church congregation. They had met when Josh was a curate at her church in Norfolk, and you could say that it was love at first sight, at least on her part. Poor Josh was giving his very first sermon, and truth be told, it had not been all that good. But she hadn't noticed, she was totally blown away by the man. In fact, the church had been nearly blown away, as he tried to perform a stunt with candles and a cardboard cake; so lost was he in his talk, that he didn't notice the raging inferno under his nose. Charging up from the back came the fat old vicar, Mad Max, with a fire extinguisher, and he fired it at Josh with such force that not only was the fire put out, Josh landed in a very undignified heap on the dais. As it was a Family Service, the children were screaming with total delight, thinking it was all part of the talk, but the vicar turned round and sternly shouted at the congregation to leave the church swiftly and orderly, until the fire brigade arrived. 'He's called the fire brigade?' yelled Josh indignantly, as Vikki ran to the front, ignoring the icy glare of Mad Max. She helped poor Josh to his feet, which were tangled up in his surplice, making the whole manoeuvre extremely difficult. The only thing to catch fire now was Josh, whose cheeks were burning red with shame and humiliation.

The approaching sound of sirens blaring only added to his embarrassment.

'What has the silly old codger gone and called them for?' he asked, then quickly flushed even redder and apologised for using that derogatory term in church.

'That's okay, we all call him that under our breath anyway,' replied Vikki, who was now having trouble controlling her giggles, and finally she too collapsed onto the dais in a heap of laughter and tears. Church was never meant to be this good! So I guess you could say that they fell head over heels in love with each other, and were an item from that day onwards.

But now that Josh was a vicar with his own parish, marriage was a three-way tap, and Vikki found life quite a chore, as living up to people's expectations of what a vicar's wife should be like was tough. She was, after all, just a girl, in love with a guy, who happened to be a priest. That did not automatically give her 'Saint' status. It certainly didn't make her kids little angels either; in fact she sometimes felt that she was dealing single-handedly with the devil's own spawn. But they were good children really. She loved them desperately and for the most part was proud to be their mother. It was just these women parishioners who expected so much from her, and from her children. She was expected to be on this committee and that rota, the house was treated like an open-house commune, and she didn't seem to have any privacy or life of her own.

When Josh was home, he was normally locked in his study preparing sermons, and that caused its own set of problems. The children wanted to play with Daddy when he was home, so it was a constant battle to keep them from going upstairs to his study, and disturbing him. Actually, he had become quite good at this sermon lark. Very good, in fact. The church was growing and becoming quite a beacon in the local community, and Vikki was really proud of her husband.

On Friday morning, Josh was out taking communion to some of the house-bound members of the church. Today was the last day of the summer holidays, so all the children were in high spirits. Daisy, the eldest at eight, but going on fifteen, was giving Amy, aged four, a hard time. Amy was besotted with Daisy, but the feeling was not mutual, and poor Amy was in tears again.

Finn, aged seven, was out in the long rambling vicarage garden kicking a ball, yet he still managed to break the kitchen window.

'How come you have acres and acres of grass to kick about on and yet you still manage to kick your ball straight through my window, while I am trying to clear up the mess you lot have left in the kitchen?' Vikki screamed.

'*Muuummy*,' wailed Amy, 'Daisy won't play dressing up with me. She called me a baby. I'm not a baby am I?'

'Tell her to leave me alone, will you, Mum?' screeched Daisy. 'I just want to be left alone.'

I know the feeling, thought Vikki. It was only nine thirty a.m., and she had had enough already. She hadn't even managed to have a shower yet. No doubt Joan and Betty would be along any minute now with a demand to sort out the flower arranging rota. *Damn*, she thought, *why can't they sort out their own blooming flowers? They only give me sneezing fits anyway, whenever I go anywhere near those disgusting lilies. What has happened to my life? This place is a tip, it's too big to manage, and the garden looks like a wildlife park. Josh is no use, as he seems to feel it is okay to be on call twenty-four seven. Well, it might be alright for him, but it's not for me!*

With that, she sat down on the stairs, shards of shattered window in her hand, and cried, hot tears flowing through her fingers.

Ding dong!

'Great, they've started already,' she muttered to herself. *Shall I ignore it? But they know we're in because of the commotion the children are making.* She wiped her eyes and nose on the sleeve of her dressing gown, and went disconsolately to the door.

'What on earth has happened?' cried Kate, 'Have you been burgled?'

'No, it's just another day in the life of,' said Vikki, 'and do you know, I don't think I can take any more.' And with that she broke down again, sobbing in Kate's arms.

After a while, the sobs subsided, and Kate patted her back consolingly, allowing Vikki all the time she needed.

'That's the way,' she said, 'it's much better all out. You've been bottling this up for months. I'm surprised you haven't cracked sooner to be honest. All these people seem to think you are both demi-gods, with non-stop energy and ever-increasing talents. This isn't the way it should be, and I can't wait to start my job. The first thing I am going to do is to get some of these roles taken away from you, and ensure that you and Josh have some quality time.'

'Huh, then you must think you can work miracles. Who do you think you are, Jesus?' said Vikki. 'This is the way they expect a vicar and his wife to cope. It's what they have been used to. I think they forget that I have a young family. When Rev Archie was here, it was so different. He had no family to get in the way, so the church truly was his life. And also, the church was just a fraction of the size it is now. Look at all the extra families that have joined us this last year!'

'That's why the church has appointed an administrator,' replied Kate, 'and the sooner I get to work, the better. But I am not working today, so why don't I spend the day here with you? I was at a loose end, to be quite honest. I have finished all the work I wanted to do on the cottage. Well, okay, that's not quite true,' she grinned, 'I'm bored! Bored with my own blooming company. So. You are now officially off duty. No arguments please, just go upstairs, and let me organise this unholy huddle. I will start with ringing Sophie's husband. I know he's short of work at the moment, so he will be delighted to have a job to do, and he can fix the window. I will then deal with the devil's children for you! After your shower, take this girly magazine I have just brought, which shows you how bored I am! I will give you a whole hour to pamper yourself, and then I will bring you a nice cup of coffee and biscuits. How's that sound?'

Vikki started sniffing again, so Kate passed her another tissue.

'Too good to be true,' she smiled, and took to the stairs two at a time, just in case Kate changed her mind and took away her dream of escape.

Daisy, Finn and Amy were all huddled in the playroom, aghast at hearing their lovely mum in such a state.

'Mummy had snot coming out of her nose,' said Amy in wonder. 'Is that snot that comes out of your eyes when you cry?'

'Don't be stupid, it's just water from your eyes,' stated Daisy, but even she was shocked to see Mummy in such a state.

'It was my fault for breaking that window,' said Finn miserably.

Kate came in with a bright smile on her face.

'Ooh, don't you all look like a set of Mr and Mrs Miseries,' she laughed. 'Come on, your mummy's fine, she is just a bit tired, and don't we all get grumpy when we're tired?'

'But it's only morning,' said Daisy, 'how can she be tired already?'

'Well, grown-ups don't go to bed as early as you,' said Kate, 'plus, she thinks of all the jobs she has to do at night-time, so she doesn't get to sleep very quickly. But she will be fine, and it gives me a chance to play with you lot. Now, I've asked that nice Mr Weekes to come round to mend the window, and you know he always has a magic trick or two up his sleeve, so cheer up! Let's all go into the garden and we can organise a game.'

'Not football, though,' said Finn, 'I might not be able to stop myself kicking it through another window, and she would start that snotty thing all over again.'

'No, not football, but how about swing ball? That way the ball can't go flying off in the wrong direction? And, then Amy and I can try on some dressing up clothes. Do you want to be a princess too, Daisy?'

'Mmm, perhaps...'

Vikki could not believe this, it seemed ages since she had any time on her own, without the children. Imagine having a shower with the door locked! In fact, she was going to have a bath, not a shower; a long, luxurious, deep, honey-scented bath. She undressed slowly, and put her clothes in the wash bin. Even choosing clean clothes for the day felt like a treat. Normally it was a matter of grabbing whatever was nearest the wardrobe door, or fell out first from the cupboard, or was on top of the ironing pile. *I've become a right slob*, she thought to herself. But who noticed? Josh didn't, that was for sure. He always had his head in a Bible Commentary or was talking to a needy parishioner. How did it happen to get like this? They loved each other still, she knew that for certain. And they both loved their children. It had all seemed so idyllic at the start, and it seemed so sad that she wasn't enjoying the dream they once had. The village was wonderful, most of the people that went to church were lovely, but apart from Kate and Ellie Smith, she had no real friends. It was all just church business. That couldn't be right, could it? She knew that she so wanted the church to see how wonderful her little family was, but somehow it all went wrong. *Stress, I expect*, she thought. Children pick up on stress and then act badly. She didn't need to be a psychologist to know that. Maybe it would be different now that Kate was going to be the church administrator, but she could not yet dare to believe it. It all sounded too good to be true. It would be lovely to spend more time with Josh, but did he feel the same? Maybe he did feel more married to the church than he did to her? *Is that why Catholic priests didn't get married?* she wondered.

She lowered herself down into the soft, scented water and felt every muscle and joint relax, then inhaled deeply. This, she decided, must be what heaven feels like. Warm and beautifully scented. She imagined Josh and the children, all dressed up perfectly, clean and happy and smelling nice. Yes, even Finn. No smelly socks or sticky dresses. They all looked beautifully cherubic and happy. She closed her eyes and drifted off, knowing that everything was in safe hands. She even managed to remember to say a prayer of thanks for Kate, turning up like an angel at just the right time. Bliss.

As the water cooled down, Vikki topped it up with hot, so she was probably in the bath for about an hour. Now all she had to do was to climb slowly out, not breaking the magic spell, and wrap a big, warm, white fluffy towel around her, straight off the radiator. Could life get any better? People paid hundreds of pounds to do this at a spa and here she was, luxuriating in her own bathroom. As soon as she had dried off, she was going to lie down on her bed and read trash, instead of something sensible. Grasping hold of the matching bottle of honey-scented body lotion she began to rub the rich, creamy lotion into her legs, up her torso, and on to her arms. Something stopped her in her tracks. She could not be sure what that something was, so she made her hand retrace its movement. There it was again. Suddenly cold, even though the bathroom was still hot and steamy, her hand shook as she traced a small uneven bump in her left breast. Shaking her head she abruptly put her hands rigidly down to her sides, and stretched all her fingers tight. Don't be silly, she thought to herself, I must be due on, that's all it is. But she had only just had her period. Cautiously she allowed her hand to gently massage over the lower quadrant of her breast again, but it hadn't gone away. She felt the right breast to reassure herself that this was just how they felt. But it did not feel the same. Not at all.

Okay, she thought. Let's not panic. It is probably something and nothing. After all, I am only thirty-four. Surely you have to be menopausal to have breast cancer?

She decided there and then to try and forget about it and to continue enjoying her brief morning of luxury. She got dressed, pausing to have another quick feel as she put on her bra, then shook her head as if to rid herself of unnecessary worry. She then went and lay on the bed, the glossy magazine untouched; thinking.

Suddenly, she was brought back to her senses by the creaking on the stairs. Grabbing the magazine, she started flicking aimlessly through the pages, as Kate brought in her coffee. She placed it on to the cluttered bedside cabinet, pushing aside a dusty photograph of the family and a scripture verse in a frame, stating 'God does not give you anything you cannot handle.'

'How's it going then?' asked Kate brightly. 'Have you read that article on Brad Pitt yet?'

'Um, no, I, um, I, well, I'm just browsing really, you know? I haven't read a proper magazine since... well, probably since I sat in the doctor's surgery when I was pregnant with Daisy! Now all I read when we go there is Goldilocks or The Big Bad Wolf. Anyway, I took much longer in the bathroom. I had a proper bath, not just a shower. It was lovely. Fantastic, even.' She could hear herself gabbling away like a maniac, anything but say what was on her mind.

'Well, you stay up here as long as you like,' said Kate, 'we are having a great time downstairs, and Robbie has already been and fixed the window, and cleared away all the glass. You would never know a tornado had hit the house earlier!'

'You know what? I think I've had enough of being on my own,' said Vikki. 'I think I will come and join you all. Too much of a good thing and all that!'

Vikki joined Kate and the children in the playroom, but it soon became clear that the adults were spare-parts, as the three siblings were enjoying each others' company, as they so often did now that they were growing older. When Vikki had given birth to Amy, she wondered if they had made a mistake in having a third child. Daisy and Finn had been born less than two years apart, and were the easiest of children. Amy had been a difficult child at first, but it wasn't long before they all settled down with each other, and the two eldest children were quite besotted with the new baby. Now, although they still had their 'moments' they were a wonderful family. Vikki's stomach kept rising up in her chest as she thought of her hand moving over her breast. What if? What if? What if?

'Vikki,' Kate spoke gently, 'You seem miles away. Is everything alright?'

'What? Oh, yes, I'm fine,' replied Vikki, but then paused.

'Actually, I am a little worried.'

Kate searched her friend's face. It was a beautiful face, and she could see traces of all three children in both Vikki and Josh. For a moment, Kate was swept off course by the deep dull ache of longing for a family of her own. Then her attention was brought sharply back into focus by the next words that came from Vikki.

'I think I found a lump. Well, I *did* find a lump. Oh, it's probably nothing, I am just feeling a bit low at the moment and panicking needlessly.'

'A lump. Where?' asked Kate, concern written all over her face.

'I shouldn't have mentioned it. You know, let's just forget we had this conversation.' She laughed uneasily, trying to dismiss the gravity of the moment.

'No, there is no way you can say that and not tell me more. Where?'

Vikki gently rubbed the underside of her breast as she tried to define the lump. Once again, its presence shocked her.

'It is almost certainly nothing to worry about. I might have bruised it, playing with the children. You know how we love to roll around play-fighting! Don't worry yourself, Kate. I am just over-reacting, I expect.'

'Where is your phone?'

'No!' said Vikki in alarm, 'Please don't! I can't go down the surgery. As soon as I stick my head in that place, everyone wants to know my business. Even my body isn't my own, you know? It all belongs to this bloody parish. Oh, I'm sorry, I am just tired.'

But Kate was already ringing the health centre, ignoring Vikki's pleas to put the phone down.

'...Yes, it is urgent,' she heard Kate saying in her most authoritative voice. *Gosh, she is going to be good in this administration role*, Vikki thought to herself. *In fact, she is a bit scary. I am glad she is on my side. I wouldn't like to be her enemy!* Her heart was beating fast as she saw Kate taking down details of her visit.

'Right,' said Kate, 'I have made you an appointment with Ellie, which is brilliant. You know how gentle she is. She has agreed to see you this afternoon at four o'clock. Now isn't that great? She will soon put your mind at ease, I'm sure. It's best to get these things sorted out before you have time to get yourself in a lather of worry. I'm sure it's nothing, sweetheart, but it is best to make sure.'

Suddenly, Vikki found tears coursing down her cheeks, as Kate took control of her life, and her problems. She ran over to her friend's side, and hugged her tightly.

'What did I ever do without you?' she said, through her tears. 'For so long now, it has always been me in charge of everybody. I have to take care of the children, Josh, the whole congregation; even those people who have nothing to do with the church seem to think I can sort out all their problems. All the charity cases end up on my doorstep, somehow. Josh is always working, always dealing with other people. In fact, he hardly seems to notice me nowadays,' she sobbed, 'and when he does, we always get interrupted by someone who needs 'the vicar' more than I do. I'm tired of it all, do you know that?'

'I do,' soothed Kate, rubbing her friend's back as if she were a little child. 'Come on now, if the children come back in and see you crying again, they will think I am to blame and might set about me, and that would never do!'

With that, Vikki managed to stop sobbing and even managed a wan smile. 'This is all going to be a storm in a teacup,' she assured herself. The two friends had another cup of coffee, and went off to find the strangely silent children. Where were they?

They heard giggles coming from the garden play house, and they crept up to the window. There was Finn, with a cardboard dog collar fixed crookedly under his chin, and he had to push his little neck down to hold it in place! And the girls were down on their knees in mock contrition, crying out loudly for God to forgive their sins. My little angels, thought Vikki, how could a merciful God ever let anything bad happen to them? Once more, her stomach curled in on itself, as she thought of the appointment this afternoon. Kate had agreed to stay for lunch, and then to babysit while Vikki went to see Ellie Smith. Ellie was a member of St John's, and an unlikely ally. She was a fifty-something spinster, and to some, a fairly formidable character. But those who knew her well loved her for her warmth, compassion and wicked sense of humour. In fact, Vikki, Kate and Ellie often spent hilarious evenings at the vicarage after the children were in bed, watching crazy rom-coms and enjoying a bottle of wine. But she was also a true professional, and Vikki was so glad that it was Ellie she was seeing and not Dr Razia, or Dr Vaughan. Both of them were lovely doctors, but she felt that the no-nonsense approach from Ellie would be just the thing she needed to set her mind at ease. If she could just be assured that there was nothing apart from a bit of fibrous tissue, then that would be great. Silently, she offered up a prayer, and asked for protection for her lovely little family.

Although they had a wonderful afternoon playing some pretty riotous games with the children, the hours dragged slowly for Vikki. But once half past three came by, all of a sudden, Vikki wanted the time to stop, as her heart began to flutter nervously within her chest. At five to four, Kate pushed her towards the door.

'Where's Mummy going?' asked Amy, her finger wrapped tightly round her 'blankie'. It was about this time in the afternoon that Amy became a little tired, and could become quite difficult. Vikki started to protest that perhaps it wasn't a good time to leave her, but Kate assured her that they would all be absolutely fine without her for just a little while. With that she scooped Amy up and gave her a warm hug.

'Mummy is just going to see that nice Dr Smith, to get her to listen to Mummy's heart and check her temperature, you know like we do when we play doctors? Shall we go and get your doctor's bag out and play hospitals?' asked Kate, tactfully indicating to Vikki to leave.

Amy smiled and struggled out of her arms, then ran to the playroom, yelling to her brother and sister, 'Who wants to play hospitals? I am the nurse! Auntie Kate is going to be my first patient. Get into bed, Kate!'

Kate laughed at her enthusiasm, and settled herself down comfortably on the sofa, but the next thing she knew, Amy, Finn and Daisy all launched themselves upon her.

'Hey! Hang on, I am ill! Get off me! I thought you were the doctors and nurses?' she laughed, as they all had one massive bundle and rolled off the sofa and on to the floor.

'Yes, but first we have to fight, and make you poorly,' yelled Finn, and they continued to sit on her and tickle her until tears poured down her cheeks.

'Okay, okay, I am *really* poorly now! Please get off me before you kill me!'

'Yeah! And then we can play undertakers,' laughed Daisy, 'and I will be the lady vicar and we can bury you!'

The next thing Kate knew, she was buried under a mountain of cushions ripped from the sofa with great enthusiasm. *How on earth do mothers survive the day?* she thought to herself with a smile. *It's totally exhausting having kids!*

Chapter 3

September arrived in a blaze of late summer glory and Kate chuckled to herself as she packed her briefcase and went to the garage to get her bike. This was just what she had dreamed of so often when she was stuck with her nose against someone's armpit on the crowded rush-hour tube. *How the other half live!* she thought and cycled off through the lanes, and into the churchyard. She was still smiling as she chained her bike to the railings outside the church building. Her office was to be housed in a large open room looking out on to the church yard. A beautiful place for reflection and meditation, she wondered if it might distract her from work. The room was fairly empty, apart from a couple of pieces of office equipment; a chair that had seen much better days, an old wooden desk, and a small filing cabinet covered in children's stickers. This used to be the youth room, but that had now moved to a large chalet-type building on the church grounds, which, rumour had it, had been the venue for many illicit couplings throughout the years. Indeed, the story was that it had been built for that very purpose by a past vicar in the sixties, who was partial to helping the lady parishioners out with their marital problems. But it was a lovely building for the kids to use now, and to decorate as they wished. It also meant that church services could go on without disruption from the noise of over-exuberant children, which was particularly important when there was a funeral service being held. The trouble was, Josh was too good at his work, and more and more young families were coming to church, which meant that the children's groups were growing fast and furiously. Where would they put them? No one was quite sure at this stage. It seemed an awful thing to be worried about when most churches around them were closing because of falling numbers, and here was the church of St John's positively bursting at the seams. This was one task that Kate would be dealing with, along with the youth worker and Bill Holmes, the treasurer. Money was not an issue, as they had been bequeathed a large sum specifically for the youth work a couple of years ago, but so far the exact use of that money had not yet been decided upon.

Josh had given her the keys to the church at the weekend, but just as she was putting the key into the lock a shrill voice stopped her in her tracks.

'Young lady! Just what do you think you are doing?' It was Mrs Barrow, the churchwarden.

'It's me, Kate. I am starting work today.'

'Yes, but what do you think you are doing with that key? It is only the churchwardens and the vicar that hold a key for the church,' replied Mrs Barrow in an acerbic tone.

'Well, that wasn't going to be very practical since I need to get into work every day, so Josh had one cut for me,' explained Kate, backing away from the miserable old woman. Honestly, she thought to herself, no wonder people are put off of coming to church when women like her existed.

'*Reverend* Mercer should have consulted me before doing that,' she replied, 'and then it should have been put to the PCC and the Fabric Committee to see if we felt that it was worth the expense.'

'If it makes you any happier, I will pay for the key myself,' retorted Kate. Well, this is a good start, she thought angrily to herself. So much for working quietly in God's house, I haven't even got inside the door!

'That's not the point!' exclaimed the old woman, 'We should have...' but Kate had had enough.

'I have a lot of work to do, and it is not going to get done arguing with you over some pointless issue,' said Kate. 'Goodbye.'

And with that, she turned her back on Mrs Barrow and walked into her office. The churchwarden was, for once, speechless.

But Kate knew that she had probably made her first mistake. Don't mess with the churchwardens. *Oh hell!* she thought. *Oops! Wrong thought, maybe I should just pray for the old bat and get on with my work.* But she began to realise that life was not going to be quite as sugar-coated as perhaps her daydreams had made it. These women were entrenched in tradition, and it was not going down well that a young woman had been given the key role of administrator and right-hand man to the vicar.

The day only got worse.

It was weird to think that the day Sophie Weekes had found out she was pregnant, was the day that Reverend Hillier had died. She had been in the chemist's when the commotion kicked off. There were shouts in the street outside the Yew Tree Inn, and she saw the undertaker rush round the corner. Curiosity got the better of her, and anyway, she could walk through the alleyway on her way home, which would give her a chance to hang around and see what was going on. There were people congregating around the Health Centre door, and also rushing from the church. But the drama wasn't happening at the Health Centre, but in the Merrywood's retirement home next door. Oh well, it was obviously just some old codger who'd kicked the bucket, nothing to do with her. Later on through the grapevine, she heard that it had been the old vicar who used to be in charge of the church. She had never set foot in the building, as her mum and dad were not interested in church. They had never even sent her to Sunday school as a child. Then she had been sent to the care home, where she grew up, and they never sent her to church either. However, her interest had been aroused by posters on the church notice board. There seemed to be a lot of activities for young families. Families eh! That's what she was hopefully going to be soon, a real family. Her and Robbie, and this little 'un inside her! She put the commotion that was going on at the retirement flats out of her mind, and rushed home, bladder full, ready to pee on her little plastic stick. Robbie was out and about looking for work, and she hoped to break the news to him when he came home. He had been really depressed lately, after being laid off work; it would bring a smile back to his face, she just knew it would. She went into the bathroom, took the pregnancy kit out of the bag, and carefully read the instructions, wriggling with excitement and the need to pee. Minutes went by, each one seeming to last an hour, until finally she peered down at the thin blue double line. Yes!

Robbie arrived home, smelling of beer as usual, and was in a sombre mood. This wasn't how it should be. Nevertheless, smiling widely, Sophie grabbed his hands.

'Guess what?' she asked him.

'Don't play games, Sophie, I'm not in the mood,' he replied. 'There's a heck of a carry-on down in the village. Seems that old vicar fella has gone and died. Didn't know him; well, only by sight of course, but I tell you, there's a lot of upset people around. Seems he was a right, kindly old chap, so it's not surprising.'

'Well, I can put that smile back on your face,' she said, 'I kind of think it's really appropriate, you know, new life for old, and all that.'

'What are you talking about, Sophie?'

'We're having a baby!'

'When? How? Why? What you talkin' about? I thought you was on the pill? We can't afford a nipper right now, you stupid woman! I'm on the dole, or has it escaped your attention?'

Sophie's excitement diminished, but only for a brief second.

'Listen, we are having a baby. I've just done the test, and it's really, really positive! It all makes sense, don't you see? We will get Child Benefit and the council will have to move us to a bigger house now! It will be alright, you'll see. Oh, please be excited with me.'

Tears started to form in Sophie's eyes. She hadn't expected this reaction from him; she thought he would be as thrilled as she was. Admittedly they hadn't actually agreed to have a baby quite yet, but it was the only thing she had ever wanted. A baby of her own, someone to mother, the way that she had never been mothered. She hadn't been in touch with either of her parents for years, and though she didn't miss them, she longed to have someone else to tell, and to be pleased for her. Not that her mum was ever pleased about anything, except the bargains down at the local supermarket.

Robbie wasn't a hard man, and he loved Sophie, and certainly didn't like seeing her upset, so he put his big arms around her tiny body and hugged her hard.

'Steady on, you'll crush the poor wee thing before it's had time to grow!' she laughed, delighted at this response from him.

'Hang on a mo', what's this tucked behind your ear?' And he pulled out the Queen of Hearts. 'So it's true then my Queeny, you really are going to be a mum!'

'How do you do that?' asked Sophie. She still had no idea how he managed all his conjuring tricks, a skill he had learnt whist at one of the many foster homes he had been in. Sophie was his family now, and he was going to make her happy, no matter what.

'Do you know what else?' she said. 'I am going to start going to church. It's an omen, don't you see? A life taken and a new one given? I am going to go to those family services the new vicar holds on Sunday mornings, and then when my little girl is born, I'll take her to the Pram Services and everything, and have her christened.'

'How do you know it's a girl?'

'Oh, it's a girl alright,' she answered mysteriously. She placed his large hands onto her tiny stomach, and there they stayed, each lost in their own thoughts, as her abdomen grew warm.

Vikki arrived home in a daze, after Ellie had assured her the lump was probably nothing to worry about. If only she felt so sure. But it was now just a matter of waiting for the hospital appointment, when she would have a mammogram. How can this be happening? Vikki thought to herself. She was only thirty four, and surely breast cancer was something that you get after the menopause? With that reassuring thought, she thanked Kate and let her escape back to the sanctuary of her spinster home. As a mum of three children and Josh; no make that four children, she knew that she could not afford to sit around worrying about something that probably wasn't even worth worrying about!

Kate had done a wonderful job with the children that afternoon, and they were all amazingly tired, so she did something she would not normally do, and plonked them all down in front of the television. *Mama Mia* was the film of the moment, and they were all soon comatose, as Meryl Streep pounced about on her bed, and sang dreadfully. What Josh doesn't know won't harm him, she thought to herself, and it meant that she was free to get their supper and think her thoughts. She knew she should be praying that all would be okay, but somehow it didn't seem easy.

Josh came in as they were all finishing supper, as usual, looking weary and distracted.

'What's up?' asked Vikki, reaching out for his hand.

'Oh you know, this and that,' he replied. 'Mrs Barrow has got me roped in with the Mother's Union flower show, and also with the British Legion on top of everything else that is happening this week. I told her I didn't have time, but she just sneered and told me that Reverend Hillier had time for *everyone*, and that I shouldn't spend so much time with the 'flighty, loose, young women' as she so nicely called the Young Mum's group.'

'You should stand up to her,' said Vikki crossly. 'She really is the pits that woman. What with her and Maud, I'm surprised we still have a congregation! If it was up to those two, only the over-seventies would be allowed to cross the threshold of the church. I ran in to Jo Stokes last week. You know, she has a little boy of Daisy's age? She wanted to find out about having her baby christened, but Maud barked at her when she came into the church, and she just turned around and walked out. We really have got to do something to stop those women frightening people away. You are doing so much good in the parish, yet one word from those dragons and it ruins everything.'

'I know,' Josh replied, 'but it is so difficult trying to keep everyone happy. Oh no! Look at the time! I have to go to the PCC meeting. I am not looking forward to this. I have already heard that there are rumblings about me appointing Kate as administrator.'

'Well, bloody well stand up to them!' shouted Vikki.

'Hey, keep your voice down, and please watch your language,' Josh said tiredly.

'Maybe it's about time voices were raised against those witches,' she replied, 'The church is about life and new beginnings. If we don't look after the young, well, they are the church of tomorrow. If all those old battleaxes had their way the church would cease to exist in twenty years' time.'

Josh pushed away from the table, frowning and anxious, so Vikki knew she had to let it go. He was doing such a good job here in Ashton Kirby, but the trouble was that he was a people pleaser, and if he wasn't careful he would burn himself out, and be of no use to anyone. She reached out and laid her hand on his, and Josh picked it up and held it to his mouth, gently kissing each of her fingers. Then, with a sigh, he gave her a quick hug, and was out of the door.

That night, as Vikki lay in bed, she realized that she still had not told Josh about her lump. This was awful. Parish life was of more importance than family at the moment. She tried to stay awake, but the PCC meeting was a long one, and when Josh came in, Vikki was sleeping.

Kate's first week was a mixed bag. Certainly, she came into contact with some right characters! But she was also rewarded by some lovely visitors, and hoped that her work would make a real difference to the parish church. It was clear that Josh needed some administrative help, with the church growing at an alarming rate. And there was so much to do! St John's was a beautiful old church, and was very popular for weddings and baptisms. This meant a lot of certificates needed to be written every week, and in triplicate! How glad she was that she had taken a calligraphy course all those years ago, at night school. As she fingered the heavy old parish records, she was filled with awe that they contained so much history. They were kept in the safe, as were all the documents of an important nature, and as she opened the safe, the smell of ancient history emanated from the small enclosure. If you could only bottle that fragrance, she thought to herself. But writing out certificates was just one aspect of the job. There were rotas to be compiled, services to be planned, diaries to be kept and visiting speakers to be contacted and catered for.

One particular person was a regular visitor to her office, and that was her favourite gentleman, Bill Holmes. As church treasurer he looked after the church finances and also took the minutes of the various meetings. He always gave her door a little tap before he entered, unlike some of the women of the parish, who really resented Kate having such an intimate role in the life of *their* vicar. Young whippersnapper! She was in no doubt what they thought of her, and they were not backward in telling her. They tried various ways of undermining her confidence, but she was quite used to dealing with difficult individuals, having worked in the lairs of financiers in the city. They also tried to abuse her position by off-loading all their menial tasks onto her, but Kate was not having any of that!

Sure enough, that morning, as Kate was chatting to Bill, the door was flung open and there stood Mrs Brown-hyphen-Smith in all her twenty stone formidable glory. She threw a sheaf of papers down on Kate's desk, and barked, 'I want twenty-five copies by Friday.'

Bill stood with his mouth agape, shell-shocked by the tone of this unpleasant woman.

'The photocopier will need a few moments to warm up, and then you may use it,' replied Kate, with a smile. 'Please record in the book how many copies you are making and what for.'

'But they're for you to do,' blustered the old woman, giving Kate the evil eye.

You could tell she was not used to being argued with.

'Who did them last month when I wasn't here?' demanded Kate.

Wow! thought Bill, this lady is feisty!

'But you're here now and you are the secretary, so you can do them,' replied Mrs Brown-hyphen-Smith. It was quite amusing that no one called her Mrs Brown-Smith, but always put the hyphen in between, because that was how she always introduced herself to people. It seemed to give her some kind of status, or at least that was what she thought, but it was just a bit of a laugh to everyone really.

Lord, give me strength, thought Kate.

'I am NOT a secretary, I am an administrator. Please understand that I am not responsible for the work that comes from the various groups. You operated perfectly well before me, and you are always welcome to use the photocopier whenever you wish, but I would ask that you help me keep a record of your use.'

An evil glint appeared in Kate's eye, as she delivered the next statement.

'Oh, and, we shall be making a small charge from now on; just 5p a copy. I know you all have quite a good balance in your accounts and we felt it was only fair. It takes quite a chunk out of the church budget at the moment, and I am sure you would agree that money could be better spent on outreach.'

If looks could kill, thought Bill, watching in total amazement as this young women took on the strength of the old-school church bastion.

Mrs Brown-hyphen-Smith spluttered and steamed and stormed out of the door, slamming it for good measure. In the silence that ensued, Bill and Kate grinned like a couple of Cheshire cats.

'High five?' giggled Kate, and the pair clapped hands and threw their heads back and laughed.

'You've set yourself up with an enemy there,' said Bill. 'You had better watch your back.'

'Oh, don't worry Bill; I've eaten more than two of her for breakfast before now!'

Chapter 4

The radiographer apologised to Sophie when she placed the cold gel on her tummy, but Sophie didn't care! Not a jot. This was the most exciting day of her life. Well, apart from the day she had discovered she was pregnant. So yes, it was the second most important, and exciting day of her life. But then, every day felt great, and though she was looking forward to meeting her little girl, Sophie was simply revelling in being pregnant. She wasn't even showing, but she had already brought a lot of loose smock tops from the local charity shop, and practised her new look by putting a cushion up beneath them. Yes, it definitely suited her. Sophie felt as important as the queen, and everywhere she went, she felt as though people must know she was special. On the bus, she was sure that everyone knew; in the supermarket, she strolled around, spending hours at the baby counters, picking up packets of nappies. She would happily have put a large sign on her chest, declaring, 'I am pregnant!' A delirium of happiness and joy encompassed her, and she wondered why no one had ever told her just how wonderful it was to be carrying a child. For sure, she had suffered a little with nausea in the early weeks, but that had all cleared up now that she was twelve weeks. She had read all the literature that the doctor had given her, and also spent hours on the internet down at the library charting the baby's development.

Once Robbie had gotten over the shock, he was as delighted as she was, and watched over her with a paternal ferocity. They didn't have much money, but he was forever coming home with little treats for her. He had managed to secure work with the local council, supplemented by the odd jobs he did around the village. People trusted Robbie, and when he told them their good news, he soon found out how generous people could be; the old ladies started knitting little bootees and bonnets, and the younger women gave him casts-off from their own children's wardrobes. These he proudly took home to Sophie, who lovingly washed them and put them away in a cupboard, already earmarked for the baby's things.

'You all right, Princess?' Robbie asked, as Sophie lay on the hard radiography table. Truth be told, he couldn't make head nor tale of what was happening on that screen, but he still smiled and nodded when the young woman pointed out bits to him.

'That's our little girl there. Say hello to her then, Rob.' Sophie grinned at him. Robbie waved to the screen bashfully.

'I don't think she can see that, you numpty!' she laughed, but all the same, she too waved delightedly at the screen.

'Everything looks fine, for your dates, Mrs Weekes,' said the radiographer. 'I can't tell you yet what the sex is, but would you like a picture of your baby?'

'Yes please!' replied Sophie, 'and I know she's a girl, anyway.'

'Well, we should be able to make that definite at your next scan then, and we shall see if you're right!'

She handed Sophie a fistful of tissues to wipe off the goo, and then waved them goodbye. It was lovely to see enthusiastic young parents, the radiographer thought to herself. So often she had young girls in here who were horrified to discover they were expecting a baby. She scrunched up the paper covering the bed, and pulled out a fresh sheet, ready for the next patient. It was a lovely profession to be working in, when everything was going well.

Robbie now had a council van, so they didn't have to catch the bus to and from the hospital. On the way home, Sophie told Robbie to drop her off at the church.

'What, again?' he exclaimed, 'You were only there yesterday. You're not gonna turn into a religious fruit cake are you?'

'Don't be so daft, Robbie. I just want to go and show Kate my baby pictures. She will be so excited. She has been really good to me. Do you know, she is buying me a little baby product every week in her shopping. How kind is that?'

'We're not a charity case, babe,' he said, frowning.

'No, I know that,' she replied, 'but I think she is really pleased for us. I wonder why she has never bagged herself a fella and had kids. A beautiful lady like that...'

The truth of the matter was, Kate was a little jealous of Sophie, but she would never have admitted it. She really liked the young girl, and admired her tenacity. She knew that they struggled financially, and Kate took real pleasure in buying the odd bottle of baby lotion or packet of nappies for them. The more time she was spending with Vikki and her children, the more she was regretting not settling down and having her own family. There was still time, but there had never been that 'Mr Right' in her life. She had certainly had her share of boyfriends, but no one who she felt she would want to spend her life with. Kate often thought it was because of her parents' marriage, which certainly did nothing to persuade her to settle down. She enjoyed her independence and financial security.

It had been really lovely welcoming Sophie into the church. The young girl had appeared at her door on the first day Kate had started in the post, and it was clear she had never set foot in a church before. She had whispered and looked petrified. Kate did her best to make her feel at ease, and dispel the myth that church was a fearful place. Goodness, she had had enough of grotty churches in her childhood. She felt that part of the remit in her new post was to help make the church open and available to all, and not just the chosen few. But it was a battle, as there were certain members of St John's that wanted to keep the rabble out of church.

Maud, the verger, was one of the worst types of churchgoers. She had been a self-appointed door keeper since forever! A thin, stick-like creature, single, of course, she was determined to prevent the art of Christian kindness ever being practised in the church. Maud had frightened off many a prospective member, and stood at the back of each service, looking daggers at anyone who dared to look as if they were enjoying themselves.

One of Kate's first challenges was to improve the welcome of visitors to the church. This was all very well at the Sunday services, when they had sides-people to meet and greet everyone who came into the church, as they handed out the weekly newsletters. But the problem occurred when the church was not in use, and Maud would hang around, ready to pounce on anyone who dared to set foot inside. Often this would be young couples who were looking to get married or have their babies baptised. Josh and Kate had discussed this problem at their staff meetings on Monday mornings, and they had yet to come up with an answer. The only hint of light on the horizon was the fact that Maud was coming up to retirement age, but how could they convince her to relinquish her duties? It was not an easy situation.

Sophie had been on the receiving end of Maud's acerbic tongue, but thankfully Kate had overheard the conversation and gone to rescue her. In actual fact, she need not have worried, for although Sophie only looked about fourteen and had the appearance of a scrawny canary, she was feisty. When Maud started to attack her, Sophie stuck out her chin and was about to launch into a tirade of un-choice words, when Kate forced her way between them.

'Thank you, Maud, I have this sorted,' she spoke firmly to the old verger, who went off with an angry mutter, and a few dark glances over her shoulder.

'Sorry about that. If I had known you were coming in, I would have been at the door to meet you. Take no notice of her; she's a bit set in her ways.'

'What an old bat!' exclaimed Sophie. 'I saw her at the back of the church on Sunday, when I came to the Family Service, and I thought she looked well mean!'

'You came to one of the services?' said Kate, obviously delighted with her new friend. 'That's wonderful! Did you enjoy it?'

'Yeah, I did, actually. I mean, I didn't think I would; as you know, I'm not used to church, but it's not as stuffy as I thought it would be.'

She hesitated for a moment, before explaining to Kate how she felt led to joining the church. She thought that it might seem a bit gruesome to mention the old guy who died, but of course, Kate was totally fine about it.

'He was a really kind old soul, and he loved little ones, so I am sure he would have been honoured to think that his dying brought you to the church. In fact, if you have a little boy, perhaps you could use Archie as his middle name.'

'Oh no, I'm having a girl,' Sophie explained rapidly, a huge grin on her face.

'I'm sorry, I didn't realise you had already had your scan. Can I see the pictures?'

'Well, they haven't confirmed it with the scan yet; it's a bit too early. But I know. I just know.' And Sophie looked off into the distance with a strange and knowing smile.

Kate decided that it would be premature for her to start looking out for pink bits and pieces for the new baby. So they talked for a while about the forthcoming baby, and about the services that were coming up. Sophie enjoyed singing the modern songs. They were so simple, and yet seemed to convey such love. They were far removed from the miserable old hymns she used to sing at school.

After Sophie left, Kate started to plan her day. Their little talk had reminded her that she had to register the church with the Christian Copyright organisation, as technically the church was acting illegally. They had ditched the old hymn books for the newer style of overhead projectors, but no one before had thought of the implications of this. Every week a new song was used, and every week, they were violating the law!

And that wasn't the only law they were breaking. She knew that she had to bring up the issue of child protection. Anyone who taught children, or looked after them on their own in any way would have to apply for a Criminal Records Bureau certificate, to prove they were safe to work with children. Now *that* was going to go down a storm. She added that to her list of items to broach at the next Parochial Church Council. The PCC members mainly consisted of the 'old school' of parishioners. What fun this job was turning out to be! She also had to bring up the issue of safety and security, and was going to suggest that cameras and water sprinklers were installed. You just couldn't be too careful nowadays.

As she was thinking of all the old battleaxes she would have to tackle head on, the door opened and in stepped the triplets. Well, they were not actually related in any way whatsoever, but they were never seen apart. The three triplets consisted of three elderly widows, Felicity Broome and the two Celia's, as they were affectionately known. These three women were not battleaxes, but the sweetest, most helpful ladies Kate had come across since her arrival in Ashton Kirby.

They peered around her door like a trio of meerkats, all grinning shyly.

'Oh, hello, dear, I hope we're not disturbing you?' Felicity asked. She must have been a beauty in her youth, for although she was now in her late seventies, she was still an attractive woman. With her grey hair swept up elegantly into a chignon at the back of her head, and her stunning blue eyes, she had many of the gentlemen falling over themselves to offer her a seat next to them. But where Felicity went, the two Celia's went. Little Celia was diminutive in stature and mouse-like in attitude, while Big Celia was Amazonian, but identical to Little Celia in her character.

'Not at all. It is always a pleasure to see you, and that is what I am here for, you know? You can come and chat to me any time, about anything. And it doesn't have to be about the flower arranging rota!'

'Well, it isn't actually about the flower arranging,' replied Felicity, 'We wanted to ask you a favour.'

'Ask away,' said Kate, 'I can always say no!'

'As you know, we run the Willows group in the retirement complex, and we wondered if you would come and talk to us?'

'Do you want me to talk about working here as an administrator, or about my church background?' asked Kate worriedly. *The former I don't feel I have been in long enough to talk about yet,* she thought to herself, *and the latter would make their permed hair turn straight!*

'Oh no!' they cried as one. 'We would like you to talk about corporate banking and the financial crisis. Our members would be so interested!'

'They would?'

'Oh yes. Just last month we had a former prostitute come and tell us about her life as a lady of the night during the sixties.'

These village dormice would never cease to amaze, thought Kate.

'Of course, I would love to help you out then. Although I don't think I will be anywhere near as interesting as your lady of the night...who was that, by the way?'

'Judith Hall,' replied Felicity, with a grin.

'Well, I'll be darned,' mused Kate. 'Judith!'

Chapter 5

'Post has arrived,' announced Josh, as he walked into the kitchen, sifting through the pile of letters in his hand. 'Mostly junk mail of course, and a load of church stuff. Oh, there's a couple for you.'

Vikki's heart skipped a beat when she saw the hospital postmark. That was quick! She only saw Ellie a couple of days ago. As the noise of the children faded into the background, she quickly scanned through the letter. They wanted her to go for a mammogram and ultrasound on Friday. Today was Monday and she hadn't yet mentioned it to Josh.

'Anything interesting?' he asked absent-mindedly whilst reading his own correspondence.

'Um, no. Um, can I have a few moments of your time once I've got the children off to school?'

'Darling, you don't have to make an appointment to chat with me!'

Oh, but I do, she thought to herself.

'Well, will you still be here just after nine?'

'Yup, I'm hoping to work on my sermon early this week. I am getting fed up with somehow always managing to be rushing around on Friday afternoons, putting it together in between children and youth meetings and diocesan chapter meetings. It's not how it's supposed to be, is it? Surely preaching should be the most important part of my job, you know, shepherding the flock and all that?'

'Yes, and your family,' retorted Vikki.

'Well, that goes without saying, surely?' he asked with a hurt look on his face.

'Please be here when I get home,' said Vikki, flying out of the door as she grabbed Amy from the table. 'Pass me a baby wipe. I can't take her to nursery looking like this.'

'That's what she normally looks like,' retorted Josh with a grin on his face. 'See you later then.'

'Daisy! Finn! Get down those stairs now! We're going to be late for your first day back!'

There followed a thumping of feet down the stairs, and a tumble of bags and bodies as they all jostled out of the front door. Thankfully, school was only around the corner, so they could afford to leave it late. Even Amy's preschool was on the main school site, which made life so much simpler. There was a Montessori school in the next village, which a lot of the 'yummy mummies' swore by, but Vikki had made the decision to keep life as simple as possible. With their hectic lifestyle, and the fact that she couldn't rely on Josh to be around, or more to the point, for the car to be available, she was quite happy for Amy to attend the local nursery.

As the children jostled along happily, Vikki had tears in her eyes, and a huge lump in her throat. This simple life could all change soon. *Please Lord*, she started to pray silently, and then found that she couldn't think of what or how to pray. Being a vicar's wife and on the prayer ministry team, she had prayed for many, many people in dire circumstances; but now it was personal, she found she didn't know what to pray. Her thoughts and concerns were not primarily for her, but for her children. What if it is cancer? How would the little ones handle their mother being poorly? How would Josh cope? *Hell!* she thought, *it just couldn't be.* She didn't have the time to be ill, and anyway, she felt fine. This whole thing was ridiculous, and would all be a storm in a teacup.

Reaching the school, she bent down and gave her children a kiss and cuddle. Finn was not impressed.

'Mum, don't do that here,' he whispered angrily. She laughed at him, and ruffled his hair as he slipped away from her. Daisy and Amy willingly allowed themselves to be hugged and petted. Thank God for little girls, she thought. We can still kiss and cuddle right through to when they are all grown up! Another dark shadow crossed her mind, but she angrily dismissed it. We WILL still cuddle when they are grown up, she shouted at the demons in her mind.

Slipping through the back gate and into the kitchen, Vikki could hear voices.

'Oh, hi, Vikki.' It was Tom Stoppard, one of the churchwardens. 'Alright if I pinch Josh for a bit? I need a hand moving some of the old pews around in the chapel.'

'No, actually, it's not,' replied Vikki. 'We have important family matters to discuss.'

'Well, I ought to just...' said Josh, looking a bit sheepish.

'Goodbye Tom,' dismissed Vikki, and Tom left, with a perplexed glance backwards.

He wasn't used to people saying no to him, especially the young vicar or his wife. He would have to have a word with Reverend Mercer next time, and make sure he explained to his young whippersnapper of a wife that he was there to serve the church first and foremost. Being a vicar wasn't just a nine-to-five job, but a vocation, a calling to God's work, and Tom, as churchwarden, was allowed to dictate just what that task entailed. Honestly, young women today! They really should know their place. He made his way through the churchyard, and bumped into Mrs Barrow, the other churchwarden. At least he felt sure she would agree with him.

'Wow! That was a bit brave of you, Vikks,' said Josh. 'Are you sure you should have spoken to him like that? You know we really shouldn't make enemies of people like Tom and Mrs Barrow. Our life will be much easier if they are on our side.'

'I don't really care whose bloody side they are on,' cried Vikki.

'Please try to curb your language,' sighed Josh, but then he saw the tears running down Vikki's face.

'Hey, babe, what's the matter?'

'I've got to go to the hospital for tests. I found a lump last week,' she sobbed.

'What?! When? Why didn't you tell me?'

'I've tried, honestly I've tried, but you're always too busy, or the children are around. I'm sorry, Josh, I know I should have told you, but I'm telling you now. Please help me out here!'

With that she fell into his arms, and finally faced up to the fear she had been holding in for days.

'What if it's cancer?' she cried.

'Hush, my darling, it won't be. You'll see, it will be okay.'

'But, it might be,' she snivelled, wiping her nose with the back of her hand.

'Come on through to the study,' said Josh. 'Let's talk this through properly. Plus I've got some tissues in there.'

'Oh, yes of course, you're well used to crying damsels in distress aren't you?' laughed Vikki through her tears. 'I never thought I would be on the receiving end of your professional shoulder to cry on.'

'Hey, you. This isn't your problem. This is our problem. We're in this together, remember? I am not your vicar now. I'm your husband. You come first.'

'Well, if I'd have known this was all it takes to get your attention, I would have tried the cancer card earlier!'

This was how Josh and Vikki dealt with most things in life, with a wry and slightly wicked sense of humour. Even though he was a man of God, he was still a funny, caring and deeply loving husband. He felt like he had been dealt a serious blow to his solar plexus, but for now he knew he had to be strong for Vikki. If anything happened to her, he didn't know quite how he would function. She was his world, the mother of his children, and his lifelong companion. How could this be happening?

'I think we should pray for peace and strength right now, don't you?' he suggested, and so they did. They had always been able to pray together, and this was a huge comfort now to Vikki, who just hadn't been able to find the words, or the faith, to pray on her own. Her husband was her strength, and she was his. Theirs was a truly modern, equal partnership, even though at times his attention was taken by the needs of a busy parish. The bottom line was that Vikki came first in his life, and as they prayed he asked for forgiveness for letting church business take priority over family.

They sat together in silence for maybe ten minutes, drawing strength from each other, and coming to terms with the elephant in the room.

Vikki was the first to move. Everything felt more positive now that she had shared her burden with Josh.

'Come on,' she said as she heaved him out of the chair. 'I know you've got plenty of work to do, and it won't get done with you lazing around like this.'

Josh reluctantly agreed. The week beckoned, and although his life had suddenly been brought to an abrupt halt, it didn't alter the fact that parish life continued outside of these four walls.

'Don't say anything to anyone yet, will you?' said Vikki. 'Kate knows, but that's all. And I don't want the children to get wind of anything either. Hopefully it will all be a storm in a teacup and we can get back to normal without them ever knowing.'

As Josh went off to the church, Vikki made the other call that she knew she should have made last week; to Sam. Sure enough, her twin brother went off at the deep end. As is often the case with twins, they had developed a sixth sense about each other, and Sam had been feeling worried about his sister over the weekend. Now he knew why. If only he had acted on his instincts and given her a ring. To think that she had been dealing with this on her own! They arranged for him to come over at the weekend. She would know more on Friday when she went for her appointment, and it would be good to have him around.

Although it was still early September, there was a biting autumnal wind, so Vikki dug out her coat, and walked over to the parish office. She felt so much better now that she had finally told Josh, and she wanted to chat to Kate.

She nodded hello to Maud, who was waiting at the door like a vicious Rottweiler, and went through to the office. Her friend was sitting at her desk, buried under what looked like a mountain of paperwork, but that did not prevent her from getting up and giving Vikki a big hug.

'Have you told him?' was her first question, and Vikki nodded.

'Thank goodness for that,' said Kate. 'Now I've checked his diary for Friday, and shuffled a few things around, so he will be free to go with you. Do you want me to be on standby to pick up the kids if the appointment overruns?'

'Trust you to think of everything. Thank you so much, Kate. But no, the kids are fine, thanks. Daisy has ballet after school, and she is going home with her friend Freya; Finn is going straight on to youth group with Edward, and Amy is going to play princesses with the twins! You know how much she loves Bella and Bethany. So that's everything taken care of. I just wish I didn't have to go. You know I keep on feeling the lump, and wishing it would magically disappear under my fingertips. But of course it doesn't.'

'I can't imagine how you are coping, Vikki,' Kate said. 'I think I would just fall apart. You are so strong.'

'Oh, but I'm not!' cried Vikki, 'I just have to hold it together, 'cause of the kids. And if they aren't around, then there is always some parishioner who is. The time I have on my own is so rare, and when I do have time, I am having to plan meals, or washing or some other mundane task. I guess it's good that I don't have too much time to think about it, or I would go stir crazy. Oh, by the way, Sam is coming at the weekend. I would really love it if you could come over for supper.'

'Really?' asked Kate. 'Do you think that's a good idea?' The atmosphere between Sam and Kate hadn't improved any with time. They just seemed to rub each other up the wrong way.

He was so fiercely protective of his twin sister, and still viewed Kate as part of the 'wicked women' group that made life so difficult for Vikki.

'Really,' insisted Vikki. 'You are the most important people in my life, and I would really appreciate it if you were there, either to commiserate or celebrate. Do you think you two could try and get along, please?'

Kate realised how vulnerable her friend was feeling. She really must make more of an effort to be friendly with her brother.

'Okay, I'll be there. Can I bring anything?'

'A bottle of your finest Pinot would be good,' joked Vikki. 'Maybe if I get you two drunk, you might be more appealing to one another.'

'I think it might take more than one bottle to do that!' laughed Kate.

As Vikki walked home, she felt more positive than she had felt for days. She was so blessed; a good marriage, healthy kids, good friends and a loving brother. She would get through this, and all would be well.

Chapter 6

The day of the PCC dawned, and Kate woke with a feeling of dread. She knew that a lot of her proposals were going to be met with hostility. When she thought of some of the deals she had made in the City, this should be a piece of cake, but long-term parishioners would not welcome the changes she was about to enforce on the church. And they had to be made; the church was not immune from the law, and child protection was an important issue. Of course, they would take it as a personal slight on their character. She knew that already. How was she to persuade some of the old ladies that ran the crèche and the Sunday schools to apply for CRB clearance? And she had to explain that the cost of the Christian Copyright licence had to be made a priority.

She walked into the hall and surveyed the members seated around the room. Dear Bill was there already, and he gave her an encouraging smile. He even winked at her, as Mrs Brown-hyphen-Smith walked in, her evil eyes searching out Kate. She seated herself directly opposite Kate, and next to her cronies, Tom Stoppard and Mrs Barrow. *See no evil, hear no evil, speak no evil!* thought Kate to herself, as she looked at the troop of evil monkeys. George Pinker entered the room and looked around, and when he saw Kate, he grinned leeringly at her. He couldn't help himself; he was an out and out creep, and he honestly thought that he was God's gift to young women. Yuck!

Betty Coates arrived and whispered slyly into Mrs Barrow's ear, with a glance at Kate. Last to enter was Josh, and Kate was shocked to see how haggard he looked. He had obviously taken Vikki's news quite badly, and could really do without this battlefield tonight. She shot up an arrow prayer that somehow the agenda would go more smoothly than she was expecting. Fat chance!

The meeting was called to order and opened with prayer. Strange, thought Kate to herself, how some of these people can piously pray, and then go on to be so evil in their attitudes. It started off with the usual fabric committee queries; about loose tiles and vandalism. Then there were the Harvest celebrations to discuss, and some further discussion about the graveyard.

Any other business came all too rapidly for Kate, and her heart was beating far too fast. But then she just reverted to her usual trick of imagining fearsome men in their underwear, and a huge grin broke out on her face, as she thought of Mrs Barrow's enormous knickers!

'Do you want to share the joke with the rest of us, Ms Hartwood?' asked Mrs Barrow.

'Er, no, I was just er, it was nothing,' she stuttered, mad with herself for being caught out. *Be sensible*, she reprimanded herself. *You've got a difficult twenty minutes coming up.*

Sure enough, her thoughts and feelings on child protection issues, the CRB checks, and the CCL went down like a lead balloon, but she maintained her professionalism, and insisted that it was not only the correct thing to do, but the church would be breaking the law to continue as it was now that these matters had been brought to their attention. She presented it not as an option to be voted for; rather as rules to be enforced. Follow that, she thought to herself. In the silence that followed, Kate was sure that they must all be able to hear her heart beating, it was so loud.

As Josh stood up to close the meeting Mrs Coates said that they had another item to bring to the committee. 'A group of long-standing members of St John's have been giving the matter some thought, and they feel that the role of administrator should be held by someone with gravitas. A man, perhaps, of some years standing? Someone who knows the church, and the village well. Not that they wished Ms Hartwood any ill, or to leave her without a job. Perhaps she would like to be in charge of keeping the porch tidy? Or of putting flowers in the lobby? That would be nice, wouldn't it, and very suitable for a *young newcomer*. What did the committee think?' She peered over the top of her glasses, grinning malevolently.

Suddenly there was a loud crash, as Josh stood up and pushed his chair back so forcefully it fell backwards. Angry and red-faced, he banged his fist on the table. There were startled faces all around.

'This has gone far enough!' he shouted. 'Kate is doing a sterling job, and has made my life so much easier. This has to be a church fit for the twenty-first century, not the nineteenth century, and if anyone here does not wish to be part of such a church, then please feel free to go now!'

There was silence... some shuffling of feet and of papers... then a quiet voice said 'Hear, Hear.'

It was Bill, bless him. Then another voice echoed, this time from Celia, and then another, and another, as the triplets raised their timid voices to stand up for Kate. She felt close to tears at this kind show of support, and knew that, although she had enemies in the church, she also had some wonderful friends.

'Well, I think that pretty much concludes the meeting tonight,' said Josh. 'I would like to thank Kate for bringing these important topics to our attention, and now I feel we should allow her to get on with her job. Thank you.'

He pushed back his chair abruptly once more, and marched out of the hall.

Everyone stared in shock; usually the vicar would stay and share a cup of tea, and listen to the various viewpoints of the committee, but Kate alone knew that he needed to get back for his wife. She reached out and grabbed Bill's hand as a way of saying thank you. She didn't trust her voice, and knew if she opened her mouth, she would probably cry.

'Will you need me to write you out some cheques?' he asked her.

'Thank you, Bill. I will let you know when the invoices come in, once I know how many people we need to get registered for CRB checks. The CCL will need to be done with a direct debit, so I will let you have the details of that. Can I come round and see you and Harold later on in the week, maybe?'

'Of course, my dear. You know that you are always welcome. We don't get many visitors, but attractive young ladies are always the most appreciated!'

It was a very well kept secret, known by none except Josh and Kate, that Bill and Harold were gay. Harold had once been married, long ago, but Bill had looked after his mother until her death about fifteen years ago, when it had seemed sensible for Harold to move in 'as a lodger'. They were both very private men, and no one would ever have suspected a thing. Bill had told Kate, during one of their unexpectedly close moments, how difficult it had been for him when he was in the Army, when he had realised he was not like the other men. He had invented a girlfriend, just to protect himself, for he had seen the attitude of soldiers when they talked of 'queers'.

How this dear man had survived, she just couldn't imagine. He was so gentle, so kind, and she would trust her very life to him, and she considered it a great honour that he had confided in her. He had also looked to Josh for help and guidance, but Bill knew that, although it was a sin, he could not change his ways, and he loved Harold with a passion. Harold was quite frail, now in his eighties, and Josh felt that the kindest thing he could do as a priest was to give these two old gentlemen the respect they deserved, and to protect their secret from the eyes of the church. It could sometimes be a very cruel world, even though it masqueraded as a caring environment. Josh's viewpoint was always, '*what would Jesus do*?' and he knew in his heart that Jesus would love these men, as indeed they loved Jesus.

Kate headed for home along the dark alley, too weary even to be fearful, as she sometimes could be. Even in a small Hampshire village like Ashton Kirby, one had to be alert to danger. She opened the door and threw down her keys, grateful to be on her own in her little cottage. Her mind was racing, and she knew it was going to be difficult to sleep tonight. The incident at the PCC meeting seemed inconsequential when she thought of what poor Vikki must be going through. She just kept praying and praying that it would be nothing. Kate knew the statistics; most breast lumps were benign. And especially given her age, it probably wouldn't be cancer. But what if it was? She couldn't even go there in her mind. Her friendship with Vikki was one of the best things that had ever happened to her. Josh and Vikki were such genuine people. Having grown up in the kind of church that frowned upon enjoyment of any kind, she was so grateful to this happy couple who had transformed the church into a lively, interesting place that welcomed people from all kinds of backgrounds. The church was becoming a beacon in the village. She could hear the talk when she was out and about. Everyone wanted to get involved. The children had somewhere to go after school. The youth had a meeting place instead of hanging around in bus stops causing trouble. The elderly felt cared for. There was something for everyone. She had even heard the term 'exciting' used when people spoke about coming to church! Surely this would surprise even the hardiest atheist. She felt so grateful to be part of this wonderful community, even if it did have one or two diehard pain-in-the-neck miseries!

She yawned and made her way upstairs. Taking a face wipe out of the pack, she took her makeup off, all the while praying for her friends. She cleaned her teeth and also prayed for young Sophie. She lay down, tucking the pillows under her neck, and within minutes, surprisingly, she was asleep.

Sitting in a corridor in Queen Anne's hospital, Josh and Vikki held hands and talked. They spoke of their children, of parish life, of their families, and even managed to joke about the situation they now found themselves in.

'What if they can't find anything?' said Vikki.

'Well, that's good, surely?' queried Josh.

'No, I mean, what if I haven't got any boobs?' Vikki said, jokingly.

'You are a total idiot, do you know that?' replied Josh, squeezing her hand.

'Mrs Mercer, please,' a young woman in a white coat called.

Vikki stood, and walked towards the radiographer. 'Gosh, you're tall!' exclaimed the radiographer, looking up at Vikki and smiling. They went in through a door marked X-Ray. 'My name is Helen, and I will be performing your mammogram. Have you had one before?'

'No, I have never had this particular pleasure,' said Vikki. She always turned to light banter when she was nervous. The radiographer recognised this and squeezed her arm reassuringly.

'Okay, if you would strip to the waist for me, while I just set up the machine. Don't worry too much. I'll explain it all as we go along. It will be uncomfortable, but not unbearable. It is also a little awkward getting into the right position, but just relax, and let me guide you. Is there anything you want to ask me?'

'Will you be able to tell me straight away if I have cancer?' asked Vikki.

'No, I'm just the radiographer, and I have to report the findings to the consultant, I'm afraid. I realise you must be anxious, but try and relax and we'll get this bit over and done with as quickly as possible. Now come over here, and stand in front of the machine. Just a bit more forward; that's it. Now turn to me slightly. Just a little more, and keep your arm over to the side. That's it. Now the plates will squash down on your breast, but it will be very quick. That's it. Sorry! I know it's uncomfortable. I'll be as quick as possible.'

After a couple more highly uncomfortable and painful x-rays were taken, Vikki was asked to get dressed and take a seat, but not to go back to the waiting room quite yet. She sat nervously twiddling her thumbs round and round, until the radiographer came out of her office.

'Em, I wonder if you would mind waiting here for a minute longer while I just show these to my colleague?'

'No problem,' replied Vikki, her stomach churning within her. She couldn't read anything on the radiographer's face; she was obviously trained in the *'school of inscrutable facial expressions'*.

Within minutes she had returned, and asked Vikki to follow her down a long corridor, through some double doors, and into a dimly lit small room. How was she ever meant to find her way back to Josh?

'This is Miss Khan, one of our consultant radiographers,' Helen informed her.

'Hello, Mrs Mercer,' greeted the young Asian consultant, holding out her hand to shake.

'Hi, how are you?' asked Vikki. *What am I doing?* she thought. *She's the one supposed to be asking me how I am. I just can't keep my mouth shut when I'm nervous.*

'So when did you first find this lump?'

'Only about a week ago. I was just drying myself after a shower. At first I thought it was nothing, but a friend told me I should get it checked out. I'm sure it is nothing, but my GP insisted I come and have a mammogram. I mean, I'm too young for it to be anything sinister aren't I? Sorry, I tend to ramble a bit when I'm nervous. Sorry, I'm doing it again!'

'There is nothing to apologise for, Mrs Mercer, please. I am glad you agreed to come. Now, we are a bit concerned about this lump, so what I would like to do is to take a look with the ultrasound. You've had one of these before?'

Vikki nodded wordlessly.

'Good. So, what I may do, if it is possible, is to insert a needle into the lump, and draw out a little of the fluid, so we can have a better look. I will inject you with some local anaesthetic, so it shouldn't be too painful.'

Yeah, right! That's what they said about the mammogram, and that blooming hurt! Vikki thought to herself, but she climbed up onto the bed obediently and allowed Miss Khan to coat her breast with cold gel, then watched as she applied the steel wand over her body. She didn't mind this too much, but it was when she injected the anaesthetic that she nearly leapt off the bed.

'Ouch!'

'Sorry about that. I am just trying to get a good sample. I think I may also try to have a look at the lymph nodes in your armpit, if that's alright? Same procedure, but hopefully it won't hurt as much.'

'Okay. What is that for, please?'

'We just like to look around to see if there is any risk of cells spreading to the lymph nodes.'

Vikki laid there, her mind racing. Cells? What type of cells? She wished she had paid more attention to her biology classes now. She felt completely ignorant and hadn't got a clue what a lymph node was, when it was at home. She would have to do a bit of Googling when she got back home. Another needle was injected into her underarm; this time it wasn't quite so painful, or maybe she was just getting used to the pain? Her poor boob was going to take some time to recover from all the horrible things it was having done to it.

The procedure was completed and Vikki was handed some paper towels and told to get dressed. Miss Khan promised her that she would be informed of the results as soon as possible.

She touched her shoulder sympathetically and told her to try not to worry too much.

'Should I be worried?' she asked.

'We'll know more once we have the results of the biopsy. Have you got someone with you today?'

'Yes, but I can't remember where I left him!'

The consultant smiled and promised her that an assistant would walk her back to the waiting room.

As she followed the young man back down the endless maze of corridors, her mind was racing. How on earth was she going to cope with the wait? She was so ignorant! For some stupid reason she thought she was going to find out if it was cancer or not today, but she was no wiser than when she first arrived. If only she had done a little research, or asked Ellie a few more questions. But she had been in a state of shock, and would not have known what to ask. One look at Josh's face, and she realised that he was expecting answers today, too.

'It was just a load of tests. I don't know anything, love. I'm sorry.'

'Come here and give me a hug,' Josh said. 'It's going to be alright, you'll see. I've been sitting here praying my socks off.'

She looked down at his feet.

'Well, you couldn't have been praying hard enough, because they're still on your feet!'

'What am I going to do with you?' he grinned as they walked off, hand in hand. A young vicar and his young wife. The future uncertain.

Chapter 7

Kate had been digging through some papers in her cottage on Saturday. She was determined to try to find out more about her aunt and why her mother and father hated her so much. Kate had always found her to be such a lovely and kind, slightly wacky lady. She must have been a real laugh when she was a young woman. The photos she had sifted through showed her with long flowing hair, and colourful, hippy kaftans. Valerie resembled a younger, happier version of her own mother, even though she was four years older. But that was where any resemblance ended. Valerie had spent her life travelling, and living in communes before settling in this lovely village of Ashton Kirby with her partner, Ray. They never married, which caused Valerie's parents great anguish, but as they had refused to have anything to do with her for years, Valerie never allowed this to bother her too much. Ray had died just five years after they had settled in the village together, and Valerie lived the rest of her life alone. It was all quite sad really. Kate and Melanie had both kept in touch with her throughout their teenage years, but as Melanie had spiralled down into her substance-fuelled existence, she had lost contact. But Kate had loved to spend time with her aunt, hearing tales of her exotic travels. However, she had always seemed a little reluctant to talk about her family. Obviously their lifestyles were so extremely disparate, but surely whatever had passed between them couldn't have been that bad?

The boxes of photos hidden inside the large old chest were just a jumble. Kate started to sort them into some kind of order, but many of them had no dates on them. She tried to judge the time-frame by the fashion, and found she was totally engrossed in the task.

Suddenly, she looked at the clock. Damn! She was supposed to be at Josh and Vikki's for supper ten minutes ago! Jumping up, she quickly pulled a brush through her hair, and looked briefly in the mirror. Saturday jeans and a tee shirt would have to do. She had no time to change. She opened the cupboard tucked under the stairway and looked into her 'cellar'. Mmmm, two bottles of red, and one warm bottle of white. It would have to be the red. She glanced at the label, and hoped against hope it wasn't a bottle that Josh had brought to hers when they came to supper.

She pressed in her alarm code, and waited for the bleep. Why did it seem to take so long when you were in a hurry? No! It hadn't taken. She must have keyed it in wrong. She tried again, impatiently, and this time was rewarded by the long tone indicating that the alarm was now set. She pulled her bike out from under its cover, and cycled off. As she was peddling furiously, she suddenly remembered that she hadn't got her lights with her. Where had the time gone this afternoon? She would have to ask Josh to run her home, and leave the bike at the vicarage. She cursed herself for being so disorganised. This was so out of character for her. It must be the influence of the ghost of Auntie Val!

The vicarage door was open, so she went through and called out. Vikki stepped through from the kitchen, and greeted her friend with a warm hug.

'I was just getting a little worried. Is there a problem?'

'I am so sorry,' said Kate, 'I was going through some of Val's photos, and the time got away from me.'

'That's okay. You're not that late, it's just so unusual for you! It's good to know that you're human! Come on through, the children are still up, I'm afraid. They wouldn't go to bed until they had seen their favourite administrator.'

They walked into the inferno that was the family kitchen. The children were all in their night clothes, and there appeared to be far more than just three of them. How did they have so much energy at this time of night?

'Hi, Kate,' they shouted in chorus, and then they peeled away from the table as one, and threw themselves at her waist, her legs, her arms, indeed any part of her they could reach. She was gripped by a surge of love so strong it almost brought tears to her eyes.

'Hi, you lot,' she replied. 'Hi, Josh, sorry I'm late. Oh, hi, Sam. How are you?'

'Starving, actually, how are you?' he replied acerbically. 'If we're not being interrupted by parishioners, we're being held up by them.'

'Now that's not fair,' scolded Vikki. 'Kate is never, ever late for anything. And she's not a parishioner. She's my friend, how many times do I have to tell you?'

'Pardon me,' replied Sam sardonically, and turned to Josh to continue his conversation, effectively blocking Kate out.

That man is so rude, thought Kate. How could he possibly be related to her, let alone be Vikki's twin? She must have got all the kind genes, and he had been left with the psychopathic ones.

She squeezed into a chair next to Finn, and Amy leapt up onto her lap, and wrapped her arms around Kate's neck.

'You lot have ten minutes,' said Vikki, as she bent down to look into the oven. 'Then it's up those stairs, and straight to bed.'

'Can Kate read me a bedtime story, please?' yelled Daisy.

'You're joking, young lady! You've just had about one hundred stories read to you by Uncle Sam. You do try it on.'

'But...'

'No buts, and don't push your luck, or your ten minutes will become two. Now be quiet and let the adults talk.'

Kate grinned at the kids. She often felt she was more on their side than the adults. Goodness, if she had children, she would be a useless mother. She would spoil them rotten, and never ever make them go to bed. She just loved their company, and their unconditional love.

She also felt far more comfortable when they were there if Sam was around. The tangible dislike that emanated from him was very hard to deal with. She felt that whatever she said, whatever she did, he disagreed with. It was almost as if he were jealous of her relationship with Vikki, and maybe he was. When she thought of this, it helped her put his attitude into perspective. I must try to be more amiable, thought Kate, always the pacifist.

'When did you get here then, Sam?' she asked him cordially.

'Long before you did,' he retorted.

'Well, yes, and I have already apologised for that.' Hell, this man truly was despicable.

'Actually, I was delving into the history of Wisteria cottage. My aunt lived there before me. Have you ever been there?' She tried again.

'No.'

'Well, perhaps Vikki could bring you over some time,' she continued. 'It is a lovely old cottage. Almost as if it's caught up in the wrong century.'

She sat there waiting for some kind of response, but of course, he wasn't going to join in the polite return of conversation.

'It is a lovely cottage, and Kate has made it into a really welcoming home,' said Vikki.

Kate smiled gratefully at her friend, and the two of them continued their conversation, effectively blocking Sam out. Well, that was his own stupid fault, she thought. He can't say I didn't try.

Once the children were bundled up the stairs, and the wine had been poured, Vikki brought a plate of heavenly garlic bread to the table, and they all fell upon it hungrily. As their appetites were satiated, and the hunger diminished, the conversation turned to Vikki's health.

They were all a little disappointed that she had no real idea still what the outcome would be. Kate watched as Sam quizzed his twin. His face was filled with concern, and she couldn't help but feel sorry for him. He had such a lovely relationship with his sister, and it must be so hard for him to watch her go through such a tough situation. He had even offered to pay for her to go privately, but Vikki had assured him that it wouldn't be any quicker. Indeed, she was shocked by the speed of things, and felt sure that her friend and GP Ellie Smith probably had a hand in this.

As the evening progressed, the atmosphere grew more relaxed and friendly, and Kate felt that she had finally made a little ground in breaking down Sam's hostility. They even managed to share the odd joke and smile. There was some hope then. It mattered to her greatly, as she was spending more and more time with this wonderful family, and she really couldn't bear to have anything upsetting Vikki, especially with everything she was going through. It was important that they all pulled together to make this as easy as they could for her.

At the end of the evening, they had all had a little too much to drink, and were all feeling a little fuzzy round the edges. Through her alcoholic fog, Kate suddenly remembered that she had no lights on her bike. *Damn!* she thought. And Josh wouldn't be able to drive her home either, as he too had been drinking.

As she wrapped her coat around her shoulders, she wondered if she should try and be brave, and walk home on her own in the dark.

'Sam will walk you home,' stated Vikki, breaking into Kate's thoughts.

'Oh no, that's fine,' stuttered Kate. 'I have my bike with me.'

'Yes, and Sam has already seen that you haven't got your lights on,' grinned Vikki. 'Bad luck! You're not walking home on your own at this time of night and that's the end of it. Josh is going to clear up this mess, seeing as I did all the cooking. I don't care if he's got a sermon to preach tomorrow morning. I'm going to bed, and that's the end of it. Give me a hug, my friend, and no more arguing.'

Trust that blooming man to have spotted I haven't got any lights, thought Kate. *What is he, some kind of policeman?*

The two friends said goodnight, and Kate gave Josh a hug, looking mournfully at the pile of washing up he had to do.

'Night night, Kate, see you bright and early tomorrow,' he said, as he tied on his apron.

Sam was pulling on a big woolly jumper, and Kate couldn't help but think how fit he was. How come he was still single?

'Come on then,' he said grumpily, 'I'm tired and I've got to walk back yet.'

That's why he's still single then, she thought, *he's a grumpy old misery!*

They walked along, with a wide distance between them. The graveyard had never felt so cold and unwelcoming. Kate thought she would have been more comfortable with the ghosts than with this man for company.

They quickly reached the cottage, and Kate smiled and said her thanks. Sam had been silent throughout the walk, but finally he turned sullenly to her and grunted goodnight. Without warning, he bent towards her, and kissed her, before walking away into the night.

Her cheek felt as if it had been branded, and she stood there for some minutes, shocked and stunned. Had that really happened? Why had it left her so shaken? She pinned in her security code, and unlocked the door, her fingers still touching her burning cheek. That man confused her.

Chapter 8

Life in the office had settled down to a basic daily routine. It was a mixture of joy and irritation. Some folks loved her, others hated her, or rather, hated the position she held, but Kate tried not to irritate the opposition too much. This could be hard at times, but she kept her head down and carried on working. There was always plenty to do, that was for sure. On a Monday morning, she normally had a bunch of the young mums come by, as they had their toddler group in the youth hut. She also had to distribute the various funds from the weddings, baptisms and funerals. Bell ringers had to be paid, as did the organist, the choir members, and the flower arrangers. There were always queries arising from the Sunday services the day before. These were normally petty problems, but seemed to take the most time to sort out.

Kate was trying to educate the congregation to allow her a time of contemplative worship during the Sunday services, and to deal with administrative issues during office hours, but it wasn't working! As soon as she bowed her head to pray when she arrived in the church, there would be a tap on her shoulder.

'Can I give you the ticket money for the ladies' lunch?'

'Have you got the flower rota ready yet?'

'When can I arrange to see you about the cleaning rota?'

As each person came up, Kate would politely suggest contacting her about it in the morning. She had even tried to put something in the parish newsletter, but they seemed to have developed word blindness. Maybe she would have to ask Josh to make an announcement at the start of the service for a few consecutive weeks.

But Kate was reluctant to come down too heavily on people. She had been through so much misery and hard-hearted discipline in the Truth Brethren church, and she loved the refreshing and friendly atmosphere here at St John's.

She had spoken to her parents over the weekend, and honestly, they sounded so unhappy. Her sister had disappeared and they hadn't a clue where she had gone. This often happened when she went off on a drink or drugs bender. Kate was so cross with Melanie, but what could she do? She knew that she was only reacting to the strict upbringing they had both suffered from. But whereas it had made Kate want to have a decent life away from the church, it seemed that Mel had gone so far off the rails, she couldn't find a way back. Kate had even offered to have her sister to stay for a while at the cottage, but Mel wasn't interested. It was too far from all her drug contacts, that was the problem. Her mum and dad were really struggling with her, and this was, of course, made worse by the Brethren. Such behaviour was obviously frowned upon, and Gillian and Jim were held to account every week, and punished by the elders who hauled them up to the front, where they were made to repent of their poor parenting. The church prayed constantly for her sister, as if by their miserable petitions, they could change Mel's attitude, and she would repent and return to the fold. Some hope!

Kate had repeatedly asked her parents over for the weekend, so that they could attend St John's, and see how much love could be found in a church, rather than the constant haranguing and punishment at the Brethren. But they would not come anywhere near Ashton Kirby, as it was tainted by Valerie's sinful relationship. They could not believe that she had chosen to live in sin. Kate sometimes felt that she would have been more easily forgiven if Val had murdered someone! What bigoted people her parents were. She hated going home; it felt so claustrophobic and restricted. She felt that whatever she said was wrong.

Kate returned her thoughts to the here and now, and settled down to the tasks she had outlined on her to-do list. She pulled out the cash box, and started to divide up the 'spoils' from the weekend weddings. Maud was out the front viciously sweeping up the confetti. If it was up to her, she would ban confetti! Then again, if it was up to Maud, she would probably ban weddings altogether. She hated anything that made people happy. In fact, the only time Kate saw her anywhere near happy, was when a funeral was being held in the church. She loved the solemnity of such services! Miserable old boot!

As if her thoughts had become reality, Maud was suddenly standing in front of Kate.

'I said, did you want a coffee?'

For some strange reason, Maud had accepted Kate's presence in the church with alarming approval. She kept her fed and watered with coffee and doughnuts, from the moment she stepped into the church building. The trouble was, Kate wasn't used to the real, strong coffee that Maud proffered her, and by midday she was usually feeling quite shaky from all the caffeine she had consumed. She was also not used to so many sticky, sugary doughnuts, but when she tried to decline the kind offerings, Maud told her she was far too thin, and they would do her good. Talk about pot, kettle, black! Maud had the build of a stick insect!

'Sorry, I was miles away,' said Kate. 'Thank you, that would be lovely.'

She would accept the first cup of coffee, and after that, suggest that she made Maud a cup. This way, she could help herself to a camomile tea. She had left the box of herbal tea bags in the kitchen, but Maud refused to use them.

Sure enough, Maud returned with a large, sticky doughnut on a plate, complete with a paper napkin.

'Thank you so much, I will eat it later if that's alright with you?'

'Look at you,' muttered Maud, 'reckon you've got that eating disease, the size of you.'

'No, really, I only had breakfast a little while ago,' retorted Kate, but Maud had already slunk away, still muttering on about 'bilirubinia' and 'anoxia.'

The phone rang, and Kate picked up the receiver, licking her sticky fingers as she answered, 'Parish office, Kate Hartwood speaking.'

It was Ellie Smith.

'Kate, is there any chance we could all get together sometime next week? You, me and Vikki?'

'Sure,' Kate replied. 'What day is good for you?'

'Well, I think Vikki will have had her appointment through by now, and it will be good for us to support her. So, perhaps Monday evening? I know Josh has a meeting that evening, so we could arrange to go over there, and take some food, so she doesn't have to do anything. I just wanted to catch you before you get too booked up, 'cause I know how busy you are.'

'Monday evening will be fine. I'll arrange it with Vikki, shall I? I know she'll appreciate it, Ellie. Thanks for that. We'll probably see you over the weekend, anyway.'

'No, that's the problem. I'm off for a few days; flying over to see my parents. Bad timing, I know, but it's been planned for some time, so I wanted to arrange something now. Whatever the outcome, she will probably want to talk it through, and I know Josh isn't always able to give her his time and attention!'

'It's a date then, I look forward to seeing you next week. Bye for now.'

As Kate put the phone down, she realised she had left jammy fingerprints on the handset. But her mind was only partly on the sticky implement. She realised that this time next week, her dear friend would know her fate, one way or the other. 'Oh Lord,' she prayed. 'Please, please, PLEASE let it be benign.' She really didn't feel at all like eating the wretched doughnut now, so she wrapped it in a tissue, and placed it in her bag. She couldn't throw it away in the bin; Maud would find it and rail at her about waste.

Chapter 9

The alarm rang and woke Kate out of a very long, complicated dream. She reached out her hand to press the off button, but the noise continued. Then she realised it was her phone. What on earth was the time? It was just seven a.m. Kate looked at the screen and answered the call.

'Hi, Kate. Sorry to call you so early. Were you asleep?'

'No, of course not,' she replied, putting her hand over the phone to hide her yawn.

'I've got a letter from the hospital. They want to see me on Friday. Friday! Why that soon? Oh, I just know it's going to be bad news! What am I going to do? What am I going to say to the children?'

'Hang on a mo'; you don't know anything for certain yet.' But Kate had a sinking feeling in the pit of her stomach. Ellie had already given her an indication that things were not good.

'How am I going to cope until Friday? I'm a nervous wreck already, and I only got the letter ten minutes ago. I've got to phone them to let them know I can make it. It's such short notice. Oh, Kate,' she wailed, 'please help me!'

'Okay, I'm coming over now,' said Kate, climbing out of bed and pulling on her jeans. 'I don't need to open the office until a bit later. I'll pop a notice on the door on my way over to you.'

'Are you sure? I would be so grateful. The trouble is Josh has gone off early to a deanery conference. I don't know how to cope with this and the kids.'

'Put the phone down, and I'll be there in a flash.'

The children were so excited to have Kate at the breakfast table when they came downstairs. Thank goodness she had put her jeans on, and not her work clothes! As Amy climbed on to her lap, with a sticky piece of chocolate spread on toast, Kate felt the now familiar pang of intense love for this beautiful child. Her fine blond hair stuck out at all angles; the children called it 'bed head'. She smoothed it down with her palm, and Amy pushed deeper into her lap. The child was still sleepy and not yet her normal bouncy self, but give it ten minutes and she would be firing on all cylinders. Even Finn and Daisy were far more subdued than she had ever seen them before. It must be a morning thing, she thought.

Vikki looked like a small animal caught in headlights. The fear was tangible. Kate reached out and held her hand tightly.

'Hi, my friend,' she whispered. 'Hang on in there. We'll get this lot sorted and then sit down with a nice strong cup of coffee.'

'Thank you.' Vikki replied. 'Thank you so much.'

The hour flew by in a cloud of children, clothes, toothbrushes and school bags, but eventually they managed to get them all out and to school on time.

'Can Auntie Kate come by every morning?' asked Daisy. 'It's the only time I've ever been first at school.'

'Don't push your luck, young lady,' said Vikki. *Am I really that disorganised on my own*? she wondered.

As they walked back to the vicarage, the two friends were silent, both caught in their own thoughts.

'So, Josh doesn't know you have the appointment date through, then?'

'No, he went off really early this morning, as he had to catch a train from Basingstoke. Then he's away for three days. What bad timing!'

'Never mind. How about if I come and stay? It's no trouble for me, and it's just as near for work. Nearer, even! It's not like I've got anyone at home, is it?'

'Wow! The kids will go mad! They will never let you leave, you know that don't you? They will probably suggest Josh move into your house, and you move in here permanently! Seriously, would you really stay for a few days?'

'No problem. So let's get this call made to confirm you can make the appointment. Have you checked Josh's diary yet, to make sure he's free? If not, I can check, and ensure he has no appointments. Is it morning or afternoon?'

'It's early Friday, thank goodness. At least I don't have to wait all day.'

'Oh, by the way,' Kate remembered. 'Ellie suggested we do a *girls night in* on the following Monday? We're bringing the food and drink, so you don't have to go to any bother.'

'That will be perfect,' said Vikki. 'I would love to have the chance to discuss things with Ellie. I know I could make an appointment to see her, but that's only a ten minute session. She will know all the answers to any questions I have, won't she?' She looked to Kate with an air of desperation.

'She may be your doctor, but she's also your friend,' said Kate, 'and I'm sure she will be a great help. Do you think I could jump in your shower? I've brought some clothes over with me, and I had better get back to work, or the old bats will have me fired. And I'd better not go to the office looking like this, had I?'

Vikki looked at Kate and they both collapsed laughing. She had chocolate fingerprints all across her tee shirt and jeans, and even had toast in her hair.

'What is it with you and my kids?' laughed Vikki. 'One look at you, and they go wild. They never do it with anyone else; well, with the exception of Sam.'

Kate bit her tongue, as she wondered how that crabby man ever got *'down and dirty'* with the children. Vikki obviously saw a different side to her brother than the one he showed to her, that was for sure. Without thinking, she found her hand going to her cheek, remembering how he had kissed her briefly. She shuddered involuntarily. Now what was all that about?

Before opening the office, Kate set off to the undertakers, to collect money from the two funerals that had taken place last week. Old Rob Bolton, the undertaker, was a lovely man, but she did have to chase him for their cash. When she opened the door, he greeted her with a wide smile. It was quite funny to see him smile, because she was so used to him looking so solemn; for the punters of course.

'It's pay up time, Rob,' she joked, 'or I come and take the coffins!'

'Not again!' he laughed. 'I always seem to be giving you money. Are you trying to fleece an honest undertaker?'

'Now you and I know there is no such thing.'

He pulled open his drawer, and she was amazed yet again at the mess he seemed to keep his finances in. She just hoped he wasn't as disorganised when it came to his customers. It must be a funny business, always dealing with the bereaved, but he had a really lovely, kind and caring attitude, and was always the perfect gentleman. His son, who was also called Robert, was getting more involved in the day-to-day business management. Rob was probably going to have to retire in a few years time, and it was nice to think the firm was going to continue in the family. She looked around at the sombre surroundings and shuddered. Thankfully she only had to come here with her business hat on, and never for personal reasons, and she hoped that it would stay that way.

She headed back to the church office to find Bill Holmes waiting at the door.

'Oh no! I forgot! We have a date, don't we?'

'Don't panic,' said Bill. 'I've only been here a few minutes. I was just admiring the flowers. Did you put the pots here?'

'Yes, I had a few left over from when I was doing the garden outside my cottage. I thought it would be nice to dress up the entrance to the office a bit. Make it a little more welcoming, you know? Try and redress the unwelcome image Maud gives!'

'Well, I have to say that I haven't stood out here before, and it is very friendly. Especially with that little sign you've put above the door, *'Welcome, Jesus Loves You'*. Very nice indeed. It's so typical of you, Kate. You have made such a difference to this church; you do realise that, don't you?'

'Well. I am trying,' she said, 'but thank you for your kind words. Now come on in. I might even be able to rustle up a cup of coffee. It's getting a bit chilly in the mornings now, isn't it?'

As they settled themselves in the now cosy little office, Bill put his ever present wicker basket down on the seat beside him.

Kate's former boss Donald had finally forgiven her for leaving, and had been supplying her with second-hand office goods, much to her delight and amazement. It made such a difference to have decent chairs and a proper desk to work on. She even had some fairly modern filing cabinets now. The churchwardens had raised their eyebrows when they saw the transformed office, but were made to eat their bitter words when she told them that it was costing the church absolutely nothing. They would have to look for something else to moan about!

'I was wondering if you would like to help me find a house for the new curate?' asked Bill. 'We have a small budget, and I haven't looked at house prices for many, many years, so I have no idea what sort of property we will be able to afford.'

'House-hunting. What fun!' she exclaimed. 'Of course I'll help. Do you want me to start looking at some properties online?'

'Can you do that?'

'Oh yes, you just put in what kind of price you want, here, do you see? Then which area, how many bedrooms, etc. And voilá!'

'That's amazing! There are quite a few around Ashton Kirby, aren't there?'

'I'll print off this list and then we can contact the estate agents about the ones we wish to view. I guess it would be sensible if we can get one that is fairly near the church, preferably. We don't know if the new chap has a family, or if he can drive or anything yet, do we?'

'I think we will be interviewing shortly, so perhaps we had better wait until then,' said Bill, 'but I would really value someone else's expertise.'

'Well, I wouldn't call myself an expert, but I have acquired a house recently, so that makes me more of an expert than you, Bill!'

'Now don't get cheeky, young lady,' he laughed, just as the door to the office opened. Maud entered, with a scowl on her face.

'Could you two keep the noise down,' she hissed. 'This is a place of worship.' And then she left as rapidly as she had arrived.

Bill and Kate giggled like two naughty school children.

'I don't know how you work here with her,' he said.

'Oh, she's alright,' said Kate. 'She seems to like me, most of the time, so I think I'm quite lucky. If she doesn't like you, then woe betide.'

'I know,' he said, darkly. 'She doesn't like me.'

'How can anyone not like you?'

'I'm afraid that I am not to everyone's taste,' replied Bill. 'I rather think she knows more than she lets on.'

Kate knew that Bill was referring to his homosexuality. She, Josh and Vikki were the only people Bill had told, and that was how he wanted it kept. But there were bound to be people who might wonder at Bill and Harold's living arrangements. It must be so tough for the old gentlemen.

Bill and Kate stopped to listen to the sound of laughter emanating from within the church. The laughter got nearer, and then the door burst open and three, smiling young women entered.

'Now what's all this joviality?' asked Kate, as Sophie came round the side of the desk to give her a hug.

'Rosie was just telling me about her daughter, Ella. Apparently, she poked a lolly stick up Maud's backside as she went past! She was furious! Can you imagine?'

And the girls fell about laughing again.

'But if that wasn't bad enough,' said Rosie, 'when Maud turned to see who had poked her, Ella stuck her tongue out and said "I don't like you." I was mortified!'

'She deserved it,' said Sophie. 'Why is she so horrid? How can she claim to be a Christian and act like that? She's the sort of person that turns people off coming to church. I know before I met you lot, I just thought everyone in church was like her.'

This really upset Kate. It was the truth though, and something she would have to bring up with Josh at the next staff meeting. Maud was sixty five now, so officially she should have retired, but each time they suggested it, she informed them that she would never be too old to serve her God. But maybe her God wasn't the same God they were trying to raise the profile of in the village? Her God had all the same characteristics of the God her parents seemed so afraid of, and that was not good news. It was no wonder the secular world had such a bad opinion of church when Maud was so eager to frighten them all away.

The other two young mothers said goodbye, leaving Sophie in the office.

'Shall I come back later?' she asked. 'You two look busy.'

'Not at all. I think we are all but finished here, my dear,' said Bill.

'I think so,' replied Kate. 'Thank you ever so much, Bill. I will email you when I have further information, and then we can get together again.'

The old man doffed his hat to the two ladies, picked up his basket, and left.

'Ah, he's a lovely old guy, isn't he?'

'He certainly is,' replied Kate. 'They don't make them like him any more, I'm afraid, more's the pity. Anyway, what can I do for you? Oh, I almost forgot. Look what I picked up at the craft market last week!'

She handed Sophie a beautiful set of hand-knitted baby clothes; a little matinee jacket, bootees, and mittens.

'Wow! And they don't make things like this any more either! Thank you so much. You really are too kind to me. Robbie's worried that we're beginning to resemble a charity case.'

'Don't be so daft. I love looking out for bits for you. It's not like I've got children myself, and my sister hasn't got any, so, think of me like a surrogate mum. Although I'm not old enough to be your mum, so don't go spreading it around, or I'll get a bad name! I can't have people thinking I'm older than I am already!'

'Oh, so you're not so worried about being a single mum, then. It's just about being older! I never put you down as vain, Kate. You shock me!'

'Well, that's a first then, isn't it? I'm sure you had me down as a boring 'older' woman.'

'No, I think you're well cool. In fact I wish my mum had been half as kind to me as you are. She was a right old cow.'

'Sophie! You can't say that about your own mother!'

'You don't know my mum, that's all I can say. I tell you, I'm better off without her.'

'Can I... is she, I mean...'

'No, she ain't dead, she just scarpered off when we were little. Me dad had already gone off with his woman, and my mum was always with one bloke or other. Anyway, the last one obviously gave her an ultimatum. Him or us. She chose him,' she said simply.

'Ouch. That must hurt?'

'Do you know, I never really gave it that much thought,' said Sophie. 'I quite liked being in the care home. It wasn't as bad as people think. I always imagined that I was at boarding school, and I had like, really, really rich parents, who worked overseas. Missionaries or something, you know? Like in Mallory Towers.' Kate smiled at the innocence of her young friend, considering all she had been through.

'And I was with my sisters, so they didn't split us up. It was okay.' She shrugged her shoulders, and Kate had the feeling that it probably wasn't okay, but knew it was better not to dig too deep.

'Be having my next scan soon,' Sophie said. 'Look I'm getting quite a bump now. And I felt her kicking! Dead exciting it is. Trouble is every time I try and get Robbie to have a feel, the little devil stops. I think she is going to be a real mummy's girl.'

'Well, I know you're going to be a brilliant mum,' said Kate. 'I am really proud of you, you know that?'

Sophie had been going to all her checkups, and attending parenting classes. She seemed determined to do the very best for this baby, and now Kate knew a little of her past, she could see why. It was strange, really. Your upbringing could push you one way or the other. You either became like the bad parent, or you went out of your way to become the best parent you could possibly be. It was also good that Sophie had found her niche in the church family, and now had so many good friends. The other mums took great care of her. It was almost as if anyone who came into contact with Sophie had the urge to mother her. She looked so young and fragile, but Kate knew that she had a core of steel.

'Anyway, I wanted to book a place at the Women's Quiet Day on Saturday.'

'Are you sure? Can you keep quiet?' laughed Kate.

'Hey, who taught you to be so lippy? I reckon it will be cool, sitting in silence and thinking. Sue Crompton gave me a CD of posh Mozart music, anyway, to play when I'm in the bath and things. For the baby, you know? It's meant to be really good for 'em. Makes their brain grow, or something. I've been getting that many books out of the library on baby care, Robbie says I will be able to take a degree in the subject.'

'That is so amazing. Good on you, Sophie. Will you have a baby shower? Maybe we can club together and buy you some books as a gift; that way you can have them permanently to refer to, once the baby comes.'

'Ah, that's so thoughtful. What's a baby shower, when it's at home?'

'Well, I think it's an American idea. I'm not really the person you should be talking to, but I can find out from the girls for you, and maybe we could throw one here at the church? I'm sure the young mum's club would love a chance to get together for an evening. Let me have a word with the girl in charge; Jenny, isn't it?'

'That's right. Cool, Kate. Anyway, I'd better let you get on. You must be pretty busy. Don't forget to put my name down, will you?'

That is one plucky girl, thought Kate, as she settled into her morning's tasks. She knew life was pretty tough for the couple. They lived in a council house at the edge of the village. Robbie worked every hour he could, but they still struggled to make ends meet. They had always shunned going on benefits, even when the work was short; they didn't want to be classed as scroungers. But Kate was going to investigate what benefits they would be entitled to once the baby came, and try to persuade them to get a little extra help financially.

The phone interrupted her thoughts, and when she heard Bill's anguished voice, all thoughts of Sophie flew out of her mind.

'Kate, it's me, Bill. I don't know what to do! Maud has found out about us. My life in Ashton Kirby is over!'

Chapter 10

'Hang on, Bill. What do you mean, found out about you? I mean how? Who told her?'

Her head was reeling at the enormity of what Bill was telling her. Maud couldn't have found out, surely? But if she had, she knew that it would spread around the church like wild fire. She understood Bill when he said his life would be over. He would never cope with the gossip and the pointing fingers. Damn!

'I had just got home after seeing you, and Harold was still in bed. He's been poorly, you see.'

'Yes, I know you told me he's been feeling unwell. So what happened?'

'Well, I went into the bedroom to see him, and he was lying there asleep. It was just natural for me to lay down beside him, just for a hug. He had been asleep when I got up this morning, and I just felt like being close to him. Anyway, I had left the front door unlocked, as always.'

Kate knew that a lot of the old villagers still left their doors open during the day. She was always trying to tell them that it wasn't safe to do so. There were too many dodgy characters around nowadays, but it was hard to get them to change.

'Go on,' she prodded him gently.

'I'm getting a bit deaf you know,' he said, 'and I didn't hear her knock. I didn't hear her call, for goodness sake. The next thing I know, she is standing in the doorway to our room, staring down at us. Just standing there, staring. She didn't say a word. But I could see from the look on her face. She stood there, and then suddenly she was off. What can I do, what am I going to do?'

He started sobbing on the phone, and Kate felt tears running down her face. *This could kill him,* she thought. *He will be unable to deal with the fall-out.* She had no idea what to say to make him feel better. Anyone else but Maud, and they might have been persuaded to keep quiet. But there would be no silencing her. Maud would feel that it was her *Christian duty* to inform as many people as possible.

'Bill, listen to me, just for a minute.'

A loud siren screamed through the village, making speech impossible.

'Hold on a minute, my friend. Just wait for this noise to stop.'

Think, Kate, think, she instructed herself. The siren continued to wail.

'Look, I can't hear myself think,' she shouted down the phone. 'Don't do anything for a bit until I have had a word with Josh. See what he suggests we do. Can you hear me, Bill?'

'Yes,' he sniffed, 'just about. Please help me, dear. I don't know what to do. I just don't know.'

She replaced the handset, and sat there with her head in her hands. It must be a police car outside, she thought. But she didn't have time to worry about that now. Her main concern was for Bill.

It was lunch time, so she could close the office without anyone wondering why. She grabbed her coat, locked up, and went out to fetch her bike. She could see the flashing lights across the green. It was an ambulance. She just hoped that no one was badly hurt. She pushed her bike through the church yard, and then jumped on and cycled off down the road. As she reached the main road, a police car came roaring up.

Must be a bad accident, if the police have been called as well, she thought to herself. *I hope I can get across to Bill's. How very selfish of me! There is someone injured, and I'm worrying about how it will affect me! But I have to get to Bill's, and calm him down, before he does something stupid.*

She had to cycle quite a distance past the scene of the accident before she could cross to the other side of the village where Bill and Harold lived, tucked quietly away from the main road. It was a beautiful, grand old house, but far too big for the two old gentlemen to look after, now both in their eighties. So for a while now, they had lived just on the ground floor, making a downstairs bedroom out of the huge dining room. Probably when they both passed on, it would be sold to developers and made into flats. There weren't many people who could afford a property of that size. The grounds were also enormous, but Harold employed a gardening firm to maintain the gardens, which were always beautifully kept. He had told Kate that when his parents were alive, they had planted out hundreds and hundreds of roses. They knew the names of every one, and would open their garden to visitors in the summer. This had continued even after his father had died. But as his mother disappeared deeper into dementia, Bill had stopped opening to the public, as it had left her confused when she saw strangers wandering around. His need to keep everything neat and meticulously tidy had led him to close off the upper floor of the house. Due to their somewhat secretive lifestyle, he did not want strangers in to help, so he did all the housework himself. And he did a wonderful job of it. Kate was amazed at the effort he went to. There were always cut flowers in the large welcoming hallway, and the kitchen was spotlessly clean. How she wished she could turn back time, and prevent Maud walking in on their secret life!

As she walked up the pathway, and let herself in (for the door was still unlocked, even after his last unwelcome intruder), she offered up a prayer. '*Dear Lord, you know how dear Bill and Harold are to us. Please protect them from the fall-out of this unforeseen disaster. Please, Lord, please...*'

Harold had obviously got up from his bed, and was now sitting with Bill in the kitchen. He was dressed in smart paisley pyjamas and a striped dressing gown, and looking at him, Kate could see what a handsome man he must have been in his youth. He still had a thick head of hair, but now it was pure white, and he was almost like how she imagined God would look, if he was human; kind, caring and beautiful. But now he had such a crestfallen expression on his dear face, that Kate nearly started crying all over again. On the opposite side of the table sat a crushed, broken version of her dear friend Bill. She ran over and wrapped her arms around his frail shoulders, at the same time reaching her hand out to grasp Harold's.

'Darling girl, how did you get here so quickly?'

'I came as soon as I put the phone down, Bill,' she replied. 'I would have been here sooner, but there's been a bit of an accident on the main road.'

'Yes, we heard the ambulance,' said Bill. 'It puts our problem into perspective a little.'

But his face belied any sense of relief. She had a feeling that Bill probably wished he could throw himself under a bus, if it wasn't for having to love and care for Harold. The older gentleman would be lost without him, both physically and emotionally.

'So what are we going to do?' he asked her, with his hands out in front of him, beseechingly.

God knows, thought Kate, *because as sure as hell I don't.* But out loud she said, 'We can sort this. Please don't make yourself ill, my friend. I'm sure I can have a word with Maud. She likes me, remember?' She tried to put a little humour into her voice.

'Yes, and she doesn't like me, for good reason,' retorted Bill. 'She has always suspected we were gay, and now she knows for sure. And so does the whole of the parish by now, no doubt.'

'No, I will talk to her. Explain to her, and tell her how poorly Harold has been. She will understand.'

'She has always had it in for me, because I won't go to church,' piped in Harold. 'I used to, but it's bigots like her that put me off. Dear Bill here won't have a bad word said against anyone, but I tell you, half the people who call themselves Christians will end up in hell, because of their hateful attitude.'

'Now, now, Harold,' said Bill, 'you can't say that any more. You haven't been for a long, long time, and I told you, this new chap, Josh, has got the old school tamed. There are a lot of decent people there now. It's watered down the acerbic contingent no end.'

'Humph. Well, I don't know about that.'

'No, it's true,' said Kate, playing for time. 'The church is a much warmer place to be now. And you remember the two Celia's and Felicity Broome? Well, they're still attending. They often ask after you, you know.'

'They do?' he asked incredulously.

'Now, Harold, you know they do. I'm always telling you I've spoken to them, and they send you their love,' said Bill.

'How about you make me a cup of tea please, Bill?' Kate was trying to think on her feet, but she couldn't really see a solution. The longer she kept Bill's mind off the problem, the better. She was seriously worried about his health. He looked ashen, and was shaking considerably more than he usually did. She could have offered to make the tea for him, but felt he was better keeping himself occupied.

She watched as he filled the kettle, meticulously wiping the spout as he did so, and fetched the cups from the wooden dresser. He even put biscuits out on a plate. As if any of them were going to feel like eating! But he was a true host, and there would never be short measures from Bill. As they listened to the kettle boil in the silence, Kate came up with a plan.

'I think, if it's okay with you, I would like to let Josh know what's happened,' she suggested. 'I believe that if we have him on board, if and when any tongues start wagging, he would be able to stop them faster than anyone else.'

'I guess you're right,' Bill agreed reluctantly. Although Josh and Vikki knew about Bill and Harold, Bill obviously felt very uncomfortable discussing his personal life with them. Of course he would! He was an extremely private man; of the old school, and he didn't go round airing his dirty washing in public. Indeed, if anyone tried tittle-tattling around him, he would tell them in no uncertain terms that it was wrong. Although a gentle and courteous man, he disliked bad manners and gossiping, to him, was the height of rudeness.

'So, how about I give him a little ring, then? Shall I do it now, as I feel the longer we leave it, the more anxious you are going to be? I can't make any promises, but I really feel that with Josh in our corner, life will be a bit easier.'

'I don't know, Kate. It's probably too little, too late. Oh my Lord, what are we going to do?' And he bent double as though crushed by a huge weight.

Hell! She thought. *He's going to keel over any minute.*

'Come on, old thing,' she said, leading him gently to the chair. 'Let's get this over with, shall we?' She pulled her mobile out of her bag, and dialled the vicarage.

'Hello, Vikki? Can I have a quick word with Josh, if he's around, please?'

'Oh, Kate, thank God it's you!' replied Vikki. 'I've just run round to the office and you weren't there.'

'Whatever's up?' said Kate, alarmed at the panic in her friend's voice. Thoughts of the hospital appointment swam violently through her mind. Or maybe something had happened to the kids? The accident on the road! Surely not, they were all in school, weren't they? 'Are the children okay?'

'Yes, yes, they're all fine. I'm fine. No, Kate, I'm sorry to have to tell you, but there's been a terrible accident... out on the main road... It was one of those large articulated lorries going through to the depot... It's Maud, I'm afraid. She was killed instantly. Apparently, she just came out of nowhere, so some of the witnesses have said. The poor lorry driver didn't stand a chance.'

Chapter 11

As Kate prepared the service sheets for Maud's thanksgiving service, she reflected on what had happened last week. She could never be thankful that someone had been killed, but she was grateful that Bill and Harold could now get on with their lives in peace. It had been a terrible shock to the whole church, but apparently she had just darted out across the road. It was obvious she was on her way to tell Mrs Barrow what she had discovered, as she had phoned her from the call box just minutes before the accident. Mrs Barrow was distraught. She had lost a long-term friend, and fellow gossiper. Who would now supply her with all the inside information she so greedily devoured? The truth was that she was more upset at the loss of this information than she was of the terrible end poor Maud had met.

It was hard putting a service together for the old verger. She had no family that anyone knew of, and the only people who would be attending were some of the old-time church members. Who on earth could give a eulogy, and be honest about her? Kate was ashamed at these terrible thoughts, but it was true. There were very few kind words that could sum up Maud's life. In the end, Josh had agreed to sum up her life by recognising the endless hours of devotion she had given in her work as verger. But the truth was, there was a new sense of lightness around the building, now that it was no longer haunted by the mean old woman. Even in death, it was hard to conjure up one kind sentence about her.

Kate had been over to Rob Bolton's to sort out the funeral arrangements, as Josh felt that it was only right that the church took full responsibility for the cost of the burial. Kate had the task of going to her small council flat, and sorting out her personal belongings, as no one on the PCC felt that they could do it. So much for her friends-in-crime, then. It was a pitiful task. The flat was sparse, unfriendly and poorly furnished, with just a hard upright chair in the living room, placed opposite an old 'Bakelite' radio. So she didn't even have a television. In the kitchen, she found just four of everything. Four dinner plates, four bowls, four cups. Her fridge was pitifully empty, and now Kate felt a terrible pang of guilt as she realised that the only life this miserable woman had was when she was down at the church. It looked as if the only food she ate were the doughnuts she brought with an almost fervent regularity, as there was no freezer, just a fridge with not enough food contained within to feed a mouse.

I'm as evil as the next person, she thought to herself. *I've condemned this old lady, yet never noticed how lonely she must have been. Why didn't I make more of an effort to get to know her, to make friends with her? Maybe she was bitter and twisted because she was so lonely. Maybe this is what life holds for me? A spinster, living on her own, with nothing to do but spread malicious gossip. God forbid! I would rather get run over...stop it, Kate!*

She was appalled at how evil her mind could be, but she just couldn't seem to stop the thoughts flowing. What would have happened if Maud hadn't been killed? The church would be in a desperate state, with the gossip going round about their dear treasurer. She thought back to how she had prayed desperately just before she had gone into Bill and Harold's house that fateful morning, feeling a sudden heady responsibility for Maud's death.

'This is ridiculous,' she said out loud. 'Maud was already dead when I said that prayer. I had passed the accident on my way there. Now, I have to stop this guilt trip, and also stop thinking bad thoughts of the dead. I am going to be the bigger person, and leave all the judgement stuff to God. I'm just going to pray for her soul, and hope that she is in a better place, and finally at peace.'

She closed the door behind her, placed the key into her handbag, said 'Hello' to the old lady who lived opposite Maud, and headed to the council office to return Maud's key.

'Please sit down, Mr and Mrs Mercer.' The consultant looked slightly uncomfortable. He was a young Antipodean, probably from New Zealand judging by his accent. Vikki looked down into her lap and saw that her hands were shaking. She then glanced at Josh, and saw that he was sweating profusely. This was not like her husband, who was always in control, always able to deal with the world's problems in a passionate and gentle manner. He didn't look like a man in control now, and would not make eye contact with her when she tried to get reassurance from him.

'I have your results. Now, let me just familiarise myself...'

Why the heck didn't you do that before I came in? Vikki thought to herself.

'Ah, yes. So, you had, um, a mammogram, and um, an ultrasound with biopsy?'

'That's right, it was early last week.'

'Yes, right, well, I um, have to say that the results, um, are not good.'

Get on with it! she shouted silently. *I can't stand this.*

'The lump in your right breast is malignant.'

'No,' said Vikki.

'I'm afraid so,' he replied.

'No,' she said again. 'It's not my right breast. It's my left.'

'Oh, yes, left breast. Um, as I was saying, we have found malignant cells. We have also found that cells were present in your lymph nodes.'

'So what does that mean?'

'Well, we stage cancers (*he has said the word cancer!* thought Vikki) by how they have spread. With a case like yours, we would say it is a stage three at present.'

'Why at present?'

'Well, stage two would be if we only found cells within the actual breast lump. But because of the size of your tumour and the fact that we have found cells in your lymph nodes as well, we would call this stage three.'

A nurse had come discreetly into the room behind them.

'Ah,' said the consultant, looking somewhat relieved. 'This is Jan Phillips, and she is one of our breast care nurses. She will discuss your options further with you.'

'What do you mean options? Aren't you just going to remove the lump? I'm quite happy to go ahead, you understand. I just want it gone.'

Josh nodded mutely beside her.

'I'm afraid it's going to need a bit more than just removing the lump.' He looked down at his notes, then back up at Vikki and across to Josh. 'You are going to need a mastectomy.'

'Okay,' said Vikki quickly. 'I'll do that.'

'Now hang on,' Josh had suddenly found his voice again. 'You're going to remove her whole breast? Are you sure that's necessary?'

'In this case, I have to say yes. We won't know until we remove the tissue just how aggressive the tumour is, but I am almost certain that this particular tumour is going to need to be treated fairly aggressively.'

'So what happens next?' whispered Vikki quietly. She felt shell-shocked, dizzy, weak.

'Perhaps you would like to go with Jan, and she'll be able to provide you with all the information you will need. I will arrange to see you on the surgical ward as soon as possible. Are you able to come in at short notice?'

'Well, I've got the children to consider, and Josh is a vicar, and he's got a very busy diary...'

'I really do urge you to treat this as a priority, Mrs Mercer. The sooner we perform surgery, the sooner we can get on with the rest of your treatment.'

The breast care nurse ushered them out of his room and into the adjacent room. As Vikki stepped out into the waiting area, she felt as if the whole roomful of patients was looking at her with sympathy and interest. They seemed to know that she had just been delivered devastating news. Maybe it was the length of time she had been in with the consultant, and the fact that they left with the breast care nurse that gave it away.

The room they were now in was actually far less clinical than the doctor's room. This one had a plush and comfortable sofa and pretty pictures on the wall.

'Very nice,' remarked Vikki, looking around.

'Yes, we're very lucky,' said Jan, 'we often get given donations by various breast cancer charities, which allows us to provide a patient's room.'

'Very lucky,' repeated Vikki, quietly.

'So, what do you know about breast cancer?'

'Not a lot.'

'So, we can start with the basics. When the surgeon performs a mastectomy, we can do several things.'

Note the word we, thought Vikki. I have become part of a system.

'You may wish to have an implant, and I can show you some of those in a minute.'

'What, like the ones that have caused all those problems, and burst inside women's chests?' said Josh, ironically.

'No, the implants we use are of far higher quality,' she reassured them. 'But this may not be suitable in any case, if Vikki has to have radiotherapy; which is quite likely.'

'So, what? I just wake up without a breast?'

'Yes, but we can provide you with a prosthesis, and again, I will show you what's available. To begin with, you would just have a temporary soft pad, but once your wound has healed, we can sort out a better, more realistic one.'

'So I will be juggling breasts by the sound of things,' said Vikki.

'Sort of,' smiled Jan. 'I'm sorry, it's so much to get your head around, but we will take it bit by bit. I don't want to drown you with information today. You have enough to get on with, for now. So I will give you this folder. In it you will find all the names and contact numbers you will need over the coming months. There is also a list of email addresses. Please feel free to email me with any query, no matter how trivial. It's always easier for me to pick up an email than a telephone call, but if you need to speak to me, then I will call you back, so don't hesitate to ring. There are two other breast care nurses, Sally and Brenda, and we will always be happy to help.'

'I can't take any more for now,' said Vikki, feeling close to tears. She kept thinking that she had to walk through that dreaded waiting-room again, and didn't want to go to bits quite yet. It was all a bit of a public drama being acted out here.

'That's fine. I am so sorry you've had to go through this,' said Jan sympathetically.

'Don't be nice to me,' said Vikki, her eyes stinging with unshed tears. 'I'll be okay.'

She stood up abruptly, and pulled at Josh's shoulder.

'Well, 'bye for now. I'll be in touch when we have a date for you; you may wish to chat in more detail when you've read some of the information I have given you. Do you use the internet?'

'Yes.'

'Try not to read too much at the moment, or it will overwhelm you. If you need any information, stick to tried and trusted sites, such as Breast Cancer Care or Macmillan's.'

They left with as much dignity as they could manage, and headed to the coffee shop, where they sat drinking scalding, sweet coffee; an untouched muffin lay on a paper plate between the mugs.

'You do realise I will never be able to wear double-breasted jackets again?'

Josh spluttered his coffee as he laughed, looking shocked.

'You are such a silly cow, you know that?'

'Yes, a cow with a faulty udder!'

They looked at each other; years of love, laughter, and happiness shared between them. Now they had a new dimension to their relationship. Cancer. There. She said it in her mind. *I. Have. Cancer. That's not so bad. I don't feel any different.*

'Do I look different?' she asked him.

'What do you mean?'

'Well, now I have a label. Do I look different now I have cancer?'

'You know what? I think you do actually... yes, now I can see. You look even more beautiful than you did half an hour ago.' He reached out and took both her hands, kissing each one in turn. 'Yes, you are truly more beautiful.'

And he really did believe this statement.

'So why aren't I in floods of tears?' she asked him as they drove home.

'I guess we all react differently; it may come later,' he replied.

'Don't go all priestly on me,' she pushed him in the arm.

'You know us,' he said, 'we tend to joke about everything, even if it's not funny. It's just our way of dealing with it.'

'What are we going to tell the children? Do we have to tell them anything?'

'We will have to when you go into hospital, and they are going to notice when you have a huge shark bite where your boob used to be.'

'That's it! We can tell them I got eaten by a shark! Finn will love that. Imagine the kudos he would get from his school friends. I'd be taken in for show-and-tell, and everything.'

'Be serious for a minute, Vikki. We have to tell them. I know Amy won't understand, but I think the other two will.'

Suddenly, thinking about the children, Vikki started to cry. How could she do this to them? She was only thirty four! How could she possibly have cancer? But she had, and they had to deal with it.

The first thing she had to do was find out what she was dealing with. Know your enemy, that's how she was going to get through this. She was not going to sit back and be overwhelmed. She was going to go into this battle well-armed. Thank goodness she was having supper with Ellie and Kate. They would be her army, and stand with her during this fight. The biggest battle she had ever had to deal with. She picked up her phone and dialled Kate's number.

Kate was finding it very hard to concentrate on her work this morning. She kept trying to imagine what was happening at Queen Anne's hospital, with Vikki. It had been ages since her appointment, but she knew hospitals were notorious for their delays. What could be keeping her? She knew Vikki would ring her as soon as she got home.

With that the phone rang, and her heart fell into her stomach.

'Hello, parish office, Kate Hartwood speaking.'

'Kate, it's me.'

'Thank goodness! I was beginning to think they had kept you in. How did it go?'

'Not good. Are you free if I come over?'

'Are you sure you don't want me to close up and come over to you?'

'No, Josh has appointments here all afternoon, so I'd rather get out, if that's okay.'

It was much easier, it had to be said, since Maud's death. Kate didn't feel so guilty when one of her friends came in. She still felt bad, almost as if she had caused the old woman's demise. It was something she had to deal with, but for now, she was fully aware that the church was a far friendlier place for visitors.

Within a few minutes Vikki had arrived. As soon as Kate wrapped her arms around her, she started to sob like she would never stop.

'I've got cancer,' she said, as soon as she could catch her breath. 'I've got to have my breast removed.'

Hell! thought Kate. *Hell, hell, hell!* She said nothing, just hugged Vikki even more tightly.

'It'll be okay,' she soothed, pushing Vikki's hair from her face, and wiping the tears away with her fingers.

Vikki took a couple of deep, heaving breaths as her crying subsided.

'Right, I'm, fine,' she struggled to maintain her composure. 'Really, I'm fine.'

'Yes, and I'm the Queen of England,' joked Kate.

'Well, your majesty, it's like this...' and she proceeded to tell her everything she could remember.

'I've probably got it all wrong; there was so much stuff to remember. I couldn't understand half of what I was told.'

'I'm not surprised. It's a totally new world of information. Who would have ever thought you would need to know all this at our age,' said Kate. 'It's so unfair.'

'No, it's not. Someone's got to get it, so why not me?'

'You're always so bloody diplomatic.'

'We'll manage. I've got you, and I've got Josh. Yes, I know, that's open to debate. And of course I've got Sam, and my mum. Oh my word! I should have contacted him! He'll be going frantic. Can I use your phone please?'

'Sure, go ahead. Do you know his number?'

'That's a point. No. I've got him on speed dial on all my phones. Blast! I'll have to go back home and phone him. Well, thanks anyway, my darling friend. Must dash. I'll see you round my house on Monday night? It will probably be a bit boring, 'cause I'm going to be grilling Ellie for information.'

'I don't mind. I'm going to try to educate myself over the weekend. I can't go through it for you, but I'm going to be as helpful and informed as I possibly can.'

'Thank you so much.' She kissed her friend, and hugged her, then flew out of the door.

Poor Sam, Kate thought to herself. *I know he's a pain, but I can see how much he loves Vikki. It must be tough being a twin. Those two have such affection for each other. It's almost telepathic the way they sense what's going on in their individual lives.*

She thought about her relationship with her own sister, and wished that she had someone who understood her in the same way. What was wrong with her family? Her mother had fallen out with her sister, Valerie. And she couldn't stay in the same room with Melanie. Perhaps she should make more of an effort, and break the curse of the broken family. But, honestly, Mel was such a drug-fuelled idiot!

It was now gone five o'clock, so she put away her folders, and locked up the office. She took the heavy church key, and locked the outside door too. Putting her briefcase on the back pannier of her bike, she cycled away to her lovely warm cottage. It was getting really cold. No Indian summer this year then. She was going to have to dig out her gloves.

Chapter 12

Monday morning dawned, and Kate arrived at the church bright and early. She was so looking forward to checking out houses for the new curate. They had three to see this morning, and the estate agent was meeting them at the first property in fifteen minutes. She looked around, wondering where Bill had got to. It was not like him to be late. Then she saw his car pull into the car park. He drove a gleaming old Rover, so suited to the old gentleman.

'Sorry I'm late,' he puffed. 'Harold was a bit poorly this morning, so I just wanted to make sure he had a hot breakfast inside him.'

'Have you called the doctor?' Kate knew they were not keen on visitors, but she was getting increasingly worried about poor Harold. He was often looking frail and out of sorts.

'I said I would see how he was when I got home at lunchtime. If he hasn't picked up by then, I will call Dr Vaughan.'

'Are you sure you are happy leaving him? I can look around this morning, and perhaps let you know what I think.'

'No, no, he's fine. He's got his favourite programmes on TV, and I've left him a packet of his favourite biscuits.'

Those two are so sweet, she thought. *I do hope nothing happens to either of them.* She shivered as she realised that they were both in their latter years, and so couldn't really expect to go on forever. Maybe that's why it's good not to form attachments to people, she thought. Because it hurts. But although she had no partner to love, and didn't have strong family ties, she did have some amazingly close friendships. And they were all suffering at the moment, which meant that Kate suffered too.

He opened the car door for her, and they drove off. The first house wasn't far from the church, which would be just perfect for a curate's house. But when she went inside she took an immediate dislike to it. It was dark, dank and dirty.

'Of course, it does need a little work,' gushed the estate agent, 'but for the price you do get a lot of house.'

'A little work! Now there's an understatement if ever I heard one,' chuckled Kate.

'Well, it is cheap,' retorted the estate agent.

'I wouldn't call two hundred and fifty thousand pounds exactly cheap,' replied Bill acerbically.

'Have you brought a house recently, sir?'

'No, but I am intelligent enough to read a newspaper and keep up to date with what's happening in my own village,' he retorted.

'This is a very desirable village, you have to remember,' she said.

He had obviously ruffled her feathers, but Kate couldn't help smiling. People were often fooled by Bill's meek demeanour, and were shocked when he came back with a sharp riposte. He was nobody's fool.

The next house was marginally better, but only had two bedrooms. They didn't yet know which candidate would be chosen, as they were inviting the three short-listed curates back for a further interview next week. Two of them were married, and one was a single guy. Both the married couples were childless so far, but that could change of course. It would be no good choosing a house they would outgrow in the three years they would be at St John's. They needed to have a room for a study, so they either had to have three bedrooms, or a room that could be used as a study downstairs.

It was the third house that stole Kate's heart. It was perfect! Okay, it needed some work, but it had two huge bedrooms upstairs, and it had a wonderful extension downstairs, with a lovely conservatory and a little 'snug'. It would be perfect for a study, as it looked out on the small garden.

She looked at Bill and could see that he felt the same way. Just a few minutes away from the village centre, it would be just right. The price was a little less than the previous properties, so that would be a good selling point for the PCC.

They returned to the parish office, and settled down to discuss the situation. Kate and Bill decided to call an emergency PCC meeting, as they were worried that the little house would be snapped up. The PCC would want to go and view it themselves, so Kate texted Josh and told him to book the date. She just hoped that they would see the potential of the house, too. There would obviously be a few PCC members who would disagree simply because Kate had something to do with the choice, but when they realised that it was the cheapest on offer, and also had vacant possession, they would have to agree it was the best deal.

That evening Kate grabbed a bottle of wine and headed over to Vikki's. She also carried a rich strawberry trifle brought from the supermarket. She hadn't had time to make anything, but she was sure the girls wouldn't mind, anyway. The evening was not about the food. They had other, more serious topics to deal with. She had booked a taxi for eleven p.m., as she didn't want to worry Josh for a lift home. Ellie was going to share the cost with her, which meant they could both have a drink. The evening would probably be a little more bearable with a drop of alcohol to blur the edges. Kate had spent the weekend researching and printing off articles. It terrified her, reading through the ramifications of Vikki's diagnosis. Hopefully it had been caught early, and she would lose nothing more than a breast. That was horrific enough, for goodness sake! She knew she had to be strong for her friend. It was only in the privacy of her little cottage that she allowed herself to cry at the enormity of the situation. The whole church was going to find out soon enough, and Kate knew how fiercely Vikki guarded her private life. But they were going to need all the help they could get, and she knew the church family would pull together, and provide that help. Vikki had so many young mums who would pick up the children at the drop of a hat. Then the older ladies would make sure that there was always food on the table while Vikki was convalescing and recovering from her operation.

But Kate had darker thoughts, reading through the various breast cancer websites. From what Vikki had told her, she was pretty sure she would have to have further treatment in her battle against this monster disease. How would she cope with chemotherapy, and losing that fantastic head of thick, wavy copper hair? It sounded so petty when compared to saving your life, but it mattered to women. She kept trying to imagine how she would feel if she was going through this terrible predicament, but her mind baulked at the idea. She hoped she would be as brave as Vikki was being. Yes, she'd had a good cry, but the way she joked about it! Kate was more worried about Josh; now he didn't seem to be handling it very well. Maybe it was because he was used to being the one people turned to in a crisis. Who did Josh turn to? There were plenty of men in the village. They all met in the Yew Tree Inn for their men's get-togethers. But who was he close to? She couldn't think of a single person Josh would call a close friend, and she knew him better than most.

Maybe he would be able to talk to someone at the Deanery Chapter meetings. He really needed to, for he was suffering as much as Vikki. He didn't seem to be functioning at all well, and several people had come into the parish office complaining that he had forgotten an appointment, or that his sermon didn't seem as good as they had come to expect. It would probably be easier next week after they had made an announcement in church, and then Vikki was going in for her operation the following day. Sam and his mother were coming down for the first couple of weeks to help with the family. Now how many men would take two weeks off to look after their sister's kids? she wondered. They were certainly a close family. Again, that pang of envy crept in. *How could she envy her friend, who was now fighting cancer? Get a grip, Kate!* she scolded herself. *You really are a very selfish person.*

Poor Josh was going to have to pull himself together tomorrow, when they had the interviews for the curacy. It was going to be a tough call, for all three candidates were highly suitable. They were having supper together in the church hall, with the churchwardens, Vikki, Josh and Kate, before facing their individual interviews. She was not taking part in these, as she did not feel that was in her remit, but she was beginning to regret that decision now, with Josh appearing to be so preoccupied. Would he be able to make the right call?

She turned the corner into the vicarage at precisely the same moment Ellie Smith appeared from the opposite direction.

'Oh, Ellie, I'm so glad to see you before we go in. This is a right old mess, isn't it?'

'I know, Kate. It must be hard for you, being so close to them all.'

Kate shrugged this off. She wanted no sympathy for herself; this was about Vikki and her little family.

'It is treatable though isn't it?' She pleaded with her eyes for a positive answer.

'I don't know,' Ellie replied, gently taking Kate's hand and holding it to her cheek. 'I just don't know, and that's the truth.'

They turned to each other in the rapidly fading light, hugged quickly and then headed for the front door. This was opened before they even touched the knocker. Three cheeky faces greeted them, freshly washed and scrubbed in readiness for bed.

'We were watching you,' Amy screamed. 'Come in, Auntie Kate, I want to show you the painting I done at nursery.'

'It's the painting you DID,' corrected Finn, at eight now the expert in grammar.

'I know I did!' she retorted, 'that's what I said.'

'No you didn't, you said done!'

'Oh shut up, you two,' shouted Daisy, 'or Daddy will remember we should be upstairs, and I won't be able to show Kate my doll's house.'

'She's seen it before! You show her every single time,' said Finn, belligerently.

‘So! Just ’cause you’ve got nothing interesting in your bedroom.’

‘I don’t want girls in my bedroom. Ugh!’

‘Finn’s got a girlfriend! Finn’s got a girlfriend!’ Amy sang as she danced up the hall, her fingers waving from her ears.

‘Shut up! I haven’t,’ he shouted as he gave chase.

‘Right, you lot. Bed!’ shouted Josh, coming out of his study.

‘See? I told you that would happen,’ sulked Daisy. ‘You didn’t listen to me, and now the very worst has happened.’

Oh, if only that was the very worst, thought Kate unhappily. Poor kids.

‘Tell you what,’ she whispered. ‘If Ellie takes the food through, I’ll sneak upstairs with you, look at the dolls’ house, and read you a very quick story. Just one story,’ she reiterated, as Amy already had her hands full of about eight books.

Once she had done her duty with her adopted nieces and nephews, she headed back downstairs.

‘Bye,’ shouted Josh, as he went out the door. ‘Have fun, ladies.’

Vikki had already uncorked the wine, and poured three large glasses.

‘I won’t be able to do this next week,’ she stated, ‘so I’m making up for lost drinking time!’

‘Here’s cheers, then.’ Ellie raised her glass to the other two and they clinked together, condensation glistening on the glasses, like mini tears.

‘I guess this is what they call drowning your sorrows,’ said Vikki, ‘I think I can understand why people become alcoholics. Every time I think about Monday, I panic, and feel like pouring another glass. Josh keeps telling me off, saying it won’t help anything. I don’t know what’s up with him. He’s not himself at all. Typical! He's always so good and understanding with everyone else's problems, but he just can't seem to deal with trouble when it's under his nose, in his own household.'

'I think that's quite a common reaction,' said Ellie. 'He is probably feeling so bewildered. I mean, you've always been such a strong team, the both of you. He relies on you more than you realise, darling. He doesn't know what to do when his source of strength is having her very own crisis.'

'You reckon? I just always imagined he would be, well, you know, strong for me. I find it quite odd that I'm having to be the strong one at the very time I feel more terrified than I've ever felt in my life.'

'I'm sure you are, but look, you've got us, haven't you? We can be your strength. We're not as close as Josh, and can stand back and see the situation a little different from him. I'm sure that once the operation is over, and you know a little more about what the future holds, he'll be there for you.'

'I hope so, because, to be truthful, I am so scared. I keep waking up in a hot sweat, thinking I will call the hospital and cancel the surgery. I don't know if I can go through with it, Ellie, you know? I have hardly ever been sick my whole life! I only go to the doctors with the children. I have only ever been in Queen Anne's once, and that was when Finn nearly cut his finger off in the shed. Can you believe it? I'm thirty-four, and never been to hospital. Never even had my tonsils out. So how can I be ill? I don't feel ill! How stupid is that? I will be going into hospital feeling perfectly well, and come out sick. Bit perverse, isn't it?'

'Shoot, Vikki, when you put it like that, I agree with you,' said Kate, shocked. 'I hadn't really thought further than you having the op. How poorly will she feel, Ellie?'

'Everyone reacts differently to surgery,' said Ellie, tactfully. 'Some people sail through, while others can't cope with the anaesthetic, or the psychological aspects of surgery. You won't know till you come round, and get through the following few days.'

'Will it be painful?' asked Vikki, biting her lip, and looking worried.

'It will probably be a bit, but they are very good nowadays with pain relief. I shall be in making sure they do the very best for you, you know that. Goodness, you've coped with childbirth three times over! You must be an old soldier when it comes to pain.'

'Yeah, and I had an epidural with all three, because I'm such a wimp.'

'Well, they're going to knock you out when they perform the operation, too, you know. They're not going to make you go through it awake!'

'Gee, thanks for that, Ellie,' she laughed. 'I feel so much better now. One good thing that will come out of this is that I should lose a few pounds at least. How must does the average breast weigh? Perhaps I'll have both off, and lose even more.'

'Trust you,' said Kate, 'anyway, you're skinny enough already.'

'I wish. Perhaps they can make a new boob with my tummy.' She pulled up her tee shirt, and revealed a very small roll of fat. 'Honest, Kate they can, you know. I read about it on this website! They can make a new one with this.'

'I don't think you've got enough there to replace the average pimple,' laughed Ellie. 'Anyway, let's not get ahead of ourselves yet. Have you decided if you'll have an implant?'

'It depends on whether or not I have to have radiotherapy. If I do, they can't do an implant. So I'll have to wait. I don't think I like the idea of a plastic chicken piece inside me, anyway, so I don't think I'll go for that option.'

'I don't know how you can talk about it so calmly,' said Kate with a shudder. 'I can't bear this happening to you.'

'It is happening, Kate. And I just have to deal with it. Anyway, there are far worst things that could happen.'

Kate couldn't really think of anything worse than having a disease that could wreck a young mother's life. Just thirty-four for goodness sake!

The evening passed in a blur of alcohol and information. Ellie was full of useful tips and facts, and it seemed that as Vikki gleaned knowledge, she became calmer. *If anyone could cope with this, she could. What an absolute hero of a woman!* thought Kate.

It was only in the taxi on the way home that Kate realised Ellie was crying.

'Hey, it'll be alright. You were just telling Vikki all that positive stuff, remember?'

'I know,' she sniffed, pulling a small delicate embroidered handkerchief out of her purse. 'I suppose I am just aware of the times it doesn't work out fine. Blast, Kate, why Vikki? Why, oh why, oh why?' And the friends sat there, wracked in depressing thoughts, as all hope flew from the car. They would both have to hold it together for Vikki and Josh, but right now, well it didn't feel good. Not good at all.

Chapter 13

Kate had spent another rushed week at the office. She was amazed to see the weeks flying by since she had taken the post, and it felt like she had been there forever. She was glad of the chance as the weekend neared, to have a break from church work, and do a few personal tasks. She had the office running like a smooth machine, and had even trained the more stubborn members to do their own photocopying without complaining, which was no mean feat! She was aware that there was still a small band of people who begrudged her working for the church, but on the whole, she was welcomed and loved.

The best part of the job was when she was able to welcome folk from outside the church community. It was good to break the taboo that the church was full of miserable hypocrites. Okay, so maybe it was, but no more than those who didn't attend church! Josh and the churchwardens had managed to agree on the candidate suitable for the curacy, and they were all looking forward to him coming. In fact it really couldn't have been better timing, what with Vikki's illness taking up so much of Josh's time and attention.

Kate had to admit she was really worried. Not so much about Vikki, but Josh, who really did not appear to be coping. On the surface he seemed to be functioning normally, but she knew that he was forgetting half of what she was asking him to do. And it was taking a toll on his sermons, which were becoming lacklustre. It must be so hard for him, but she fervently hoped that he would manage to hold it together, for Vikki's sake.

Vikki was going into hospital tomorrow, and Sam and Irene were now settled in the vicarage. It felt really strange to Kate, as she usually felt so at home over there, but she now felt like a visitor rather than a close friend of the family. She had tried to be a bit more amiable around Sam, she really had, but he was just so damned difficult! If she said something was blue, he would say it was red! They couldn't seem to find any common ground on which to have a friendly discussion, except about Vikki's welfare. When he spoke about his sister, he seemed to melt and become nearly human. She could see the love and concern on his face, and it hurt her to see him suffer.

She had a little package of goodies to take round for Vikki during her hospital stay. It consisted of a tiny bottle of her favourite perfume, a beautiful Paperchase pad and pen, a new flannel, face wipes and sweeties. She also picked up a couple of bottles of expensive pomegranate flavoured water, the sort of thing Vikki would never treat herself to. The friends had gone shopping for new night clothes and slippers last week, and Kate had also treated Vikki to a couple of the latest 'chic lit' books. She didn't need anything heavy or difficult. What she was going through was tough enough.

The house purchase seemed to be going through without any problems, and now Kate needed to get a team on board to organise the cleaning and decorating. She had been able to go round and see it a couple more times since they had agreed on a price with the estate agents, and had taken photos of every room, so that she was able to see what needed doing. The church had a team of men and women who made up the Fabric Committee. The majority of the work would be done by them, but it was going to need a few more volunteers on board, so Kate had put an advert in the newsletter. She knew that most folk had busy lives already, so the more people they were able to recruit, the easier the load would be.

She had managed to persuade the PCC that Sophie's husband Robbie would have a paid role in doing a lot of the garden clearing, as he also had access to a lorry. This would work really well for both parties concerned, as Robbie and Sophie could do with the extra cash.

Kate had also managed to persuade a young woman who had recently joined the church to help with design and colour, as she had been an interior designer before she had her family. Joanne Morgan was a lovely woman, but oh, so shy! It had taken forever for her to pluck up the courage to join the women's group, but she would still sit on her own a lot of the time, or could be found washing up the cups rather than having to socialise. It was fine if you didn't really like to mingle, but Kate could see that in Joanne's case, she was held back by fear and embarrassment. Her children were a little bit older than a lot of the young mums, but she wasn't quite as old as the flower arranging group, and so she didn't appear to fit in anywhere. Kate thought that she must try and invite her round for supper one evening. Perhaps she would be more comfortable on a one-to-one basis. Maybe when Vikki was in hospital, as Kate would have a bit more time on her hands then. Normally, she would have had more of a role with Vikki's children, but with Sam and Irene there, she was a little surplus to requirements.

Kate had arranged to go and visit her family the following weekend. Now that was going to be fun. Her mother had told her that Melanie had returned home after her latest disappearing act, and looked terrible. Could Kate have a word with her, please? She couldn't think what good that would do. One word from Kate usually sent her sister rushing in the opposite direction.

However, with Vikki's situation uppermost in her mind, and observing the way Sam was suffering, she decided she must make more of an effort with Mel. If only she could get her away from those so-called friends. It just seemed that Mel was so easily led astray. She had always been that way, even at school. *Perhaps if she'd had a different bunch of friends, life would be quite different now. Who knows?* Kate wondered to herself.

What Kate wanted to do was to tell her to get a grip, and be thankful she didn't have cancer, but she guessed that wasn't quite the right approach. She must try to be more tactful with her younger sister. Try and win her round with love, instead of seemingly winding her up.

On Monday morning, she hurried though her work, as she had to be over at Merrywoods' at lunchtime for her talk with the elderly residents. They were such an amazing group of people. Mainly consisting of women, with the odd lucky gentleman thrown in for good measure, she found them all rather interesting. She was aware that the public perception of old folk was of a group of doddery, demented, bent figures. If only they would spend more time getting to know them, there were benefits to be had on both sides. They had stories to tell that one could only begin to imagine! Stories of war, espionage and crime; of heroes and villains, family feuds and brave soldiers. And they could enjoy a good joke, as long as you remembered to speak loudly enough!

She looked through her planned talk, and made a few amendments. If she knew the Merrywood clan, she wouldn't get through half the stuff she had written down, as they would constantly interrupt and ask non-stop questions. Still, it didn't harm to be well prepared. She had even produced a hand-out showing a mock print-out of the type of figures she used to deal with when she was in corporate banking. That would make their eyes pop out of their heads!

That evening, Kate walked across to the vicarage to wish Vikki good luck. She rapped at the knocker, and waited for the rush of children to fly through the door. Instead it was opened by Sam.

'Oh, it's you.'

'Nice to see you too,' she replied.

He stood at the door.

'Well, do you think I could come in? It's getting a bit chilly out here.'

'For sure,' he said, stepping aside. 'It's just, well, I was expecting it to be Tesco's with the online delivery.'

'Well, I'm sorry to disappoint you. I've just popped by to see Vikki, if that's okay with you?'

Blast! she thought, *why oh why did she have to be so churlish? Just because he behaved like an oaf to her didn't mean she had to do the same.*

'Yeah, come on through. It's all a bit chaotic in there.'

'I'm well used to it,' she said with a smile.

'Yes, I had the feeling you are always round here.'

'What's that supposed to mean?' she snapped. So much for being the bigger person!

'Nothing, I was just saying.'

'I don't come round to get in the way. I come round to see Vikki, to help with the kids, and to work with Josh.'

'Of course you do, you're the 'parish administrator',' he said, with his fingers wriggling in the air, emphasising the commas.

'Do you have to work at being such a pig, or does it come naturally?' she asked him, just as Vikki came down the hallway. Damn! This wasn't what she needed right now.

But thankfully Vikki hadn't heard the sharp retorts going on.

'Hi, Kate! Come on in to the mad house. Thank God I'm going into hospital to have a rest! Just think, four days at least lying around in bed, without my brood going mental.'

'Think again!' Sam replied, 'we will be bringing them in at every opportunity. You're not getting off that lightly.'

I bet he means it as well, thought Kate bitchily. She pasted on a smile, as if everything was hunky dory, when truthfully it was far from it. A lump formed in her throat at the wonderful way her dear friend was coping with this terrible situation. How could she be so stalwart? Well. If she could be, then Kate would follow by example. She looked across at Sam and gave him the broadest smile she could manage.

'Let's go, Sam,' she said, grabbing him by the arm. The look on his face was payment enough for the effort it took. He followed her through into the kitchen, where his dear mum sat at the table looking slightly out of her depth. She was in her seventies, a tiny little lady who had lost her husband just a year back, now. This family was all she had. But you did need more than a little energy to handle the Mercer crew, as Kate knew to her cost, and she was still young and relatively fit.

Daisy noticed the arm-in-arm look straight away. Nothing, but nothing escaped her astute gaze.

'Kate loves Uncle Samuel, Kate loves Uncle Samuel,' she chanted, which of course was soon taken up by the other two.

'Pipe down you lot,' said Sam, more sharply than he intended, Kate felt, as she observed the worried looks on their faces.

'Don't shout at us, please,' said Amy. My word, that child could put you in your place with a chilling glance.

'No, I didn't mean to shout. I'm sorry, it came out all wrong. It's not you I'm cross with,' he said glancing crossly at Kate.

'Are you angry with Auntie Kate then?'

'No, and she is not your auntie, she's your friend.'

'She is our auntie, isn't she, Mummy? Please tell him!' Daisy pleaded.

'Well, technically she isn't,' said Vikki, grinning at the discomfort Sam and Kate were going through.

'What's technically mean?'

'It means that Uncle Sam is your proper uncle, because he's my brother, you remember I told you all of this last week? But Kate is like a sister to me, because we're such close friends, so that's why you've got in the habit of calling her your auntie, I suppose...' She trailed off, feeling drained by the children's questions. They never let you say anything without demanding long, drawn out explanations!

'So, if Uncle Sam married Friend Kate, then she would be a proper auntie,' shouted Finn, jumping up and standing on the dining table.

'Yeah, when hell freezes over,' muttered Sam, as Vikki shouted, 'Get off that table! How many times do I have to tell you? A table is for eating, not for feet!'

Shoot! That was a horrid conversation, thought Kate, as Amy crawled into her lap, the customary thumb stuck in her mouth. She smoothed the child's soft fair hair down, marvelling once again at the perfection of her little head. Everything about this child was perfection, in tiny, miniature form. God, she loved these kids like her own!

Chapter 14

Josh and Vikki had decided that it would be best to make a public announcement in church about her forthcoming hospital stay, and thus avoid rumours flying round. It was met with gasps of horror and surprise. During coffee afterwards, Vikki was inundated with good luck wishes, and offers of help. Those offers included making meals, helping out with the children, and taking some of the burden of parochial duties from Josh. This was when being part of a close church family came into its own. Kate, in her usual efficient manner had drawn up three lists for people to add their names to. There was a great danger in times like this, of either having no help on one particular day, or of being swamped with casseroles. It was so good of them all to offer, and it seemed a terrible shame if any of the food had to go to waste, so this was by far the most sensible way of doing things.

They had asked for people not to visit Vikki while she was in hospital, and also not to keep phoning the vicarage for updates. Kate was going to post information on the newly designed church website. For those members who were not computer savvy, she also posted details on a news board in her office. This way, it would protect Sam and Irene from being constantly interrupted while they were caring for the children. She was also doing it to protect the parishioners. She knew only too well what the sharp end of Sam's tongue felt like, having fallen victim to it on numerous occasions.

Irene had come along to the church service with the family, but Sam had chosen to stay at home. That was fine with Kate. The less she had to see of him, the better. It was bad enough that he would be coming to the harvest supper in a couple of week's time. Vikki had insisted that she would be fit enough by then, and thought it would be a nice way of saying *thank you* to her brother and her mum for helping with the children. Kate had a strong suspicion that Sam didn't see it as much of a gift, but thankfully, on this occasion at least, he was too polite to say so. It really was a right pain, him coming, though. This would be the first big event that she had arranged at the church, apart from Maud's funeral, of course. She had put a lot of thought and effort into it, and had been looking forward to it, until now. Never mind, she would carry on regardless and try to ignore the horrid man as best she could.

This week was going to be tough to cope with, knowing what Vikki had to endure. She also had the prospect of spending the weekend at home with her parents, which was filling her with a nagging sensation of depression. If only they would come down and see for themselves how much fun church life could be! The miserable bunch that called themselves The Truth Brethren could learn a few lessons from St John's congregation. For goodness sake, it was the same scriptures that they read from, week after week! But their interpretation was full of hate, damnation and punishment, not the love, joy and peace that was preached here. Sure, there had to be a price for being a committed Christian, but if they were to reach out to non-believers, they had to make the gospel appealing. But as Kate had learnt only too well, the same sun that melted butter, hardened clay. Josh and Vikki were so good at creating a warm and loving Christian environment. Their fresh, young and welcoming approach won over hearts and minds. She could see and hear it wherever she went in the village. Only last week, she had been waiting in the queue for her lunchtime roll in the Bakery, when she overheard a couple of ladies talking about the harvest supper. Apparently one of the ladies had lived in the village all her life, and had never stepped foot inside St John's until this year. Now, she was on every rota and every committee she could fit in to her day! The other lady had asked what had changed her mind about the church.

'I don't really know. It's all happened so suddenly,' she replied. 'It's almost as if, as soon as I went to the first service *(it had been a welcome service for newcomers)*, I felt like I belonged somehow.'

'They're only after your money, you know that?' replied the other woman, scathingly.

'No, that's the thing. They don't seem to want anything from me. In fact, everyone I speak to seems to want to do something *for* me. They're really, really caring, you know? Not at all like that poor unfortunate woman who was killed on the main road a few weeks ago. You remember? That thin one who used to strut up and down the green looking like she hated us all. No wonder they couldn't fill the pews in them days!'

'Well, I don't know, I can't see my Fred wanting me to be as involved as you seem to be. He wouldn't like it at all. Mind, I might persuade him to come along to that supper, seeing as there's free food on offer.'

Kate smiled to herself. She could never have dreamed that the role of administrator was going to be so fulfilling. The funny thing was that she had hardly had time to set foot beyond the parish boundary since she had started work. Her car was still tucked away in the garage, and she hadn't driven it in over a month. She would have to make sure it worked for her drive to Carshalton this Saturday. It was amazing how much she was saving using her bike everywhere she went, and she felt much fitter for it. Not that she had to worry about her weight, but she was a bit of a couch potato on the quiet, and sometimes she did get concerned about how little exercise she took.

She also had the wonderful feeling of a good day's work done at the end of every day. She never, ever felt like that when she worked in the City. Every day had just merged over into the next, and the tension hung around you like a noose, whether she was at work, on the tube, or even supposedly relaxing at weekends. Her job still spilled over into the weekends now, for obvious reasons, but it just didn't feel like work when you were dealing with friends. There were, of course, still the obvious exceptions. Only last week, Mrs Barrow and Mrs Brown-hyphen-Smith had accosted her in the churchyard on her way home, demanding to know why she hadn't told them earlier about Vikki's forthcoming hospital stay.

'Because it's not really any of your business,' she informed them tartly. 'Unless, of course, you are volunteering to help with the children?'

'Certainly not! Those children are SO bad mannered. I don't know what's up with the youth of today. Not enough discipline, that's what!'

'I have to disagree with you, Mrs Barrow. The children are a total delight. I have seen firsthand what harsh discipline can do to a child, and those three children are brilliantly behaved, but more importantly, they're happy.'

'Oh, so you know about raising a child then, do you? Had them yourself, have you?' Mrs Barrow grinned evilly at her friend.

'Yes, actually, I've had six, and all by different fathers. And then they were all adopted when I had to go to prison. Goodbye.'

She hopped on her bike, and couldn't help but turn back and laugh as the two women stared after her, open mouthed. 'Put that in your pipe and smoke it,' she laughed.

On Tuesday morning, Kate opened the office and went to make herself a cup of coffee, now that Maud was no longer around to do it. She still suffered huge pangs of guilt about her death, especially when she ruminated on what a miserable, lonely existence she had lived. As she went into the kitchen she glanced into the church, and saw Josh kneeling in the front pew.

Should I go and join him, or leave him alone? she wondered. She decided to give him a few moments, before offering him coffee. However, within minutes of her return to the office, Josh had joined her. He looked gaunt and grey, so she walked over and hugged him tightly.

'Oh Josh,' she asked, 'was it really that bad?'

'Worse,' he replied glumly. 'She was fine until we walked onto the ward. Then as soon as the staff came to do all her pre-op checks, she started shaking really violently. I had to wrap my arms around her to try and calm her down. Oh my God! How can this be happening?' he cried. 'I've had to leave her, and now I wish I could go back there, and scoop her up in my arms and bring her home.'

'Do you know when she's going down for surgery?'

'I think she's first on the list. They seemed to be in a hurry to prep her for theatre, poor kid. Honestly, Kate, she looked about twelve, and so scared. She's never had any operations in her life. Well, neither of us has actually. I mean, I've obviously done plenty of hospital visiting in my time, and so has Vikki, bless her. I don't know how I'm going to function this morning.'

'No one's expecting you to do anything,' she soothed. 'Your diary's clear for the morning and afternoon. I've got the parish visitors to do your Communion visits, so why don't you go home and take it easy?'

'I can't! Irene is really taking this badly, too. It's her little girl going through this. What must it feel like to see your child suffering?'

'Look, here's my key, and this is the code for the alarm,' she said, ripping off a piece of paper with the four digits on it. 'Let yourself in, and make yourself some coffee. There's even some carrot cake on the table. I must have known I was having visitors!' She smiled at him, trying to lift his mood. 'No, seriously, I've been comfort eating for England. I'm not handling this well either, so I can only imagine how you feel.'

'Wow, Kate, that is so thoughtful of you. I must admit, it's great having Sam and Irene here to help, but the place doesn't feel like my own. It's bad enough without Vikki being there. Now it's filled with other people's belongings, and I can't find a quiet place of my own. I know I've got my study, but you can imagine how difficult it is when you can hear guests pottering about. You feel obliged to socialise somehow.'

'Well, you will have total peace in my cottage. Everyone knows I am in the office today, so you won't get any callers or hawkers, except perhaps the Jehovah's Witnesses, and I think you can cope with those, can't you?'

He rubbed his fingers around his dog collar, scratching at his neck as he did so. 'Thank you. Give me a ring if there's anything you need me to deal with,' he said as he left.

'Just forget about the parish for now. Go pray, shout and rant at God, and give him some grief from me, too, while you're at it. He and I are not on speaking terms at present,' she grinned ruefully.

Poor Josh, she thought, for about the millionth time. *What a nightmare he is living through. God, where are you? What the hell do you think you are doing?*

Kate was able to visit her dear friend the next day. She was slightly dreading it, for she had no idea what she would say to her, but she needn't have worried.

'Look at this!' said Vikki as soon as Kate had kissed her gently, and put the fruit and drink down on her table. Vikki pulled her vest top down to reveal a long gash where her left breast had once been. All that covered it was a clear dressing.

'You are something else, you know that,' laughed Kate. 'Why haven't you got a bandage on it?' she asked, fascinated and appalled in equal measures.

'My surgeon doesn't believe in bandages,' she replied. 'I must admit I was expecting to be wrapped up like a mummy when I woke up, but I looked down and there it was... gone! Howzat?!'

'Oh, stop it, you crazy women. Seriously, how are you?'

'Well, I was pretty sore yesterday, and quite sick after the anaesthetic. They gave me some seriously strong painkillers, though and I felt totally out of it. Maybe I ought to source some cannabis from the local comprehensive. It's a cool feeling.'

'You are incorrigible,' laughed Kate. 'I can't get over you making a joke out of having your breast removed. You must have something wrong with your brain.'

They could banter like this with each other because of the closeness of their relationship. Everyone who knew Vikki understood that she used black humour as a method of coping. People who *didn't* know her sometimes thought her flippant, but that was far from the truth.

'I'm just relieved it's all over, to be honest with you. It doesn't actually hurt today as much as I thought it would. I've even been up and had a wash in the bathroom. Thank God I've got an ensuite. I couldn't face wandering round lop-sided in front of all those male patients.'

'It's very strange, having mixed wards still,' said Kate. 'I thought they were all banned now?'

'Well, they're not strictly mixed. They have male and female bays, but yeah, you do have mixed bathrooms. Not very good is it?'

'No, especially with something as intimate as a mastectomy. What are the staff like? What are the patients like? Share the goss', girlfriend.'

'The staff are very nice, but oh, so busy. You ask for something and have to remind them about ten times. I have to keep ringing my bell, because the old dear in the next bed keeps trying to get out of bed, and calling for Harry. Apparently, that's her husband, but he's been dead ten years, poor soul. It must be horrid getting old.'

'You'll never be old,' reassured Kate. 'Well, not like that, I mean, not on your own. I mean, oh dear! I'm digging a hole here. Help me out, won't you?'

'I know what you mean, silly,' said Vikki. 'I'm hoping they'll let me home on Friday.'

'That soon?'

'I should think so. I mean, I'm up walking and self-caring, so I can't see why they would want to keep me in. I've got a couple of drains in, and providing they are not filling up too much, I can either have them taken out, or go home with them still in, and the district nurse will come round and manage them.'

'Hey, this is a whole new language you're speaking here. What's a drain when it's at home? I thought it's something the water emptied into.'

'Similar. Apparently they drain all the pus and blood from the wound site.'

Kate lifted her hand to cover her face. 'Okay, too much information. I could never be a nurse. I think I may faint just listening to you talking about it.'

'You do look a little pale; well, paler than you usually do, which is saying something. Sit down and take the weight off your feet.'

'I might just do that,' she said, and she gratefully lowered herself into the plastic covered chair. 'Have the children been in to see you?'

'Oh yes. And guess who climbed onto my bed and nearly shot me through the roof with pain?'

'No! Poor Amy, she wouldn't understand would she?'

'No, she acted like she always does. It was the other two I felt sorry for. Their little faces were so serious, and they were so quiet. Not like them at all. Apparently Finn had a fight today at school. Sam had to go in and see the headmaster.'

'What on earth was that about? He's never been in trouble before, has he?'

'No idea. He just won't talk to me.'

'That is so awful, poor Finn. What about Daisy?'

'She won't even look me in the eye. I had little presents for them and everything, for when they came to visit me, but she just stared at the floor. That's another reason why I want to come home. They need me there. I mean, I know Mum and Sam are doing a great job, but kids need their mum, don't they?'

Kate bent over and carefully gave Vikki a hug.

'We all need you, darling,' she said, meaning it. She needed Vikki to lighten her mood when she was feeling depressed. She needed her to share the gossip and to have a bitch about the old boots in church. She needed her friend to be well and whole again. But she would never be whole again. She was a broken angel, but still every bit as beautiful.

The hour sped by, but at the end of visiting time, Kate could see Vikki looked tired.

'Are you in pain?' she asked.

'A little bit, but they will be coming round with the drugs trolley in a moment.'

'Oh, I'll stay for a quick fix then, shall I?' laughed Kate.

After a few more warm words, she walked off the ward, as the bell rang down the corridor. She shivered as she went out into the cold night. It was the end of September; winter was on its way. She pulled her coat tightly around her tiny frame, and hurried to the car.

Chapter 15

Saturday morning dawned and it was pouring with rain, as Kate backed her car out of the garage. She hated driving down to her parents at the best of times, and the M25 was horrendous when it was raining. Once more she felt the familiar cloak of depression settle around her shoulders at the prospect of spending two days at her childhood home. She knew that if she had not escaped to university, and got away from Carshalton, she would probably have suffered true clinical depression, for it was never far from her psyche. The traffic was quite light this early in the morning, but it was slow going, as the rain made driving decidedly hazardous at times.

As she drove into Plough Lane, and pulled up outside number four, she found all her movements were slow, as if wading through treacle; the dread was spreading through her like a tide coming in. There would be no welcoming party at the door. They didn't do welcoming here. Any show of emotion was considered frivolous. How she hated this dump!

She still had the key, so she rang once on the doorbell, and let herself in.

'Mum, Dad, I'm home,' she called out. No answer, but then that's what she expected.

She walked through to the kitchen, and found her mother baking, her hands covered in flour.

'Hello, dear,' she said in that sad, simpering voice.

'Shall I put the kettle on? I'm parched! It's teeming down outside, and the journey was horrible.'

She may as well start the conversation, for she knew better than to wait to be asked.

'Your father's in his study. Best not disturb him till after his prayer time.'

No change there then, she thought. Out loud she asked, 'How are you, Mum?'

'Oh, you know, dear. Blessed, truly blessed.'

'Well, you don't look it,' Kate muttered.

'Pardon?'

'I said, glad to hear it. Where's Melanie?'

'Up in her room, sleeping.'

'What, just for a change?'

'She was late home last night, so I don't expect she'll be down for a while.'

Kate's mother continued to knead her hands into the dough, never looking up to make eye contact with her. This woman was so controlled and restricted, it was simply horrendous to see someone so lacking in emotion. Her father was the same. If you were to see him, you would think him hen-pecked, with an overbearing wife; but this was not so. It was an overbearing church that had caused such damage to these two weak people.

Kate turned away from her before she said more. She knew it was pointless. Her parents were so tightly in the grip of the Brethren that anything she said would not reach through to their emotions.

She bounded up the stairs, desperate to get away from the stifling image of her repressed mother, and knocked on Melanie's door. She didn't wait for an answer, simply turned the knob and walked straight in. The smell of alcohol and dirty clothes hit her as soon as she stepped in.

'Mel! It stinks in here!' she exclaimed. 'How can you let yourself get like this?'

Mel revealed her tousled head from under the bunched up duvet. She squinted her eyes together as daylight assaulted them.

'I didn't know you were coming up,' she muttered, rubbing her hands over her eyes.

'You probably did, but just forgot, as usual.' She started to pick up the strewn clothes from the floor, making a small pathway through the debris of the room.

Mel yawned and stretched. 'Give me a few minutes to get up and showered, and I'll be down.' She assumed Kate would leave the room, so started to nestle herself back into her pit.

'Oh no you don't. You're getting up now, not this afternoon.' Kate pulled off the duvet, revealing Mel's frail body, still in her day clothes from the bender last night.

'Up! Up! Up!' She pulled at her sister's arms and hauled her into the shower. She was tempted to turn it on to cold, but felt that may have been going a step too far, considering she had not seen her sister for many months. 'Come on, sis. Let's try and spend some quality time together, eh? I've missed you.'

'Have you? Have you really?' Mel looked as if she was starved of kind words and Kate immediately felt guilty. It must be a miserable existence living here under the shadow of the Brethren, with Mum and Dad slaves to their stupid rules.

'I have, honestly. Look, I'll set about tidying your room while you're in the shower, and then maybe we can get out of here before lunch, and go for a coffee down at that new place in the high street.'

'I haven't got any cash.'

'Don't worry about that. It's on me.'

Kate switched on the CD player, and tried not to judge as she put the clothes in the washing basket. None of them were fit to hang back in the wardrobe, but she appeared to have her entire wardrobe on the floor! She then set about clearing the dressing table, which was cluttered with cigarettes, lighters, tablets and caked-up eye shadows. What a way to live. Her heart went out to Mel. She couldn't possibly be happy like this, could she? *Thank you God*, she prayed silently. *At least I managed to escape and find you properly.* She looked at her hands, sticky and grubby now and rubbed her fingers together. She was going to need a dishcloth to wipe the tops down.

Walking down the stairs, she passed her father's study. *Blow it!* she thought recklessly. 'Hi, Dad,' she called out. *No answer. Of course not. Stuff you, then!*

Gillian was still in the same position that Kate had left her. Smoothing and kneading, looking down at the table. It's like a bad caricature of a Stepford Wife, she thought sadly. She thinks she has to look busy all the time; to be constantly caring for her family. How was she going to stand this for forty eight hours without cracking up?

Trudging upstairs, she could feel her energy sapping away, and knew that she could be sucked into this grim existence if she wasn't careful. For some strange, inexplicable reason, she imagined bringing Sam here. What on earth would he think? His family were all so vibrant and happy, even his dear, quiet mum, Irene. She may not have as much energy to cope with the little ones, but she loved watching them, and was obviously so proud of her grandchildren. Kate wished she could magic herself back to the vicarage; to see the children, of course. She shook her head slightly to shake the image of the bustling kitchen table back in Ashton Kirby, full of longing. For the children. Of course.

Kate was amazed to see her sister had scrubbed up quite well, and was now looking jauntier than she remembered seeing her for a long time. They walked down to the coffee shop arm in arm, reminding her of long-forgotten memories, when they were school girls, and Mel was unaffected by alcohol and drugs.

'So how are you?' she asked tentatively. 'Really?'

'I'm sorry you caught me in a bad way this morning, but honest, Katie, I really am doing okay.'

'Really?' Kate looked at her in disbelief. What she had seen and smelt this morning didn't look much like *doing okay* to her.

Mel was the only person in the world who was allowed to call her 'Katie'.

'I've met someone.'

'What?'

'I've met someone. He's really special, and he wants to help me get clean.'

'That's something only you can do, sis.'

'I know, but he works at the rehab centre. I haven't used for over five months. Even the alcohol I'm getting a grip of.'

Kate looked at her enquiringly. 'Well, go on, spill.'

'I hated him at first. He was such a prig! But you know, he is the only person ever to stick by me, even when I've failed. Anyway, it's gone past just being a professional relationship. Last night, well, it was a one off. Honestly, Katie.'

'That's what you always say.'

'No, I was invited to a thirtieth birthday bash. I shouldn't have gone, I know that now. But there were drugs there Katie, and I walked away! I think I was so shocked at my ability to refuse them, that I grabbed a drink. The rest is obvious. But I will get there. He matters to me. We're taking it slowly, but we're good. You'll have to meet him.'

Kate looked at her sister, and noticed that her eyes were actually sparking and alive, something she had not seen for years.

'I'd like that, Mel. I really would, and I do hope it works out for you. You're thirty-one, for God's sake; you have to pull yourself out of this hole you've dug for yourself. Get yourself a job, and a place away from Mum and Dad.'

'Now that would be good,' sighed Mel.

'Honest, sis, it's not healthy living here. I could feel the depression and oppression fall on me like a cloak when I walked through the door. It's a sick house. The Truth Brethren is a sick cult.'

'How did you manage to get away?' asked Mel wistfully.

'I was lucky, I guess. But if you manage to get yourself sorted, you will have to bring your new man down to see me. Make it a goal, eh? Hey, I don't even know his name?'

'Jonathan. His name's Jonathan.'

'That's a nice name,' Kate said, reaching over the table and taking her sister's hand in hers.

Kate somehow endured the weekend, but the effort took its toll on her, and she felt drained and low, longing to get back to her cottage in Ashton Kirby. The house was dull and uninteresting. Pictures and ornaments were frowned upon as unnecessary frills; a sin even. Food was plain and heavy; again, spending money on nice food was positively evil! What kind of god would invent a world full of colour and imagination, yet forbid his children from enjoying any of it? She had tried to talk about her life and activities in St John's, but her parents appeared uncomfortable even talking about such things. By the time Sunday afternoon came, she was on her way, not a minute too soon. But she couldn't leave without one small dig.

'Mum, I've found some papers at the cottage.'

Her mother's head snapped up sharply, fear showing in her eyes.

'Talk to me about Aunt Val. Please tell me something about your sister. What did she do that was so evil? She didn't kill someone, did she?'

'Just leave it,' barked her father.

'Mum?'

'Don't go meddling in things you know nothing about,' she answered sadly. 'Val is dead, and that's that.'

'But you wouldn't talk about her even when she was alive! What skeletons are in the cupboard that I should know about?'

'You don't need to know anything,' she pleaded. 'There is nothing to know. She just left, that's all.'

Yeah right! thought Kate, but she could see she would get no further. Maybe she would find out more at the cottage. If she could find time, that was.

Vikki had been released from hospital and was now recovering at home. She was still receiving visits from the district nurse to check the wound and to empty the drains. The children had been fascinated and disgusted in equal measure at the weekend, when she came and poured the bloody fluid into a jug. Thankfully they were at school on the day Vikki had her drains removed. That would have been too much! But the relief of being able to walk around without her bag of bottles was enormous. She felt so free, and was surprised at how little pain she was in. Apart from a gaping wound on her chest, she didn't really feel a lot different. She was able to get up and dressed during the day, and had found some beautiful scarves to drape over her scarred chest. She had never been over-endowed on the breast front, so thankfully it wasn't that obvious she was slightly asymmetrical. It would be a few more days before she could wear her 'softie'; a flesh-coloured pouch filled with stuffing. The children had managed to deface it already, and had drawn a nose and eyes on it with felt pens, and carried it around, calling it their pet mouse, and had even named it Maisie. Vikki couldn't be cross with them; it was the sort of thing she would have encouraged them to do! And it was very amusing, especially the thought of tucking Maisie into her bra!

The house was very crowded with Irene and Sam, but she was so grateful for their help. Irene was finding it very tiring, but Sam appeared to be relishing every second, winding the kids up at every opportunity. Poor Josh was finding it very difficult to study in his room, and was spending more and more time over in the church, trying to write his sermons.

Vikki had started to help prepare meals, and put the children to bed, but she was still having an afternoon nap, while Sam went to pick the children up from school. Lots of her friends had come to visit her, starry eyed and in love with her brother Sam!

'Can I borrow him as my au pair once you're better?' asked Jo Stokes. 'He can service my needs any time!'

'You're disgusting,' laughed Vikki. 'That's my twin brother you're talking about.'

'Twins! I didn't realise! No wonder he's so dishy. You are such a good looking pair,' she gushed.

'Shut up, you,' barked Vikki, embarrassed. But it was true. Everyone found Vikki stunning. Her Amazonian stature, and long, flowing auburn hair were captivating. It was so tragic that she had to go through this horrid trauma, but she didn't appear at all depressed by it. The tears would flow in private; the church congregation would not see her pain. That was her plan, anyway, but who knew what the future held?

Chapter 16

It was Saturday evening and the harvest supper was due to start in forty-five minutes time. Kate had been up since dawn organising, and helping with the catering. The church looked resplendent in glowing hues of red, yellow and orange; flowers, fruit and vegetables. In the centre of the altar sat a huge plaited loaf brushed with a golden glaze, donated by the Bakery.

At the front was a large flower display, and all around the church there were smaller posies of flowers at every window, and at the end of every pew. The sights and smells were heady, overwhelming the senses. The day had dawned hot and sultry; they were finally getting the promised Indian summer, and the whole church was filled with a sense of anticipation. Autumn may mean the end of summer, but it was Kate's favourite season, as it held the promise of new life. Seed heads fell to the ground, apparently dead, settling in to the soil for the winter, yet bursting forth in the spring. It was as if nature was snuggling under a duvet for a long sleep.

The young people were providing the entertainment, in the form of a quiz and a short cabaret. There was so much talent among them; some of the singers and musicians would be heading off to university after the weekend, so there was a sense of sadness as they joked and practised together, possibly for the last time. Who knew if they would return from their studies to a quiet village life in Ashton Kirby? Kate recalled how she yearned to escape forever when she headed off to study, but would she have felt that way if she had belonged to this vibrant church? Probably not.

The tables in the hall were placed in long rows, and laid with flower garlands, plates and glasses. Daisy and Finn were allowed to stay up, but Amy was being looked after by one of the young people, who had kindly sacrificed her evening for Josh and Vikki. *That's the way this church worked, they really care for each other*, thought Kate. She smiled as she took out the quiches from the oven, wiping her head with the back of her hand. Gosh, it was hot!

The family of St John's began to file in, and seat themselves with their friends, the chatter filling the hall and rising to the rafters. Children ran around, laughing and screaming, and being told off by parents to keep the noise down. But this was a time for celebration, so no one really minded. A team of women brought the food over to the tables, and Kate glanced across to Vikki and Josh's table. She saw Vikki waving and gesturing to her, so she walked over.

'Here! We've saved you a seat,' she told her, pointing to an empty chair.

Great, she's saved a chair next to Sam, Kate realised, but she couldn't appear ungrateful. She hadn't got as far as thinking where she was going to sit, knowing that anywhere would be next to friends. Tears sprung unexpectedly as she thought back to the miserable weekend with her parents. What a contrast! She offered up a prayer of thanks, as she settled down and greeted everyone at the table.

The food was good! Kate hadn't realised how hungry she was; no, not hungry, famished! Thinking back, she had not eaten since coffee and a cake at eleven this morning. She fell upon her food with great gusto, and listened to the rise and fall of conversation all around her.

Once the food was cleared way, she began to relax. Her work was now over for a while, as the young people took on the entertainment section of the evening. There were a couple of girls singing their own arrangements, and then a young, talented musician played a saxophone. The music wafted around the hall, sending sleepy vibes over the tables, as people, stuffed full of good food, were embraced with gentle melodies and soft jazz.

Then the young folk started handing round paper and pens ready for the quiz, and everyone started to perk up. They really loved their quizzes at St John's! The master of ceremonies called for attention, as Matt and Sue, the youth workers, bounded their way to the front.

'Right you lot,' they yelled, 'you have ten minutes to grill the person on your left! The questions are on the back of the sheets, and you have to answer all the questions honestly. No cheating, and no jumping to the next question! At the end of ten minutes, John will sound his sax, and you have to swop round, and then the questioner becomes the questionee. Get it? Right.'

Then John gave a great blow on his saxaphone, and the quiz got underway.

Kate's heart sank when she realised that she had to pair up with, of all people, Sam!

'So who's going first?' he grinned at her. 'I think that as the lady, you get to be questioned.'

She looked down at the sheet of paper. Daisy and Finn had attached themselves to Sam, and were looking up at her in eager anticipation.

'We all know what your occupation is, Auntie Kate,' shouted Daisy. 'You're the administrator.'

'Hang on, who's meant to be asking the questions?' laughed Sam. *At least he was in a good mood,* thought Kate gratefully.

'So that's what I put down for number one then, is it? Right, number two. What's your favourite music?'

'Um, Vivaldi.'

'You're joking, right?' laughed Sam.

'Stop mocking me,' she said, her face turning red. 'You're not supposed to judge me, just ask the questions.'

'Fine, but what other music do you like? Anything a bit more modern?'

'Well, I like Adele. And Duffy.' She could see Sam was having a job to stop laughing.

'What?' she asked him. 'There's nothing wrong with that, is there?'

'No,' he sniggered as he wrote it down. 'It's just, well, it's all a bit lame, isn't it?'

'You like David Grey,' yelled Finn.

'Do you?'

'She does, she's always got his CD on, honest, Uncle Sam.'

'Oh shut up you!' she said, thoroughly embarrassed now. 'What's wrong with liking David Grey?'

'Isn't that a bit, well, a bit nineties?'

'Who do you like then? Muse, I expect?'

'Muse!' he spluttered, 'Does anyone still listen to Muse?'

'Stop it!' she shouted, then looked round as everyone was staring over at their table.

'Please,' she said in a quieter voice. 'You're not meant to be judging me, just asking my opinion. And it's a free country.'

'Hey, you two. Is that world war three going on down that end of the table?' joked Vikki.

'It's your pain in the neck brother,' replied Kate, feeling suddenly like a school girl, telling tales.

'Behave yourself, Sam, or I won't let you come out with me any more,' Vikki told him, with a grin.

'I wish,' he grinned. 'Okay, next question. Favourite food?'

'Pasta, she loves pasta!' yelled Daisy.

'Who's meant to be answering this?' Kate asked. *These kids know me better than I know myself,* she thought. *I obviously spend too much time with them.* 'It's true. Pasta is my-all time favourite food.'

The questions continued until suddenly, there was a loud blast from the saxophone player.

'All change,' yelled the children. 'Your turn now, Uncle Sam.'

'Thank goodness. Now it's your turn to be humiliated. So, what's your choice of music then?'

'He likes loud music. I can hear it when I'm trying to go to sleep, 'cause his room's next door to mine!' said Finn, interrupting again.

Daisy hit him with her elbow, telling him to keep quiet.

'Alright, yes, I like um, let me see. AC/DC, Foo Fighters, Velvet Revolver, anything in that genre.'

'To be quite honest, I've never heard of any of those,' said Kate primly.

'Well, you haven't lived,' he replied slyly. 'But if you need educating, perhaps you would like to come round one evening?'

'Is that a date?' she joked, suddenly feeling hot and breathless.

'If you want it to be?' Suddenly, the room stood still, and she could no longer hear the chattering banter all around her. She held her breath.

'Next question! Next question!' shouted Finn, jumping up and down on his chair.

The moment passed, and Sam went on to spill his life story. I know nothing about him, she thought. Probably because every time his name was mentioned, she bristled and moved to another subject. So, he was an architect, was he? She would never have guessed.

'What's your favourite food then?' she asked him.

'We know that!' butted in Daisy again. 'It's pizza!'

'Well, we both like Italian, so at least we have something in common.'

'I'm sure if we asked each other enough questions, we would probably find we have a lot more shared interests,' he whispered.

He's flirting with me! she thought madly. 'Are you flirting with me?' she asked him aloud.

'Do you want me to be flirting with you?' he replied, looking at her directly, in a way she had never seen him look at her before. Her stomach flipped over, and she reached for her glass of wine.

'I think I do, actually,' she replied, shocking herself with the answer. 'I think I do.'

'Kate. Kate!' She heard her name being called from a million miles away. It was Mrs Barrow, blast the woman! 'Where have you put the black bags? I need to start clearing all this mess away. It's getting late.'

'Is it?' she asked, feeling dazed. Kate pushed away from the table, and found that her legs were shaking, and it was difficult to walk. She glanced behind her, hardly able to believe that a flirtation had occurred between them, but it had, and she had reacted violently. What was it with him, that he could stir up such strong and conflicting emotions? she wondered. She passed the rest of the evening in a fog of emotions, often having to ask people to repeat their questions.

Bill looked at her strangely. He had never seen Kate so distracted. Harold had been to see his GP and had been started on some new medication, and was looking so much better. He had been diagnosed with diabetes, and both Bill and Harold had been forced to look at their diet and make changes. It was the first time for years that he had attended a function at the church, and he seemed to be enjoying himself. Kate went and gave the old gentlemen a hug goodbye, as they made their way home. The hall looked a mess, with left-over food, half empty glasses and strewn paper serviettes. The team of men and women who had offered to clear up worked mostly in silence, all keen to get home now that the evening was over. It had been a huge success, and everyone said how much they had enjoyed themselves.

As the last of the musicians hauled their heavy equipment out to the cars, Kate stifled a yawn, as she realised how exhausted she now felt. It had been a long day! She opened the car, and piled in the table cloths and flower decorations that she was taking home. The flower ladies had presented each of the helpers with a beautiful arrangement. The church was working well, and although it seemed a strange thing to say, since Vikki's illness, there was far more love and tolerance for the young family, as the PCC and churchwardens pulled together to make life easier for Josh and Vikki. It was weird how good came out of bad.

As Kate stood up from the back seat of the car, she heard a voice behind her, in the shadows. Her heart thumped for a second, then she realised it was Sam.

'Oh, you frightened me,' she said, placing her hand over her heart. Surely he could hear it hammering?

'Sorry. I wanted to say thanks for all the hard work you've put in tonight.' He paused. 'I've really enjoyed myself. I never thought I would say that, you know. I think I owe you an apology.'

'You do?'

'Yeah, I know I've been a bit of a prat around you. Ever since Josh and Vikki came to Ashton Kirby, I've been so cross at the way their life has been invaded. I know it goes with the territory, being a vicar of a church and all that, but I just watched her disappear, if you can understand my meaning.'

'I can,' she replied quietly.

'The thing is, I got off on the wrong foot with you. I blamed you when I know I should have thanked you. Vikki has explained to me how invaluable your friendship has been to her; that's before she even takes into account the pressure you've taken off Josh, now you work at the church.'

'Please don't apologise. I know, well, I can see how much you love Vikki, and it's just a protective brother/twin thing. They are under a lot of pressure here, I know.'

'That's still no excuse for rudeness. I want to make it up to you.'

'Seriously, there's no need,' she said, but her heart was flying skywards. 'Look, it's not yet eleven. I'm too buzzed after all this to be able to sleep. Do you fancy coming round for coffee? That's if you haven't got to rush off anywhere?'

'That would be great. Perhaps you could show me your David Grey collection?' he joked.

She slapped him on the chest and they drove off, laughing.

The harvest festival the following morning was a true celebration of all God's gifts, and Kate felt such a strong sense of belonging, she was moved to tears. The church had never looked more beautiful, the singing never so glorious, and the service led by the children's groups was perfect. If only the hundreds of people who had never stepped foot inside a church could feel the love flowing round this building, she thought. It would be bursting at the seams.

She had been invited round for Sunday lunch at the vicarage, and for a change, she was looking forward to it. Sam was cooking a roast dinner, and the children and Irene had put together a selection of puddings. It all looked quite marvellous.

Suddenly, she felt a tug at her back, and Vikki pulled her into Josh's study.

Vikki pushed Kate into his seat, then pulled up a chair and sat opposite her.

'Right then, spill,' she demanded.

'What are you talking about?' Kate stalled for time, unsure of what to tell Vikki.

'He went home with you, and since then he's seemed, well, different. I've never seen him so cheerful, and I want to know what you've done to my brother!'

She slumped down on the chair. She could never hide anything from Vikki.

'Oh, Vikki, I don't know what's going on,' she sighed. 'We just sat and talked. It was almost one o'clock before I knew it. We could have talked all night. We suddenly seemed to have broken through some kind of barrier. It was just like you and me chatting together; it was finally so easy.'

'I knew it!' said Vikki, banging her fist on the desk. 'I always had a feeling his gruffness and anger around you was hiding something. He's in love with you!'

'Oh, don't be so blooming daft, you crazy woman. Did they remove your brain when they took away your boob?'

'No, no, no. I am a woman of wisdom, you see. I can see it all clearly now! How wonderful! My best friend and my brother.'

'I wouldn't go that far,' laughed Kate. 'We only talked, you know; he didn't propose marriage, you silly cow.' The two women continued to banter in the way only close friends could.

Amy came to find them, pulling at both their hands.

'Come on, Mummy, come on, Auntie Kate, it's dinner time. Can I sit next to you, Kate?'

'Of course you can, poppet,' she said, allowing herself to be led through to the dining room.

She smiled at the gathering of people, feeling so happy to be a part of them.

Sam smiled shyly at her, almost coy now that there was a cord of friendship between them.

Josh said grace, and then they all enjoyed the food and intimacy of a large family.

Chapter 17

Kate pushed hard on the small loft opening. She had not been up here since she first moved in, and that was only to put her junk away out of sight somewhere. She stood precariously on the ladder, wobbling slightly as she peered into the darkness above. So, there was no loft ladder attached then. She looked down at the step-ladder, hoping and praying fervently that it would not collapse if she pushed her weight down upon it. It was an old step-ladder she had found in the garage, splattered in paint, and rusting around the hinges, but it appeared quite sound apart from the aesthetics. She placed her hands both sides of the loft opening and pushed up with all her might. She just managed to get her legs to the top rung of the ladder, but her arms lost power before she could hoist herself all the way through.

I must start going to the gym, she thought. My arms have absolutely no strength in them. But Kate was determined, so she tried again, and again, feeling like a failed gymnast, as her arms buckled beneath her each time. Finally, she managed to push herself over the edge, and shot up into the dust and dark.

Did it! she thought triumphantly. I'm not sure if it will be any easier going down, but I'll worry about that later. She had the foresight to push the large torch up before her, so she switched it on and peered around. There was her rubbish sitting surrounding the mouth of the loft, but as her vision became accustomed to the gloom, she began to make out the blurred outlines of boxes and bags. The first bag she opened released a waft of moth balls, as she rifled through a collection of old clothes. Pushing that to one side, she came across boxes of old shoes, camera equipment and even an old slide projector, plus hundreds of slides. Now that should prove interesting! She hoped that these might be pictures of her aunt's travels around the world. Stepping further away from the light of the opening, she cautiously placed her feet on the rafters. She had heard too many tales of people crashing through the ceiling while searching through lofts, and she didn't fancy being discovered hanging there days later, by the neighbours!

She had now reached the old water butt, and could see even more boxes stacked up against the sides. Where on earth should she start? she wondered.

A small box caught her eye, and she reached over and picked it up. It was much smaller than the rest, and quite light, so she took this one over to the loft hatch, ready to be taken down with her. She stepped her way back, and searched around for a few more likely boxes and bags to take down. Four would be enough for one trip, she thought, otherwise she was in danger of cluttering up her tiny living space. She could always come back up for more, then return anything that was not needed, or dump it, depending on the contents. It was time this space was sorted out, and she really claimed the cottage as hers, anyway.

She shone the torch towards the hole, and had started to make her way back, when she saw an old carrier bag, tied with a knot at the top to prevent the contents falling out. She loosened this a little and saw piles of photos inside.

Bingo! she thought. That was definitely coming downstairs with her. She reached the hole, and threw down the bag of clothes, ready for the dump, and also the bag of photos. This meant that there was less for her to carry down, for she was already trying to work out how she was going to manage. She wriggled herself down to a sitting position with her legs hanging over the edge, then swinging sideways, managed to twist her body so that her feet found the top rung of the ladder.

Phew! she thought, *that was easier than I thought*. She stood there and reached for first one box, then the next, and balanced them on the banister, before she fixed the loft lid back in place and wiped her hands free of dust.

She was going to phone Robbie first thing in the morning and ask him if he could fix a proper loft ladder in place for her. That way, she would be able to put some of her own junk up there, and help free up some of her wardrobe space. She had been reluctant to put anything that she thought she would need away, as she knew how difficult it would be to lay her hands on it up here. Maybe he could even put a couple of shelves in, while he was at it? It was so useful knowing someone who was an all-round handyman, and she knew he was always grateful for the extra work.

Kate took all the boxes downstairs, and then sat back in her armchair, exhausted. She really was going to have to join a gym. Even going up and down those stairs seven times in a row had left her puffed out! Now that she was making inroads with Sam, she felt very conscious of what a couch potato she was. He was really into keeping fit, and ran every morning. The only exercise she had was cycling gently round the village, like the old spinster that she was! He put her to shame.

She opened the bag of photos, and was rewarded by the sight of hundreds of pictures, obviously taken in exotic locations. As she looked through them, she also discovered some old black and white photos. These had been taken at school when Valerie and Gillian were children! There were photos of them as cute little girls, dressed in identical dresses, with teeth missing and their hair tied in bunches. It was strange to see them, as there had never been any photos up at home. Taking photos was seen as a sin, somehow; a form of idol worship. Such a strange religion! As she burrowed down into the bag, and took out handfuls of pictures, she even discovered one of her parent's wedding. She had never seen these before. How did Aunt Valerie get hold of them, for she obviously hadn't been at the wedding? She thoughtfully sifted through the photographs with her fingers, as scenes of tropical islands and sunny beaches, faded now with time, passed through her hands. This was fascinating stuff. She began to form a plan of putting her aunt's life story together using the photos. Putting these to one side, she reached over to the smaller cardboard box, and untied the ribbon holding it together. She discovered a collection of old passports, certificates and documents inside. This information would probably help her piece together dates and times, and she was getting quite excited as she planned her new project. Thumbing through the papers, she found driving licences, birth certificates and even a diving certificate. So exotic! Kate paused as she studied her aunt's birth certificate, feeling sad that she had not spent more time with her. Val had died suddenly and tragically in a supermarket of all places, from an unexpected brain aneurism. It was a lovely way to go, but it had left the people who found her deeply traumatised.

Kate picked up a small certificate, and turned it over in her hands. It was a death certificate. The name on the certificate was Paul Turner. She turned cold as she looked at the details. It recorded the death of a little baby, just one week old. Her aunt had a baby? It didn't have the name of the birth mother on it, just the name of the person who had registered the death, and this she did not recognise. But Turner was her aunt's surname. This didn't make sense. The address was in her home town of Carshalton, but it was not her grandparent's address. She was going to have to force her parents to talk to her. She had to know, for surely this was her family history? Maybe this was why Val had been excommunicated? They would never have stood for a woman getting pregnant out of wedlock in the Truth Brethren, for sure. It was all quite mysterious, and left Kate feeling very unsettled. Now, instead of finding out more about her aunt, she felt as if she knew even less. She was going to have to return home and demand answers.

Kate sat on the new information she had discovered for a few days, trying to get her head around the idea that her aunt had lost a baby boy. Did her mother even know about it? Her mother would have only been about fourteen when the baby was born, and Val obviously didn't have the baby at home. Or maybe she did, and he had died at a neighbour's house? But no, because surely the death would still be registered at their home address? It was so puzzling. If only she had a better relationship with her family. She had also been doing a little online research about the Truth Brethren, but there was very little on the internet about them. No doubt computers were considered a sin to them as well as everything else! It was evident they did not belong to any of the mainstream churches. Kate had looked through the directories of Baptist, Evangelical and Pentecostal churches, but they weren't listed anywhere. In a way, she was glad about this. She hated the thought of a huge organisation spread across the UK behaving in the terrible way the Brethren did. If only she could persuade her parents that their beliefs were wrong; they were bound up by the stupid rules and regulations, and afraid of the consequences of not conforming to them. But they were so restricted and miserable, and Kate knew that this was not the Christian way of living at all. She had discussed it at length with Josh, who was horrified to hear that a so-called church was operating in this fashion. He promised her that he too would try and dig around, and find out what he could about the organisation known as 'The Truth Brethren'.

As a child, Kate had not had the sense to question what her parents were involved in, but thankfully she had the intelligence and strength to pull away from it as she grew older. Kate had also been doing a lot of research into breast cancer, and it frightened the life out of her. Vikki had now been diagnosed with a stage three, grade three tumour, and was starting chemotherapy that very week. She was so amazing about the whole situation, and kept cheerful despite the knowledge that she would in all probability be losing her beautiful hair. Kate and Vikki had spent the morning at the hair salon having their nails done and having a massage, before, horror of horrors, Vikki had her hair cut into a short, neat bob. It made sense, Kate could see that. If it was going to fall out, then it would be easier to cope with in graded stages. Sam had gone ballistic. He had never known his sister with anything but long, flowing locks, and could not get his head around the fact that she was going to lose it.

'Come on, Sam, it's only hair,' she had joked. 'It's soon going to grow back again. It's just like losing a nail.'

'I don't know how you can be so flippant about it, Vikki,' he had scolded her. 'It's your crowning glory, and it will take years to grow back.'

'Yes, but it will grow back, that's my point. Hey, this treatment is going to save my life, little brother, so what's the point of getting sentimental over a few feet of dead cells?'

'Stop calling me little. We're the same age, idiot!'

'Yeah, well, sometimes you act like you're a lot younger. You always have.'

He grabbed her by the throat and playfully strangled her.

'Get off, you're pulling my hair,' she yelled.

'Well, it's the last time I get to do it,' he said, 'so tough buns!'

'Just bring your duster next time you come over, and you can polish my head for me,' she grinned.

But Sam was crestfallen. He had struggled with watching Vikki go through the devastating surgery, and now this. It may be purely aesthetic, but surely she must be upset about losing her hair? It was just a front, and Vikki was the master of disguising her true emotions. He had returned to his home in Bristol now, and hated the distance between them. Truth be told, he hated being apart from Kate too. He recognised that he had been attracted to her from the start, but had refused to admit to it; instead he had allowed everything she did to irritate and annoy him. He knew that he had been a total jerk towards her, but now he had the chance to make it up to her. She hadn't yet had the chance to visit his flat, but she was coming down for the weekend soon. A whole weekend with her! His heart beat faster at the prospect. He had planned a whole load of things for them to do; she had never been to Bristol, so it would be fun to show her all the usual touristy bits and pieces. He sat at his workspace, overlooking the river, and could not settle his thoughts. So much had happened in the space of just a few weeks. How could he be feeling such sorrow and happiness in equal amounts? It all took such a great deal of energy, that there was nothing left for his usual creative expression. He looked at the drawing board and willed himself into the latest plans. His client was coming round later that day, and he had to have something to show him.

Chapter 18

Kate and Vikki sat in the chemotherapy suite at Queen Anne's hospital. It was a new extension, and the fresh furnishing and modern art displayed upon the walls belied the purpose of the department, whose sole aim was to poison the patients. All in the name of medicine, of course, but that was still what they were doing. Glancing around them, the two friends watched as men and women, some with hair, some without, sat and waited. The remarkable fact was that most of them looked cheerful and upbeat, even though they were frail and sick.

'That's a pretty headscarf,' remarked Vikki. 'Do you think I should ask her where she got it from?'

'Why not?' replied Kate. 'And do you think that's a wig the lady over there is wearing, or her own hair?'

'Well, if it's a wig, it's a jolly good one,' said Vikki.

'Excuse me, could you tell me where you got your scarf from? It's very beautiful.'

'Sure,' replied the lady. 'This your first time?'

'Yes, I'm a chemo virgin.'

The lady laughed and held out her hand. 'My name's Pat, and this is my last session, thank God.'

'How's it been? Truthfully.'

'Truthfully, it's been hell!' she laughed, 'but every week gets a little nearer to finishing. And you get to meet some amazing folk here, patients and staff alike. It's like a very friendly club. I will write down the website where I got most of my head gear from. It's an American site, but it's so much better than the English sites.'

'Typical,' said Vikki. 'They seem to have so much more panache and style than we do!'

A large nurse stood at the opening of a door and yelled, 'Mrs Mercer.'

Vikki and Kate looked up and shivered. Not only was her stature enormous, but in her hands she held a red tray, with not one, but three enormous syringes.

'Bloody hell!' said Vikki, 'they can't all be for me, can they?'

'There's only one way to find out,' said Kate, pulling her friend to her feet.

The nurse introduced herself as Lynn, and invited Vikki to sit down. She checked her name and date of birth, and then told her what she was going to do. The three syringes consisted of two doses of chemo and one anti-sickness drug. She took hold of Vikki's arm, and searched for a good vein.

'Are you squeamish?' she asked. 'If so, look away now.'

Vikki turned her head in the direction of Kate, and grimaced.

'There you are, all done.'

'Really?'

'Yes. You have lovely veins.'

'Why thank you, all the boys tell me that!'

'Oh, I see we have a joker among us,' smiled Lynn. 'Now, when I put the first syringe in, you will probably get a horrid taste in your mouth, so suck on this boiled sweet.'

'Sweeties as well! You're full of pleasant surprises. Does my friend get one too?'

'Vikki!' admonished Kate. 'No, I'm fine,' she said to the nurse.

She was shaking as she observed what Vikki was going through. How on earth was she being so calm about it? Kate was under no illusions that this was the easy part. She had read up on the side-effects of chemo, and they were horrendous. She knew that she was going to have to toughen up herself, to help her friend through the next few months.

As the nurse took the needle out, and gave her a swab to hold, Vikki began to turn a whiter shade of pale. The nurse quickly handed her a round paper-mâché bowl.

'Take your time, honey,' she said kindly, as she patted her shoulder gently. 'The first time is always the worst.'

'I just didn't expect it to happen so quickly,' Vikki said, as she pulled her hand through her hair. A fine sheen of sweat had broken out on her face.

'Some of that is probably down to nerves,' said Lynn. 'Hopefully the anti-emetic I have given you will prevent you actually being sick. If it's not enough, just ring us up, and we can sort you out with something stronger. Now, here's a prescription to pick up from the pharmacy. Perhaps your friend here can go and pick that up, while you have a little rest?'

'Sure,' said Kate, getting to her feet. She would be glad of something to do. She was feeling a little queasy herself, truth be told. As she walked out of the room and down the corridor looking for signs to the pharmacy, she wiped away the tears from her eyes. This was so wrong! How could dear, sweet Vikki be having to go through this evil disease? She knew that the next few months were going to be difficult, especially with Vikki having a young family to deal with. As Kate waited for the prescription to be made up, she rang Sam on her mobile.

'Hey you,' he replied.

'Hi. I just wanted to hear your voice,' she said.

'Are you okay?'

'Yes, no. I, I don't know. Vikki has just had her first treatment.'

'How did it go?'

'Oh, you know Vikki. A laugh a minute. I don't suppose the nurse has ever had a patient like her before. Oh, Sam, it was horrid. Those gigantic needles filled with obnoxious liquid. It can't be right, can it?'

'Come on, you. It's going to make her better. We all know there is no other option. I really wish I was there, for both of you, but I'm sure as hell grateful she's got you with her. Now, you've got be strong for her, you know that? Will you do that? For me?'

She wiped her tears away with her hand. 'What if I can't do it, Sam? What if I let her down and keep crying? It will end up with her supporting me!'

'You can do it. I didn't fall for a weak woman. The only reason I fell for you is because I could see that core of iron through the centre of you. Be my hands there, Kate. You know I'd give anything to just drop work and come down. But I can't, and I know she's in good hands.'

'I know. I just love her so much, and I can't bear the pain she is feeling. Thank you, Sam. I appreciate you believing in me. It's what I needed to hear. Thank you.'

She put the phone away just as they called Vikki's name, and then collected her drugs.

When she returned to the chemotherapy suite Vikki was back in the waiting room chatting to a man.

'Hi, Kate, meet Richard. He's an old hand here, and has been teaching me a few tricks.'

Trust Vikki to pick friends up as she goes along, thought Kate, as she shook hands with the young man. *But he looks too young to have cancer!*

'Testicular,' he grinned shaking her hand.

'Pardon?'

'Cancer of the testicle, that's why I'm here. It's really the first thing people want to know when they meet a new patient here. What's he got, what's she got? Well, I find it's best to say it out loud, you know? Get it out in the open. Not my balls, of course, just the word. Anyway, it's ball, singular now.'

Vikki and Kate were breathless with laughter at this handsome, young guy, exposing his vulnerability to the world. If only everyone had such a healthy relationship to the word cancer. Vikki had found so many folk couldn't even mention the word, and if they did, it was whispered in hushed tones, almost as if it were a dirty disease, or something to be ashamed of.

'I've already told him I've only one boob,' said Vikki, 'so now we're intimate friends.'

'Wow, you two are fast workers,' laughed Kate. 'Did she tell you she's a happily married woman with three kids?'

'Yes, and he's a happily married man with four!'

'No way! You don't look old enough!'

'I sure am, do you want to see my birth certificate?' he retorted. 'Seriously, these are my kids,' and he flicked open his phone, to reveal a sweet photo of four little girls.

'The last two were twins,' he grinned ruefully. 'Bit of a handful, as you may imagine.'

'And I thought I had my work cut out,' said Vikki. 'I'd take my hat off to you, if I had one. I'm one of twins, and I never really thought how tough it must have been for my mum and dad until I had kids myself.'

'You will be able to take your hat off soon, I expect, when you lose your gorgeous tresses,' he said sadly, looking at Vikki's stylish new crop.

Vikki put her hands up to her head, and thoughtfully touched her hair.

'Why haven't you lost yours then, if this is your fourth session?'

'Different chemo regimes, I guess,' he shrugged. 'Doesn't seem fair really does it? I bet you I can identify all the women here with breast cancer, because they nearly always lose their hair. My mate over there has bowel cancer, and he never lost his, either.'

They looked across at an elderly man with grey hair, and sure enough he hadn't lost it.

'Mine is a lot thinner than it used it be,' he said, handling his head thoughtfully. 'But you know, yours will grow back really quickly, and a lot of people say it's thicker when it does.'

'God forbid!' laughed Vikki. 'Mine was thick enough to start with! I've only just had this lot cut. Do you want to see how long it was?' It was her turn to scroll through her phone pictures, until she found one with the kids climbing all over her.

Richard looked thoughtfully at the photo. 'That's criminal,' he said sadly. 'Really, really criminal.'

They all sat quietly for some moments, contemplating the idea of Vikki being bald, until she jumped up from her seat.

'Come on you, I've got to pick the kids up from Sue's house. They'll be getting worried.'

They said their goodbyes to Richard, and headed back to the car.

'How are you feeling?' asked Kate

'A bit queasy,' she replied, 'but I've got a spare sick bowl here, just in case. I would hate to mess up your lovely, pristine car. You can tell you don't have kids, you should see the state of mine!'

They drove home, both lost in thought. Vikki was quieter than Kate had ever known her to be, but she was probably feeling quite rough. She dropped her off at Sue's, and then headed back to do a few tasks in the office. She was neglecting her work a little. The trouble was, she had two new situations that were taking her mind off her work. Firstly of course, was Vikki's illness, but secondly was her new relationship with Sam. They were taking things slowly, but she couldn't stop thinking of him. Their romance had happened so suddenly, and unexpectedly. She had been so wrapped up in hating the man, but now these new emotions were overwhelming. Truth be told, she knew that there had always been some sort of attraction going on between the two of them, but it had been hidden behind the animosity. She was so glad that was all behind them now; they needed to have a united front for Vikki's sake. They would be spending a lot of time together and it would have proved very difficult if they couldn't have got along.

As she flicked through the pages of her diary, filling in the next few chemotherapy dates, she realised that she was going to have to be highly organised. Christmas was looming up; the biggest date in the church calendar. There were so many services to prepare for, and it was the time of the year that many folk outside of the church family came along. Everyone wanted to attend either the midnight mass, or the carol service. This year they were going overboard with the crib services, as they had so many young families now attending. They were also going to hold a Christingle service for the first time ever. She knew this was a popular concept with a lot of churches. The idea was to give everyone attending the service an orange with a red ribbon round the circumference, representing the blood of Christ, and a candle in the centre, symbolising the Light of the world. The Mother's Union were coming on board with this event, and had agreed to make up the oranges. At the moment though, they had no idea of numbers. How would it take off? Kate knew a lot of the mums were going to invite friends to come along, so she was hoping it would be a good turnout. She flicked through the dates in her diary, realising that Vikki's chemo would go right through to the other side of Christmas. Kate had managed to clear a lot of the dates for Josh, so that he would be able to take her to most of her sessions, but those he couldn't manage, Kate was available for. It was going to be more difficult when she had to undergo radiotherapy, as this was every day for five weeks. They were going to make a rota up of friends to help with transport. She doodled on the page as she tried to think of ways she would be able to do most of the dates. She knew how much Vikki hated asking people for help. It was bad enough getting the children picked up from school every day. Vikki was usually someone who helped everybody else, and this was not coming naturally to her.

The phone rang, and it was Vikki.

'Long time no see,' joked Kate.

But Vikki was not laughing.

'It's Finn,' she cried. 'He got sent to the head's office again.'

'What! That's so unlike Finn. What on earth for?'

'Well, that's what I thought. But apparently he punched some boy in the playground. Knocked his tooth out, as well.'

'What made him do that?'

'They couldn't get him to say. Of course, it would be on a day that neither Josh nor I were available to pick him up, wouldn't it? Poor kid was so ashamed when Sue was told to fetch him. Oh Kate. I can't believe he did it. But when I asked him why, oh it's just too sad.'

'Why, what did he say?'

'Apparently, this lad was telling the other boys that Finn's mummy was going to die.'

'No! That's so terrible. Poor Finn. I would have joined him in beating up the kid, I think.'

'I know. That's how I felt. But of course, he didn't tell the head any of this, so what was she to do? He had to sit outside her office all afternoon as punishment. I have rung her and told her what he told me, and she has been in contact with the boy's parents to explain. I don't know what to do, Kate.'

'Well, I think you should sit him down and just talk to him. It's what you guys do best.'

'But what can I say? Don't you think he's too young to explain it to?'

'No, I don't. Perhaps if they knew a little more about what is happening to you, they might be able to deal with it better. I know Amy's a bit young, but the other two are more than capable. Put it in a way they will understand. If you like, I will come over and take Amy out for a bit, so you can spend time with them.'

'No, that's okay, thanks, Kate. You are so wise, you know, considering you're not a mum yourself. Josh is home early tonight, so I will be able to have some time with Daisy and Finn on my own, while he puts Amy to bed. Thank you so much for being there. I just needed to talk to someone. I can cope when it just affects me, but not when it's the kids. It screws me up really badly.'

'I can only imagine, Vikki. You are such a brilliant mum. And I think you should be proud of young Finn, standing up for you like that.'

'I know, he's such a darling. Thank you, Kate. Sorry to have interrupted.'

'Any time, you know that. Bye, Vikki, take care.'

She replaced the receiver, wondering how much more Vikki could take. 'God,' she shouted, 'what the hell are you doing? Can't you make this easier for her?'

Chapter 19

'Thank God for sat nav, that's all I can say,' said Kate, as she slumped into the deep leather sofa in Sam's flat. 'I would never have found my way through that one-way system otherwise.'

'Yes, it's a bit of a maze, I have to admit,' he said ruefully. 'You did well to get here in such good time.'

'This flat is something else,' she said, looking round. 'It's stunning!'

'Well, let me get you a drink, and then I'll show you round.'

'That's some view you've got there. It's fantastic,' she breathed, looking out on the water. 'How I would love a view like that. You must think my cottage is pretty pokey, compared to this.'

'Your cottage is beautiful, and well you know it,' he told her.

'Well, yes, but I do love this modern, clean look. I'm quite envious.'

'Don't be,' he said, 'It's just a building.'

He handed her a glass, then plonked himself down beside her. They grinned at each other.

'So, I've got a whole weekend of you, all to myself, with no Daisy or Amy vying for your attention.'

'That will be fun,' she laughed. 'But you love those kids. I can see it in your face. You let them do anything to you.'

'Yes, and I have the bruises to prove it.'

'They are great, aren't they?' she smiled. 'Vikki and Josh have done a marvellous job with them.'

'I think most of the credit goes to Vikki,' he argued.

'Of course, I forgot, you resent the church and Josh's job, don't you?'

'Well, it's true. That marriage is split between Vikki, and the congregation. I just think he should get his priorities right.'

'She knew that it would be like this when she took him on,' she chided him gently. 'A vicar's job was never going to be nine till five.'

'But they are all so demanding!' he exclaimed. 'Still, I guess you're right, and you have made a huge difference to his workload, so I will always be grateful to you for that.'

'I would never have thought that when I first met you,' she laughed. 'Do you remember what you were like?'

'Don't remind me,' he said, shaking his head. 'I'm embarrassed and ashamed at the way I treated you, I just thought you were another one of *his flock* and were being a nuisance to Vikki. I understand now just how valuable you are to her. She couldn't manage without you, you know, both as a friend, and with the way you've managed the work-load for Josh. He was a useless timekeeper before you came along.'

'I know!' she giggled, as the wine started to relax her.

He leant over and kissed her, causing her to spill her wine on the sofa.

'Oops!' she said. 'Now look what you've made me do.'

'That's the beauty of leather. It simply wipes down,' he said, as he produced a white handkerchief with a flourish.

'Now I would never have put you down as a hankie man. More the man-size tissue type of guy.'

'But I'm a gentleman, and you never know when you might need to produce one; never know when you might meet a damsel in distress. Even in your own living room.'

'Is that how you see me?' she laughed. 'And you, I guess, would have to be the knight in shining armour then?'

'At your service, dear lady. Now, try to drink the rest of that wine, while I go and see to the cuisine.'

'Something certainly smells good. I never had you down as the cooking type either.'

'There's a lot you don't know about me. And there's a whole lot I don't know about you, but I intend to find out.' He winked cheekily at her, and then went through to the kitchen.

Kate looked around at his fashionable bachelor's flat, with row upon row of CDs, and a large flat-screen TV. *When was the last time she had watched any TV?* she thought to herself. Her days were filled with work, which often spilled over into the evening. Then when she did have any free time, she either spent it with Vikki, or on the computer, researching.

She got up to wander around, and noticed a lot of photo frames on top of the bookshelf. She smiled as she saw Vikki and her family beaming out from the pictures. *He really loves his family,* she thought. She bit her lip pensively as she remembered the situation with her aunt. She had not told anyone about it yet, not even Vikki. She was almost ashamed of the influence the Brethren church had on them, and now this latest scandal! What would Sam think if he knew she was so distant from her family, and that there were so many skeletons hiding in the closet?

Peering through the doors, she spotted the bedroom and bathroom, and as she carefully pushed open the last door, she saw it was kitted out with keep-fit equipment. *Oh my word, a gym!* she thought. *If he ever gets to find out what an unfit person I am, whatever will he think?*

Just then, she saw Sam walk over to the table with a large, steaming casserole dish in his hands.

'That smells wonderful,' she said, as the aroma of garlic and fresh lime assaulted her nostrils.

He went back to the kitchen, and returned with a huge plate of focaccia and a green salad, and placed it all on the table.

'Voilà,' he said with a flourish of the tea towel. 'Now come and dine.'

After supper, Sam put some music on the iPod, and sat down next to Kate.

'Now is this Kung Fu Fighters, or whatever it is they're called?'

'Foo Fighters, you daft thing! No, I thought you might prefer something a bit more chilled.'

'Have you put all your music on an MP3 now? If so, why have you still got all those CDs?'

'I keep them purely for sentimental reasons,' he said.

'You old softie.' She poked him gently in the ribs, and he grabbed her hand away from her, twisting her body towards him as he did so. Kate was caught off-guard, and suddenly found herself being kissed passionately. As their kisses became more heated, she suddenly pulled away.

'What's up?' he asked breathlessly. 'I thought you were okay with us?'

'I am,' she stuttered. 'In fact, it's more than okay.'

'Phew! I thought maybe I was getting things wrong there for a minute. I was pretty sure we both felt the same way about each other.'

'It's just....'

'Yes?'

'Sam, I've never, I mean, I'm still...'

'Hungry? Thirsty?'

'No, no, I couldn't eat another thing. It's just, being here with you for the weekend, obviously you're expecting, and I'm expecting, well, you need to know...'

'Are you having second thoughts?' He looked crestfallen as he held Kate's hands in his.

'Oh no! Sam, it's just that, you're my first time.' She sat there with her head down, feeling rather stupid.

'You are kidding me? You're still a virgin? How come?'

'I've never felt it was right, that's all,' she said simply.

'Hey, we can take it slowly,' he said. 'I would never do anything you're not comfortable with.'

'Don't you dare stop now,' she laughed. 'I've been looking forward to this moment ever since you kissed my cheek months ago, when you still hated me!'

'You remember that kiss?' he asked. 'I couldn't stop myself, you stood there looking so prim and proper, and I just wanted to shock you.'

'So there was no passion involved then? You simply wanted to wind me up!' She slapped him playfully. 'That's not much of a chat up line, you know? Kiss me again please, Sam.'

As Sam led Kate into the bedroom, she had no qualms at all about what she was giving up to him. She knew that she had fallen in love with him, and was sure it was reciprocated.

The weekend passed in a blur of passion and fun, as they explored each other's bodies. Much later, they went out and he showed her the sights and sounds of Bristol. It was with great reluctance that she packed up her bags to head home.

'Promise me you'll come down again soon?' he asked her, brushing her hair tenderly behind her ear.

She stood on her tiptoes and kissed him on the tip of his nose.

'Try and keep me away,' she said.

He watched as she walked over to her car, and settled in for the drive home. He was overwhelmed by how much he loved this little slip of a woman. He had been such an oaf when they had first met! Just thinking how he could have ruined everything made him shudder. She had wrapped herself firmly round his heart. He went in to the flat, and realised she had left her scarf on the back of the chair. He hurried to the window, but she had driven off. Smiling, he held it in his hands and inhaled her scent. He was rather pleased she had forgotten it.

Kate had made it back in time for the evening service, and sat herself in the pew, next to Sophie.

'I'm so glad you're here,' said the young woman. 'Look what I've got!' And she showed her a new scan picture of the baby. 'They've confirmed it's a girl!'

'Well, you knew that anyway,' smiled Kate.

'I know, but it's reassuring to know I was right,' she grinned smugly. 'And I don't think Robbie quite believed me, but he does now! So we're painting the nursery pink at last. I'm going to paint some Disney characters on the walls. Really big ones!'

'I didn't know you could paint?'

'Well, I can copy off cards and stuff. That'll be alright won't it?' She looked a little unsure.

'It will be just perfect,' Kate reassured her. 'So you're half-way through now? How very exciting!'

'I know! But in a funny way, I don't want to rush through being pregnant, 'cause I actually love it, you see? I love being special, and having my baby girl close to me. I am looking forward to meeting her, but I'll have a lifetime to share her with others. Right now, she's just mine.' And she wrapped her arms round her swollen belly.

Shoot! I feel insanely jealous! thought Kate to herself, as pangs of intense pain shot through her unexpectedly. *Just be pleased for her, you miserable cow!*

Kate smiled warmly at Sophie. 'You've done so well to get through all this without feeling sick or anything. And you look amazing,' she told her truthfully.

'Well, I was a little nauseous to start with, but I didn't mind, they say it means the pregnancy is more viable when that happens. Do you want a feel? I think she's giving a little wriggle.' Sophie reached down and took Kate's hand.

As she felt a strange little wave sweep across Sophie's stomach, Kate felt tears in her eyes. She took her hand away abruptly, causing Sophie to glance at her strangely.

'Are you alright, Kate?'

'Yes, I'm fine,' she snapped. 'The service is starting.' And she bent her head, as if in prayer.

What is up with me? I've never felt this way about seeing pregnant women before, she thought. But then, she had never really been that close to anyone who was expecting. Sure, there had been women she had worked with who had gone off on maternity leave, but she had allowed Sophie to get right under her skin. Her mind was distracted throughout the service, as she kept thinking of her age, and all the tales she had heard about fading fertility. She really wanted children, she knew that now. Perhaps she hadn't before she arrived in Ashton Kirby, but spending so much time with Vikki and Josh's tribe, and now going through Sophie's pregnancy step-by-step, made her realise that time was ticking for her. *I wonder if Sam wants children?* she thought, then shook her head briefly and smiled to herself. Perhaps I'm getting a bit carried away. We are only just getting to know each other. She was pretty sure he would though, knowing the way he felt about his nieces and nephew. She then started to think about the poor baby who had died all those years ago. How sad to lose a tiny baby so soon. Her aunt must have been devastated! Surely her mum would have known something about it? She really wanted to see Sam next weekend, but it was vital she sorted out this mystery first, and laid it to rest. She looked up when she heard the last hymn being read out. Goodness! She had been so lost in thought, that she had not heard a word of the sermon or prayers. Hopefully, Josh would forget to ask her what she thought of it.

Chapter 20

Kate had been in touch with her sister Melanie during the week, and it sounded as if she was managing to stay on the straight and narrow. She had even managed to get a job on the checkout counter, down at her local B&Q store. Things were really looking up for her, and Kate was delighted. She hated being at odds with her only sibling, and it would make her life so much easier if she had a friendly face at home when she returned. It was always such a chore visiting her parents, but this time she had a sense of purpose. She was determined to find out what her mother knew about baby Paul.

She found her mother alone in the sitting room.

'Where's Dad?' she asked.

'He's down at the chapel. There's a bit of a problem with one of the young men.'

'Oh, they're holding one of their kangaroo courts, you mean?'

'Don't be so rude, Kate. It doesn't suit you.'

'And being so bloody pious doesn't suit you either, Mum.'

'Please don't swear.'

'I'm sorry. It's just...well; don't you ever wish your life was a bit less *ruled*, Mum?'

'It's the way it's always been,' said her mum firmly, 'that's all.' Her mouth set in a grim line.

'But you could be so much happier. Being a Christian doesn't have to mean punishment and rules.'

'Well, what would you know?' her mother's cheeks flared red, and she even stomped her feet. 'You're never here, anyway.'

'Yes, and you know why! It's choking, Mum. It's not the way the rest of the world live, you must realise that?'

'Christ never said it would be easy to follow Him,' she replied primly, and started to quote scriptures. 'Whoever chooses to follow Him, must lay down their life...'

'I know all that! I go to church too. I read my Bible. I say prayers too, if you must know! But I also have a life, for God's sake.'

'Please don't use the Lord's name in vain.'

'You make me swear, Mum. Listen to yourself, it's just not normal. Look, I'm sorry. I know I shouldn't swear, and I'm not mocking you, honest. It's just, well you always seem so unhappy. I just want to try and help you.'

Her mother sighed and sat down. 'Seriously, you don't understand, Kate. I have no choice. I can't expect you to understand.' She raised her hands in a hopeless gesture. 'I can't get away.'

'Mum,' said Kate urgently. 'You can, you know. If Dad wants to continue in this stifling lifestyle, that's up to him, but you don't have to, I'll stand up for you, if you like. Come and stay with me for a while.'

'I can't. I have to look after your father, and that's the end of it,' she sighed.

Kate realised that it was futile to continue; to do so would just antagonise her mother, and she wanted to ask her some serious questions.

'Let me make you a cup of tea, Mum. I've brought some chocolate biscuits with me. Is that a good idea?'

'That would be nice, dear, Thank you.'

She went into the kitchen and looked up to the ceiling, as if to find a way through to God. *Please help me help my mum,* she pleaded. *And please help me find out the answers I need. Thank you Lord. Amen.*

She returned with the teapot, and a plate for the biscuits. She never used a teapot at home, but she knew better than to dunk a tea bag in a cup here. That was probably seen as a sin! She slowly unwrapped the biscuits, and put a few on the plate.

'Mum,' she said slowly. 'I've been looking through some of Aunt Val's papers.'

Her mother's head shot up. 'Well don't!' she shouted.

'Don't be so daft. I've been meaning to clear the loft out a bit, and I've got to get rid of some rubbish. Anyway, there's a lot of fascinating stuff up there. Do you know I've even found some wedding photos of you and Dad! You looked so pretty and young!'

Her mother looked panicked.

'Anyway, that's not what I wanted to ask you. I know Val did something the church didn't approve of, and that's why none of you want to talk about her.'

'You're right there.'

'But come on! She was only a young woman when she left. What could possibly have been that bad? What about God's forgiveness?'

'Please leave things as they are,' her mum said. 'It's none of your business.'

'But it is. She's my aunt and your sister. I know that no matter what Mel does, I love her anyway. I may not always like her, but I will always love her.'

'Are you questioning my love for Val? I loved that woman more than I've ever loved anyone. She was like a mother to me, I'll have you know.'

Her mother sunk lower into her seat, her shoulders slumped.

'So leave it.'

'No, I won't,' said Kate stubbornly. 'I think I know why she left, Mum. I've found a death certificate. I think Aunt Val had a little baby. Is that why she was sent away?'

Her mother went white and started to struggle for breath.

'Mum? Are you okay?' She rushed over and put her arm around her shoulders. 'Shall I call the doctor?'

'I'm alright,' she gasped, 'just get me a cup of water. I'll be okay.'

'Tell me what all this is about, Mum. Am I right?'

'No, you're not, you nosy parker. I told you. Just leave it.'

'Well, I'll ask Dad then, shall I? Does he know anything?'

'Your father knows nothing!' she barked. 'Don't you dare mention anything to him!'

'Alright, calm down.' She was now seriously worried about her. Kate knew that she was not going to get anything out of her mother now, but she was obviously on the right trail, judging by her reaction. But why did she get so upset? Surely what her aunt had done more than forty years ago hardly mattered now, did it?

She returned to Ashton Kirby with a heavy heart. She had gleaned no more information from her visit, and had wasted a weekend when she could have spent it with Sam. They had talked for hours on the phone to each other, and texted little love messages, but it wasn't the same as physically being together. He had been so sweet when she had told him she was a virgin. Her strict church upbringing had had a serious effect on her, and although she knew it was okay to have sex with someone you loved, she still felt deep down, that sex was somehow 'dirty', and a sin. Her rational mind had broken away from every other rule the church had repressed the brethren with, but this one had managed to stick with her. She just thought that she was frigid, because she had never really wanted to make love with anyone, until Sam had come along. Now she was so glad she hadn't! It was so good having him teach her, as they explored each other's bodies. She now knew that she wasn't a prude! In fact, she felt positively naughty! And it was a good feeling. She giggled, as she thought of Vikki's reaction when she had told her.

'You and Sam! You naughty girl. He's my brother. Ugh! This almost feels like some kind of incest! We're obviously too close, you and I!'

But she had hugged her tightly, thrilled that her brother had finally found someone to be with. She had worried about Sam for years, as he went in and out of relationships, with absolutely no commitment at all. But now these two had found each other, and it was the best possible news to help her survive the long, dark months of chemotherapy.

Kate's life was rich and full, and a mixture of sheer joy, frustration and sadness. She never realised how happy she would feel, being in a relationship with Sam. It was above and beyond anything she could have ever imagined. She loved travelling to Bristol, and being cocooned in his flat, away from all the pressures of work, and her complicated family.

Christmas was approaching rapidly, and she was chasing her tail trying to get all of the service sheets printed and collated for the various services. She was liaising with the two local schools as well, as they were having their end of term services in the church. They were also taking part in the Christingle service; a first for both the schools and the church.

Kate had even managed to persuade the owners of the farm, on the edge of the village, to lend their animals for the crib service. She was so excited about the tableaux they were building up, and one of the young pregnant mums was going to act the part of Mary. She was due to give birth any day now! It had the potential to be slightly chaotic, Kate had to admit. The children were already looking forward to the animals pooing and weeing everywhere, but it was only for ten minutes. What could possibly go wrong? Yes, plenty, but it would be fun, and hopefully the word was going round the village even now. This was a chance to bring in folks who still thought of church as stuffy, boring, and not relevant in the twenty-first century.

She was also spending a lot of time at Vikki's house, helping out with the children when Vikki was feeling rough. Her treatment was given every three weeks, and it was during the first week of every cycle that she was knocked out. The first twenty four hours left her feeling nauseous and sick. After that came the dreadful leg and body pains; Vikki described it as 'having labour pains throughout the whole of her body'. Even the powerful pain killers she had been prescribed did nothing to alleviate it. As the pain abated, a dreadful tiredness would sweep over her, leaving her limp and lifeless for a few days. She did not feel too bad for the following two weeks; that was in spite of the mouth ulcers, stomach cramps, and dry, itchy skin. Even her nails were falling out! Despite all the horrors of chemotherapy, Vikki managed to hang on to her sense of humour and wit. She needed this, especially when her hair fell out. The first few handfuls came away suddenly, as she was washing her hair in the shower. As she rinsed the bubbles away, she found her fingers full of clumps of hair. It was shocking, frightening, and not something any woman should have to go through. Within days, most of her hair was gone. Vikki had asked Kate to shave the remainder off for her. The children were in bed, and Ellie Smith and Kate were invited for the Bald Supper.

After plenty of wine, and nibbles, Vikki presented Kate with Josh's shaver.

'I can't possibly do this!' she cried, horrified.

'Of course you can. Imagine shearing a sheep.'

'But I've never sheared a sheep.'

'Well then, this is your lucky day! Go for it, girl.'

'You do it, Ellie.'

'No thank you. I'm a doctor, remember. I'm the one who gives her foul medicine to make her sick and ill. I'm not going to be responsible for making her look like Kojak as well.'

'You do make me do some awful things,' Kate said glumly, picking up the shaver. 'Please don't hold it against me for the rest of my life.'

'I'll let you try on my wig. Please, please,' Vikki pleaded, comically, with her hands clasped in mock prayer.

'Oh, alright, if you insist.'

Kate turned the shaver on, and with a shaky hand held it up to Vikki's head, the gadget buzzing like an angry bee. Nothing happened.

'It doesn't work,' she exclaimed.

'Give it here, you numpty.' Vikki grabbed the shaver from her hand, and pulled a little switch down.

'You hadn't pulled the cutter down. Now try it.'

This time, it purred through the auburn locks, creating a pathway straight through the middle.

'Take a picture with my phone, please,' said Vikki, handing the mobile to Ellie.

'You can't be serious!'

'Of course I am. It's a chapter in my life, isn't it? I want it recorded for posterity.'

Ellie reluctantly got up and snapped a photo.

'Now, get over here, and I'll take a selfie of all three of us. Let me just switch the camera to face us... there!'

The two friends peered over the top of Vikki's bald pate. It was horrifying, distressing and yet incredibly comical to see her this way.

'God, you're so brave,' said Ellie, shivering. 'I don't know if I would agree to have chemo.'

'Of course you would, if it was going to save your life. Come on! You're a doctor.'

'I know, but I'm quite vain, I think. I wouldn't be as lackadaisical as you are about it, that's for sure.'

'Listen, ladies. I am going to beat this bugger of a disease. I am not going to bow down to it by crying and feeling sorry for myself.'

'Yes, you have the right attitude, I guess. I just think you're remarkable, that's all.' Ellie shrugged, amazed at the strength of character her friend possessed. She had seen enough people going through cancer treatment, and most people needed counselling to get through it. Vikki was truly one in a million!

Kate and Vikki had gone to a wig centre in town last week. The poor hairdresser didn't know what had hit her, as Vikki rampaged through the shop, trying on the most outrageous wigs, and both women fell about laughing. She had finally settled on a short, blond one, surprisingly. But it would have been very hard to find a wig that came close to her unusual, copper coloured hair, so it was more sensible to go for a style and colour totally unlike her own.

It actually suited her, and pleased Amy, who called Mummy 'her twin', for they now had matching hairstyles. Daisy had sulked for hours, feeling left out of this new situation, until Vikki had reminded her that she shared her mummy's hair in 'real life', and when her hair grew back, they could be 'twins' again. This mollified the child slightly, and she was even more delighted when she was allowed to put her mum's wig on. She looked like a grown-up version of Amy! They were all crying with laughter when Finn put it on, and pranced around in a feminine fashion. Josh arrived home, and found them all collapsed on the sofa, with Amy crying that she had wet herself.

'I don't know what happened, Daddy. I was laughing so much it hurt, and then I wet my knickers! I didn't mean to, honestly. Don't tell me off, please.'

'Come here, little lady,' he said, crouching down to wrap his arms around her. 'This won't be the first time your idiot mother will make you wet yourself laughing. She frequently does the same thing to me.'

'You wet your pants? Really? Ugh!'

He looked over at the giggling pile of love on the sofa, and found that he had a huge lump in his throat. His wife was something else. God, how he loved her! He was not going to let cancer destroy her, it couldn't. It just couldn't.

Chapter 21

Sophie and Robbie had invited Kate round for coffee, to see the nursery. Their little house was tucked into a corner on the small council estate. A plain house among other plain houses; but inside, it was a different story. In each room, you could see Sophie's character shining through. It was bright, pretty, clean and very girly! It was obvious whose personality was reflected in the decor, even though it was Robbie who carried out most of the donkey work.

'Hello, Kate, come on through,' said Robbie, holding open the front door.

Sophie waddled over to greet her. She was getting enormous!

'Look at you!' exclaimed Kate. 'How much longer have you got? Are you sure you've not got twins in there?'

'Just one little girl,' she grinned. 'Little bump in here is getting a bit crowded now.' She patted her fat stomach protectively. 'She wants to come out and enjoy her new nursery. Come and see.' She grabbed Kate by the hand and pulled her along the narrow hallway leading to the bedroom.

'Oh my word! It's totally stunning! Who did all this?'

'Me and Robbie,' said Sophie, grinning widely. 'Do you like it?'

'Do I like it? I absolutely love it! You have such an amazing gift, you know that?'

She looked around at the pink painted bedroom, with a mural of Disney characters running round the walls. In the corner was a tiny crib, covered with a pink veil of sheer gossamer lace.

'Where did you get the canopy from? It's gorgeous!'

'I picked up this old ball gown from the charity shop. It was really cheap, and after I had used the lace, I cut up the silk under-petticoats for cushion covers, see?' She held out a fat silk cushion, edged with red piping. 'I know it's a bit, well, gaudy, but I love it.'

'So do I,' said Kate. 'You ought to write a book about making something from nothing. It's very fashionable, you know. You never cease to amaze me. I know you make all your own clothes from your charity shop finds, too, but they never look second-hand. They look like they're designer fashion.'

'Aw, shut up, Kate, you're making me blush.'

'You clever thing,' said Kate getting up to give her a hug. 'I can't get near enough to you any more, with that fat belly. My arms aren't long enough.'

They both stayed in the room gazing round and chatting, until Robbie called up to say that their coffee was getting cold.

They sat downstairs chatting about the new arrival, and also about the work Robbie was doing on the new curate's house. Suddenly, Kate looked across at the clock on the wall.

'Goodness! It's one o'clock! I didn't realise how long I've stayed. I'm so sorry taking up all your morning. I have to go, as I have a couple coming to discuss their wedding arrangements.' She stood up, and handed her mug to Robbie, then went into the hall to slip on her shoes.

'It's great having you round, Kate. Please come any time, especially when the nipper's here. It will be company for Sophie, especially when I'm working.'

'Of course I will, but I have a feeling Sophie will never be without company, Robbie. She's made quite an impression with the young mums at church.'

'She makes an impression with everyone who meets her,' he said. 'I'm so lucky, you know. Sometimes, I have to pinch myself to see if all this is real.' He waved his arms around at the house, and all that it contained.

'Well, she's lucky to have you as well. There aren't many guys who are as handy around the house as you are. Anyway, I've got to dash. See you soon, Robbie.' She placed a kiss on the side of his face, and dashed away.

'She's such a lovely lady,' said Sophie affectionately.

They both stood watching her cycle through the estate, thinking how fortunate they were to have such a good friend.

'She's like the mum I've always wanted, Rob. I know she's too young and all that, but she seems so grown-up and caring, like I would expect a proper mum to be. Not that I have a clue really. This baby will never doubt my love for her. I'm going to spoil her rotten.'

'So I'm going to have to be the mean disciplinarian in the family then, am I?'

'Gosh, Robbie, such a big word! Have you swallowed a dictionary or something?'

He chased her into the kitchen, and pulled her down onto his lap.

'I love you, Mummy,' he whispered into her ear, stroking her belly.

'I love you too, Daddy.'

Chapter 22

'Am I going to see you this weekend, or are you going to Sam's?' asked Vikki.

'No, he's coming up here. I said he could stay at the cottage, if that's alright with you?'

'Who am I to stand in the path of true love?' she laughed. 'But you're not getting away that lightly, you're both coming to spend Sunday here with my horrors, whether you like it or not. You can't spend all weekend locked in your love chamber.'

'You bet we are! I'm not going to cook him a roast dinner, I wouldn't know where to start.'

'Well, then, you had better come early, and I will get Josh to give you cookery lessons. I'm not having my brother shack up with some bird who can't cook.'

Kate hit her with the magazine she had been reading. 'Shut up, you! I can cook.'

'What?'

'Um, pasta...'

'That's all, you idiot! He can't survive on pasta! He's a big, hunky bloke. He needs proper sustenance.'

'He can cook perfectly well himself.'

'And is that what your marriage is going to be like, then? Is it going to be you wearing the trousers?'

'Slow down, honey. Who said anything about marriage? Just butt out of our business, you interfering old crow.'

'You can't talk to me like that! I've got cancer!' Vikki hunched herself up, looking weak and pathetic.

'You're not using the cancer card with me, my friend. I know perfectly well it's all a sham.'

They bantered together a while longer. There weren't many friendships that could endure the stress of illness as well as theirs had, and instead of pushing them farther apart, it had brought them closer than ever.

'So, come on, spill, Kate. Where is this relationship heading?'

'I don't know,' she replied coyly. 'We're just taking it slowly. We get on so well, and it's great being able to share him with you, but, it's difficult. I've never been in a serious relationship before. I think I'm so used to my independence. And so is he.'

'Yeah, and you're both clocking on. It's about time the pair of you took a serious look at your future. You want to have kids, right?'

'Of course. I think... well, one day I expect.'

'Girlfriend, your eggs are getting old!'

This earned her another whack of the magazine.

'Ouch! That hurt. Think about it, you do love him, right?'

'That goes without saying. Anyway, it's not up to me, is it?'

'Hell, woman, this is the twenty-first century we're living in. You don't have to wait for the guy to ask you to marry him. If I know my brother, he's so laid back you'd be fifty before he even thought of tying the knot. You've got to break him out of his bachelor mould.'

'I don't know. We've both got our own lives, our own properties, our separate interests.'

'Rubbish. If you love someone, obstacles like that don't get in the way. Seriously, do it for me, Kate. Before I die. Please.'

'Idiot! You're not going to die. I won't let you! So you can lose that little bullet from your arsenal of bribes.' But a small chill had crept up Kate's spine. She just assumed Vikki would beat this disease, and refused to consider the possibility of her dying from it. She was a fighter, anyway. If anyone could get through it in one piece, Vikki could.

The kids burst through the kitchen door, breaking into her thoughts, thankfully.

'Daisy! I hear you won an award at school for playing your recorder. Are you going to give me a demonstration?'

'Sure,' she replied, as she ran back out of the room to look for her instrument.

'Mummy!' A shout came from upstairs. 'Where has my recorder gone? I can't find it anywhere.'

'Where did you leave it last?' asked Vikki, waving the instrument around in her hand.

'I can't remember.'

'Well, have a think. It's good training for your brain.'

'I had it this morning when I was going to school,' she mused, clomping down the stairs. 'Then I had breakfast....' she walked back into the kitchen.

'Oh yes,' she grinned sheepishly. 'I had it at the table.'

'I thought you would remember that quite well, after I told you three times to stop playing it at the table.'

'Ugh! It's covered in sticky marmalade. Mum, it's not fair! Amy's ruined my recorder.'

'Don't be so silly. It's your fault for leaving it lying around. Now just get a wet wipe and clean it up, and stop making such a fuss.'

Kate sat and smiled at the little scene playing around her. What kind of mum would she make? Would she be as good as Vikki? Amy broke into her thoughts by jumping up at her lap.

'Can I have a cuddle, please Auntie Kate? No one here loves me.' Her little bottom lip was stuck out in a sulk.

'Of course you can sweetheart, but you're wrong, you know. Everybody loves you; they can't help loving you, because you're scrummy.' She tickled her tummy until Amy screeched with laughter.

Josh came into the kitchen, preoccupied with the letter in his hand.

'Oh, hi there. I was going to give you a call, Kate. Are you able to help me out next weekend, please? I'm stuck for someone to lead the prayers.'

'Sure, I'll have a look at who else is available. Leave it with me.'

'I thought maybe you could do it,' he said, slyly.

'Me? I've never led before. I'm not sure I could.'

'Of course you could!' said Vikki butting in the conversation. 'You've got a wonderful way with words.'

'Thank you, but I have never led from the front.'

'Well, now's your chance. It would be great if you could, you know. I have complete confidence in you, Kate. What do you think?'

'I'm not sure,' she answered slowly. 'I'll think about it. Can I get back to you? If not, I will find someone else to do them.'

'Sure,' he replied. 'Thank you.' He reached over and kissed all the girls seated at the table.

'Bye Finn,' he shouted up the stairs.

'Bye, Dad,' came the muffled reply.

'What is he doing up there?'

'He's building a space rocket. He's got all the old toilet rolls up there to use as engines, and has stuck them to his bed posts. The imagination of that boy,' sighed Vikki tiredly.

'Are you not feeling good?' asked Kate, looking at her friend with concern.

'I'm fine, just a bit weary. I will be glad when this chemo stops, I have to admit. I'm fed up with it all.'

It was unusual for Vikki to sound so defeated. It must be bad, thought Kate.

'I tell you what; I am going to take you to the spa as a pre-Christmas treat. How does that sound?'

'Oh, that sounds wonderful,' she sighed, 'but I don't know if I can pin Josh down to stay home for an evening. He is so busy just now, as you well know.'

'That's not a problem. I will find someone to babysit for you. It's all part of the package,' she added with a flourish.

'Just what I need,' Vikki sighed. 'Thank you so much.'

'No worries. Just leave it to me, and I will arrange an evening. I wonder if Ellie would like to join us? We could make it a real girl's night out.'

'I'm sure she would love to. Do you know what? I'm feeling better just thinking about it. Just lying on those heat beds doing nothing. Mmmm, sheer bliss.'

A few days later, the three friends booked into the spa, and stripped off in the changing rooms. Vikki appeared to have no inhibitions regarding her missing breast, and Kate and Ellie were awed and inspired by her brazenness. She had chosen a smart turban to match her swimsuit, and looked rather like a glamorous 1920s model. They chased through to the jacuzzi pool like a bunch of giggling schoolgirls, and dived straight into the warm, luxurious water.

'Now this is the life,' said Vikki, as she relaxed back in the bubbles. 'Why don't we do this every week?'

'Cost, maybe?' laughed Kate.

'Mmm, that could have something to do with it, I guess. But seriously, we should treat ourselves every few months or so. Because we're worth it!'

The evening passed all too quickly.

'Who would believe that relaxing was such hard work?' said Ellie, as they climbed out of the swimming pool, and headed back to the locker rooms to get dressed.

'I have had the most glorious time,' sighed Vikki, as they walked back to the car. Vikki hung on to Kate's arm, and seemed to be dragging herself along, as if walking were a real effort.

'Are sure you're okay, darling? Maybe this was too much for you, in the middle of chemo?'

'No, no. I always wilt about this time of evening. Seriously, I wouldn't have missed it for the world.'

The smile on her face confirmed her words, and Kate felt a little happier. She would definitely treat Vikki to another session when she was fully over her treatment. She would really be able to appreciate it then.

Chapter 23

It had been decided to hold the nativity outside. It would mean that numbers would not be an issue, and neither would the small problem of animals urinating in the church. Amy and Daisy were joining the angel hosts, and Finn was to be a king, bearing gifts. The house was cluttered in tinsel and costumes, as they excitedly prepared for the big day.

But on 23rd December, Vikki was struggling to concentrate. She felt so ill and feverish. The children were shrieking around her, making her feel dizzy and disorientated.

'Please slow down,' she implored them. 'I can't concentrate.'

But the children had the Christmas bug, and there was no way they could keep quiet. They continued to scream, giggle and argue, chasing around the house in a swirl of tea towels and angel wings.

'Mummy! Tell Finn to leave my baby Jesus alone! He keeps taking all his clothes off.' yelled Daisy.

'Don't tell tales!' he retorted. 'Anyway, babies didn't wear clothes in them days. They were wrapped in bandages.'

'How did their mummy change their nappies then?' asked Amy.

'They didn't have nappies.'

'How did they keep them from weeing everywhere then?'

'Mummy! Mummy?'

Vikki lay down on the carpet, the room swimming, listening to the children's voices fading in and out of range.

'Mummy!' cried Daisy. 'What's wrong?'

Amy lay down next to her mother and cried into her shoulder. Still Vikki could not respond, as she sank further into a fog of fever.

'Call Kate,' ordered Daisy, taking the lead. 'Hurry up, Finn! Her number's on the list.'

Finn hurried to the kitchen, and carefully dialled the parish office.

Before she even had time to answer professionally, Kate heard a plaintive little voice on the end of the phone.

'Kate, it's Mummy, please help. She's ill.'

'Finn, is that you?'

'Yes, please hurry, I'm frightened.'

She could hear the fear in the child's voice, so she reassured him she would be over straight away. She clicked the receiver down, and immediately dialled 999 and requested an ambulance. It could be that the children were overreacting, but she was not going to take a chance.

Her heart was beating rapidly, as she locked up the office and flew over to the vicarage.

The front door was wide open, and Finn grabbed her hand and pulled her through to the lounge.

'What's wrong with her?' Daisy was sitting next to Amy, tears rolling down her sweet little heart-shaped face. A tousled angel hanging on to her mother's arm. Lifting her face to Kate, she sobbed, 'Don't let Mummy die, please, please.'

Kate sat down on the floor, checking Vikki's pulse. She was barely conscious.

'It's okay, Vikki,' she soothed. 'An ambulance is on its way. You're going to be okay.' She stroked Vikki's bare head, at the same time reaching out to sooth the girls. Poor Finn stood awkwardly at the side of the sad little cameo, his eyes as big as saucers, looking down at the gathering of females on the floor.

'Come here, Finn,' said Kate, reaching her hand out to him. He gladly swooped down, and joined the huddle. And that was how the paramedic found them, just minutes later.

'Blimey! That was quick,' exclaimed Kate.

'Hi, I'm Mike and I'm a rapid response paramedic,' he told her. 'I live in the village. The ambulance proper will be here in a few minutes. Can you tell me what happened?'

The children all looked mutely at the paramedic.

'I'm not quite sure,' said Kate. 'The children called me, and said that she was poorly.'

'Right then,' he said calmly. 'Let's have a look at her, shall we?'

He bent down next to Vikki, and called her gently. Getting little response, he took out his stethoscope and listened to her chest. He also took her temperature.

'She's burning up,' he said. 'Has she been unwell lately?'

'Oh, I'm sorry, I should have told you. She's having chemotherapy for breast cancer. I know she carries a card somewhere. Let me go and look in her purse.'

She rushed into the kitchen and searched through Vikki's handbag, locating her purse, and pulling out the card detailing her chemotherapy regime.

Two female paramedics came through the front door.

'Hello?'

'Through here,' shouted Mike. 'I think we're going to need a stretcher.'

One of the women ran back to the ambulance, while the children watched, open-mouthed, through the window.

'Okay, kids, we're going to take Mummy to hospital for a little check up. Now don't you worry. She's just got a bit of an infection, and it's made her feel poorly. Are you able to stay with the children?' the rapid response paramedic asked Kate.

'Sure,' she replied. 'But I ought to ring her husband, and tell him what's happening.'

'We won't wait for him, as we really want to get her seen to as soon as possible. Can you tell him to join us in the emergency department?'

They watched as Vikki was taken onto the ambulance. The children were torn between fear, and fascination that an ambulance had come to their house.

'Come on, you lot,' said Kate. 'She's in good hands, and she'll be back before you know it.'

'Can we go and visit her?' asked Daisy, sniffing, and wiping her hand across her face.

'She might not be in there long enough. We'll just wait and see. Now what were you doing before Mummy became poorly?'

Within minutes, in the nature of children everywhere, their excitement at having Kate to play with overtook their concerns for their mother's well-being.

'Look, we've got our costumes for the nativity.'

'Baby Jesus used to wee all over his mummy.' said Amy.

'Did he now?'

'Yes, 'cause they didn't wear nappies, they just wore plasters.'

'Bandages, you ninny!' shouted Finn.

'That's what I said,' she replied indignantly.

'Well, that's true, but I am sure their mummies probably used a cloth similar to a nappy,' said Kate. 'You know, it's not all that long ago that people used cloth nappies, anyway. Disposable nappies are quite a new invention.'

'What?! Did they have to wash pooey nappies then? Did all the poo go round and round in the washing machine?'

'I don't think so,' said Kate, wondering exactly what people did do. She had never really paid much attention to the business of washing nappies! She felt a pang of remorse, realising that there was so much she didn't know about having a baby. She was learning a great deal from being alongside Sophie, but she had never really had anything to do with babies, up till now.

Looking at Vikki's children, she realised just how much she was missing out on. *Would Sam want to have children?* she wondered. But hang on, surely she was getting ahead of the game! They were still in the early days of their relationship, although she knew already that she loved him, more than she had ever loved anyone before. But as to a future together?

Sam! she suddenly remembered. She was so lost in her thoughts of love, she had forgotten to ring and inform him that Vikki was ill. Perhaps she should wait until they knew a bit more, as he would only worry, and dash down.

She had called Josh away from the midweek communion service. Luckily, the communion had already been celebrated, and she knew that Bill would wind the service up for him. She longed to be able to go with him, but knew that she needed to stay with the children. Hopefully Josh would ring her soon with some information.

It was a few hours later when Josh rang. Vikki's white cell count had fallen so low that she needed urgent treatment. She was doing well, he had reassured Kate, but would need to stay in overnight.

'That's okay, I can stay here until you come home,' she told him. 'Shall I gather together some toiletries and night clothes for her?'

'Oh, that would be great, Kate. I hadn't thought of that. I was just so frantic. How much more has she got to go through?'

'I've put it round the prayer chain, so everyone will be praying for a quick recovery,' she told him.

'Thanks, Kate. I don't know what we would do without you. You're an angel, you know that?'

'Get away with you,' she admonished. 'I'm in the company of angels here, though,' she joked, looking at the girls twirling round the room to the music.

'Mummy will be home in time for the nativity won't she?' asked Amy anxiously.

'I'm not sure,' hedged Kate.

'She's got to see us!' cried Daisy. 'We've worked so hard! She's got to come home in time.'

'Listen, girls, Mummy is quite poorly. Now you know how strong she's been with all the treatment she's had to endure, and she will do everything possible to get home in time. But if she can't make it, I'll be there. How about that?'

Amy bit her bottom lip, glumly. 'I want Mummy to see me.'

'I know, darling. And I know she wants to see you.' Kate suddenly had an idea.

'But, if Mummy can't come to the nativity, we can take the nativity to her!'

'Really?'

'Let me have a word with Daddy when he comes home, but I'm sure something can be arranged. She will get to see you one way or another.'

Chapter 24

Thankfully, with treatment, Vikki began to recover. Ward 'M' South had a visit from the angel Gabriel and the full cast of the nativity, bar the animals. Kate was sure that the matron would have put her foot down at that. It was a blessing for Vikki, and a joy for the whole ward, as the children bounced around singing their songs. The nurses joined in with the singing, and it lifted the spirits of even the sickest patients. Vikki was allowed out in time for Christmas, but warned to take things easy. With Sam and Irene coming down to take charge of preparations, this was just what she was able to do. Kate was of course included in the family celebrations. In fact, they all thought of her as family, anyway. Josh obviously had a lot of services to lead, and also communion to take to the frailer members of church, who were unable to get out and about. But once lunchtime arrived, his work for the year was finally over, and he could at last relax into the family bosom.

The children were running on adrenaline, as they waited for the gifts to be handed out after dinner. Trying to encourage them to eat more than a few mouthfuls of roast dinner was impossible, and so they let them down from the table, enabling the adults to enjoy their meal at a more leisurely pace.

This was the first, proper family Christmas Kate had ever enjoyed. In past years, it was a dismal affair at her parent's home, with or without her sister, depending on what substance she was under the influence of at the time. They had been disappointed that Kate wasn't going home, but she had explained to them that her friend needed her to help with the children, so they had to be content with that.

She had loved buying gifts for her newly adopted nieces and nephews, and also for Sam. They were going back to the cottage to exchange their gifts to one another that evening, and she was dying to see his face when she presented her gift to him.

She had splashed out on a huge telescope that would be wonderful for use in his flat, with stunning views over the river and beyond. He had expressed a new-found interest in star-gazing ever since Kate had pointed out the constellations to him, so they would be able to view them together. They had many different hobbies and passions, but were keen to share and learn from each other. One thing she could not get her head around though, was his terrible music taste! He had persuaded her to go to a music gig with him, to try and convert her, but she had just stood with her hands over her ears for the most part. The volume was out of this world, and she was sure her eardrums had burst. But that was just one facet that made up her wonderful Sam, so she didn't complain too loudly.

And so began a new year, full of hope, possibilities and fears. Vikki had one more chemotherapy session to go, and then she would start radiotherapy. She had been assured it would be much easier than the chemo, but the fact that she had to travel to the hospital every single day, for five weeks, was still daunting. Kate was finding it difficult to make space in her diary to go as often as she wanted to with her friend, but she was willing to work on into the evening if needs be, and often did.

Daniel Davies, the new curate was joining the team early in the year, and he was going to be a great help to Josh. It meant that there would be another pair of hands to lead communion, and take services. They had a good team of lay people at St John's, but still the burden of responsibility fell upon Josh. It had been a tough end to the year, what with the ordinary needs and demands of a young family, and Vikki's illness. Kate had taken on a lot of the work load, but in a way, the more organised and appealing the church became, the more work it required. The church was bucking the national trend and was growing in an extraordinary fashion. For a small village, they exceeded expectations of the ratio of people attending. It was fun, exciting and hard work. It meant more baptisms, weddings, groups and visits, and that required a lot of teamwork. Kate had helped set up a team of parish visitors, who kept an eye on the elderly, lonely, and infirm. This type of outreach was important, and increased the kudos of the church to the wider community. People were curious. What was it that drew so many to the old building in the centre of the village? There were lunches, 'Welcome Suppers', kid's parties, youth groups, nurture groups and men's breakfasts to organise. The flower arranging team was made up of the traditional members, and they ran themselves without much outside help. St John's now had a large group of younger women who liked to meet socially and to further their knowledge of the Christian journey. All in all, parish life had never felt so good. Since Maud had died, they had increased the welcoming team to include volunteers willing to man the church throughout the day. Kate still had a strong sense of guilt whenever Maud came up in the conversation. She had never liked the woman, but would never have wished her to die in such a tragic way. But imagine the consequences if she had not died! Bill and Harold would not have been able to cope with being 'outed'. It would have destroyed two lives, instead of just the one lost in the accident. But the atmosphere in the church had improved considerably now. There was a large welcome board in the main entrance to greet people, and it was full of useful information and contacts. Kate had placed photos of Josh, herself, the key members of the PCC and the Welcoming committee on the board so that people would know who to look for.

Since the Christmas services, she had recieved a flood of enquires for further information about events that were taking place in the church, and she relayed this to the relevant leaders.

Kate was so glad to be part of this caring, burgeoning society. Whenever she thought of the straight-jacket that called itself a church back home, her heart broke. All those people being demonised by a so-called religion! It tore her apart to think of her down-trodden parents, and of the fear that she had lived with as a child. She had still been unable to persuade her parents to come and visit her in Ashton Kirby. They obviously considered it to be the home of the devil, judging by the repulsion on their faces whenever she mentioned it.

Now that the rush of Christmas was over, Kate felt that she might have time to resume her search for information about her aunt's life. She had managed to place most of the photos in date order. And what a life her aunt had lived! Australia, Indonesia, Kenya, New Zealand, Cyprus, Greece; the list was endless. She recalled conversations she had shared with Val when she was alive, and it had clearly been a source of great sadness that her partner had died so young. They were obviously soul mates; you could see in the well-thumbed and faded photos just how close they had been. She was going to try asking some of the older ladies round at the health centre what they remembered of her aunt, as she had worked there for several years before she died. It was part of Val's story, her history, and she wanted to know all about it. It was so sad to think she had lost a little baby. What was the story behind that, Kate wondered?

But first of all, she had to help Vikki finish her treatment, and hopefully get on with her life again, without cancer. It would all be over and done with by the end of February, then she would be able to build up her strength, and look forward to the spring.

Chapter 25

Kate had never read the prayers in church before, and was a little nervous, to say the least. She knew all the folk who normally led them. Some were great. They were succinct, caring and passionate. Then there were those who waffled needlessly, and she could hear the yawns from the pew behind! She really didn't want to get it wrong, so she went through the list of needs in the village, the wider church, and worldwide. She wrote them out so many times, that she knew them word perfect in the end. But then she panicked that she wasn't saying them from the heart. 'Oh Lord,' she cried 'please help me get this right, and let my prayers make a difference.'

She left her cottage as the bells were ringing, and walked through the ice-covered churchyard. It may have been cold out, but her face was burning, her heart pumping. She was greeted at the door by Felicity, who kissed her warmly on each cheek.

'My, you're burning up!' she remarked. 'Are you okay?'

'To be honest, Felicity, I'm not sure. I'm leading the prayers for the first time ever, so I'm a bit nervous, to put it mildly.'

'Oh, you'll be great,' she replied. 'Come on now, you can give great talks, so what's a quick batch of prayers? It'll be fine.'

'I hope you're right.'

She took a deep breath and headed for the pews, but before she was seated, she had several people come up to give her items for the newsletter, asking her for information and to arrange appointments. The whole idea of leaving her alone on a Sunday to enjoy worship had gone by the board, then!

First the songs, then the notices, than another song, then the sermon. The service sped by, as Kate nervously twisted her thumbs together in her lap. This is daft, she thought. I can do this, of course I can. Just calm down you silly woman. She took some deep breaths and looked up just as Josh announced that Kate was coming to do the prayers. She walked up to the front, and stepped on to the dais. Holding the piece of paper in her hands she looked up, and invited the congregation to join her in prayer.

Sam was walking up the centre aisle. What on earth was Sam doing here? It wasn't his weekend to come up. Kate's hand flew to her mouth, as Sam headed straight for her. An expectant hush descended on the congregation. Kate glanced back at Josh, looking for some kind of guidance. He just smiled back at her. She turned to the front again to see Sam now directly in front of her. There were a few giggles from the pews, as they watched the scene unfolding in front of them.

Sam got down on one knee.

'Oh my word!' thought Kate. *'Not here, surely?'*

But it was happening. It really was happening. Sam stayed down on one knee and looked up at Kate, a huge grin on his face. She was shaking now, no longer aware of the congregation watching them.

'Kate, will you marry me?'

'Shoot, Sam! You do pick your moments!' She looked down at his lovely, kind face, so like his sister's.

'Of course I will!' She threw back her head and laughed, and the church joined in with clapping and laughing.

Suddenly the organist started playing the old Beatle's song, *She Loves You*, and the congregation joined in, singing at full volume.

Kate pulled Sam up into her arms, and they twirled around on the dais, oblivious to the people watching.

'Hang on, I haven't given you the ring,' he said, pulling a box out of his pocket. Inside was a beautiful platinum ring, with a small line of amethyst stones.

Kate looked incredulous. How had he pulled all this off without her knowing? She glanced back at Josh, shaking her finger at him.

'You were in on this, weren't you?' she laughed. 'So that's why you wanted me to lead the prayers. You don't really expect me to do them now, do you?'

Celia Harvey walked up to the front, holding out her arms to Kate and Sam.

'It's alright, Kate. Josh asked me to lead prayers today.'

What a schemer! She stood at the front and thanked the congregation for taking part in the deception, and apologised for the 'disruption to service', which they all chuckled at.

Kate and Sam walked back to the pews, hand in hand, and as the service continued, she glanced down at her ring.

Engaged! Me engaged! It all seemed too much to take in, and it really was totally unexpected. He had never even mentioned the idea to her. They had been together for a few months, and she loved him dearly, but still, she didn't realise he was so serious. But she was delighted. They had plenty to discuss when they got home. She wondered if Vikki was in on the secret. She thought she probably was, because the twins were so close. She was sure her friend would approve, as she was always dropping hints that the two of them should make things more permanent.

At the end of the service, they had so many people come and offer their congratulations. Even the grumpy Churchwardens mumbled a 'well done' to Sam and patted his shoulder. High praise indeed!

They walked out of church, and Kate had a sense that this must be what it felt like to get married! She had walked into church single, and now walked out as someone's fiancé. She experienced a warm feeling, a glow, surging through her body.

'Come on wife-to-be, we're having lunch at the vicarage. It's all arranged.'

'But I hadn't even expected to see you this weekend,' she laughed. 'The cottage is a mess.'

'As if!' he laughed. 'You don't know the meaning of the word mess.'

'Well, you wait. I have Val's photos spread on every surface.' She hit his shoulder playfully. 'I can't believe you did this,' she said again. 'What a way to propose. Hang on,' she stood still, pulling away from him.

'What if I had said no?'

'But you didn't, and that's all that matters. Now come on, we've got a wedding to plan.'

She followed him down the path, joy bubbling up within her. She jigged along next to him, singing 'I'm getting married in the morning.'

She knocked on the vicarage door, before pushing it open. Inside, the hall was filled with balloons and banners declaring 'Congratulations!'.

Vikki came to meet them, and Kate hugged her tight.

'You were so in on this, you toad!'

'I know! Such fun! Now, when can we go and buy a wedding dress? Please, please choose me to be your matron of honour.'

'And the girls will be my bridesmaids, and Finn will be our pageboy.'

The children bounded out to meet them, grinning and giggling. Amy sidled up to Kate, and wrapped her arms around Kate's legs; her usual affectionate position.

'Are you and Uncle Sam really getting married? You will look like a princess.'

'Thank you, darling. Yes, we really are.'

'How many big sleeps?'

'Oh, we don't know yet. It will be quite a lot of big sleeps, I'm afraid. Too many for you to count. There's a lot to plan and organise.'

'But you're good at organising. Daddy always says you are.'

Kate giggled as Josh shrugged his shoulders in assent.

'I take it you two love birds are going to ask me to officiate?'

'We wouldn't dare go anywhere else,' said Sam, wrapping his arms lovingly round Kate.

'I suppose I'll even have to write out my own marriage certificate,' said Kate. 'I had better make sure I don't make a mistake on that, or I'll have to look at the error for ever after.'

'Do you think you will be able to get your mum and dad to come for the wedding?' asked Vikki cautiously.

'You know, I hadn't thought of that? I hope so. Also, I think I had better ask my sister to be a bridesmaid. Thank goodness I've got you for my matron of honour. If it was left to Melanie, I would probably be taken to a nightclub and be made to peddle drugs all night!'

'So that's two big bridesmaids, and two little ones. Ah, that's perfect,' beamed Vikki. 'I can't wait.'

'So when's the big day going to be then, big man?' Josh asked Sam.

Kate looked at him expectantly.

'Well, I obviously haven't discussed it yet with my fiancé,' he grinned.

Kate's heart swelled with pride. She was now part of a couple, and it had been made official. She was so excited, her heart still hadn't stopped racing. She realised what a lift this must be to Vikki, after the worst year of her life.

'What do you think, wifey?'

'How much is involved in planning a wedding?' she asked Vikki.

'Oh, there's nothing to it,' she laughed. 'Just got to book the church; ticked. Pick the bridesmaids; ticked. Venue for the bun fight, honeymoon destination, dresses, cake, guests....'

'Hold on, hold on. Can't we just elope?'

'No way, you're not getting away with anything but the whole nine yards, young lady.'

They continued to banter their way through a light lunch of bread and cheese. The children had already pulled on the dressing-up clothes and were playing weddings, while the adults grazed their way through the next couple of hours. Josh had to leave to take a baptism, so he said his goodbyes, and they opened a bottle of wine to continue the celebrations.

At one point, when Sam was dragged away to sort the children out, Vikki and Kate sat in companionable silence, lounging on the battered old sofa.

'I keep wanting to pinch myself,' said Kate.

'Me too; you can't imagine how protective I am towards my baby brother. I am older than him, you know. By about five minutes! I dreaded him meeting the wrong woman, and not having any say in it. But he's only gone and fallen for my very best friend! How pleased am I! It's a dream come true.'

'It is for me, too. To think of how we hated each other when we first met.'

'Yes, but I think that was because you just wouldn't admit you fancied the pants off each other.'

'Shut up you!' she threw a cushion at her.

They continued to discuss dates and venues for the rest of the afternoon, as Sam sat in the snug, watching football.

'Are you coming with me tomorrow, Kate? I've got to have my tattoo, before starting radiotherapy.'

'Of course I am. I've got Felicity to man the office for me, so there is no rush to get back. Perhaps we could go into town and have lunch afterwards? Maybe pick up some bridal magazines?'

'What a brilliant idea. It's my shout. I owe you for all the help you've given me these past few months, especially just before Christmas. Honestly, Kate, I could not have got through all this without you. The kids have such trust in you. Fancy you being the first person they phoned when they found me out of it, bless them. They knew you would make it all right.'

'You certainly had us all worried, Vikki. I'm just so glad that horrid chemo is behind you now. Radiotherapy is the last leg, and then you can look forward to building your strength up and recovering. You've been a total hero through all this.'

'Get away.' She pushed Kate lovingly, embarrassed by the praise. 'Honestly, you certainly get to know who your real friends are though. Do you know, some women who I thought were my friends, have ignored me totally. You remember Alice, who I used to go to keep-fit with? She crosses over the road now if she sees me coming.'

'How strange,' said Kate thoughtfully. 'I think some people can't cope with cancer. They don't know what to say, and it's probably more about them, not you.'

'It's the same when I see folk at the supermarket. They seem desperate to minimise what's happened to me. There's me with no hair, nauseous and fed-up, yet they insist on saying, "you look well!" Right!'

'I suppose they just don't know what else to say.'

'Yes, well, I know I'm a vicar's wife and all that, but I still feel really peeved by the attitude of some so-called friends. Some strangers have been kinder to me than mates I've known for years.'

'That's human nature for you. You never know how you will react until you're faced with it. Try not to be too hard on them.'

'Okay St Kate. I'll try harder. So when are you going to really lead the prayers in church then?'

'They'll be out of date! I read all the latest news and everything. I can't believe Josh made me go through all that for nothing.'

'But it was a fun way to propose, you have to admit. In front of all your friends.'

'Yes, it was quite perfect. I guess I had better tell my parents at some stage.'

Kate looked thoughtfully out of the window, wishing that her family was as loving and relaxed as this one.

Chapter 26

Sophie came into the office, waddling through the open door.

'You can't get any bigger, or I will have to take that door off the frame,' laughed Kate, as Sophie sat down with a huge sigh.

'Do you know, I think I'm going to pop any day now. Seriously, I love being pregnant, but I really can't carry on like this much longer. I'm so tired.'

'I'm sure you are, honey. You have done so well, and I take my hat off to you. I haven't known many pregnant women, but the ones I have known moaned from the first month. If it wasn't morning sickness, it was sore breasts, swollen feet, or other aches and pains. You have been the model pregnant woman.'

Sophie smiled broadly. 'I know! I feel so special being pregnant, and I'm frightened of losing that 'special' feeling.'

'Yes, but you'll be a proud mum then, so you'll still feel special, especially when everyone's looking into the pram and gazing at your little girl.'

'Oh, stop it. I get so excited just thinking about it. I hope I'm going to be a good mum,' she sighed pensively.

'You will be; you're a natural. And you'll have lots of help from your friends in the church.'

'I will, won't I? I'm so lucky. And you've been so lovely to me and Robbie. Will you be godmother to my little one?'

'I'd be absolutely honoured,' said Kate, meaning it.

'So, now you've got engaged, have you thought about having kids?' Sophie asked with a sly grin.

'Give me a chance to get down the aisle!'

'You don't need to wait though, do you? You've got a nice house, and you're...well, you're mature already.'

Kate threw a rubber at her friend.

'Don't be so cheeky, young lady. And anyway, we don't know where we're going to live or anything. It's still early days, Sophie.'

Sophie looked up anxiously.

'You're not going to leave Ashton Kirby?'

'Well, I haven't really given it a lot of thought. I would love to stay here, but I've got Sam to think about now. He has a wonderful flat in Bristol, and his work is there; I just don't know.' She bit the side of her lip. She truly hadn't thought the living arrangements through. It was true that she had laid down roots in Ashton Kirby and made so many friends. Would Sam want to uproot and leave Bristol? Could he? It was one of many topics they were going to have to discuss before they set a date for the wedding.

Sophie reluctantly heaved herself out of her chair. 'Well, don't leave it too long. I can save all my baby clothes for you if you like.'

'You never give up, do you? I will think about it, and you can be sure you will be one of the first to know, if and when I get pregnant. Satisfied?'

'Great! I'm off to see the midwife now. Not many more visits left.'

'Take care, Sophie. See you soon.'

Kate and Vikki found their way to the radiotherapy suite, and booked in. It was in a different part of the hospital from the chemotherapy suite, but the unit was very new and open-plan in design.

She was directed over to a waiting area, and within seconds her name was called.

A nurse showed her the huge machine, and explained what they would be doing.

'But first, we have to make a small tattoo, so that we can line up the machine exactly,' he explained to her.

'Can I have a butterfly?' giggled Vikki.

'It won't be that big. In fact, you'll have a job seeing it,' he told her. 'Especially as you have so many freckles anyway. I think even we're going to have fun spotting our tattoo on you!'

They placed her on the bed and pulled the machine over her, and they marked the area the treatment would cover. Afterwards, they gave her a sheet of paper with the whole course of twenty five treatments mapped out.

'You're lucky that there are no bank holidays to factor in,' he said. 'It tends to throw people off when they have to break for a couple of days. Now, we try to adhere to this calendar, but obviously sometimes we may have to phone you up and cancel a date, due to machine break-downs, etc. We have tried to keep most of the times the same every day, as we find it helps people to sort out their diaries, and plan their days better.'

'Thank you. Will it make me feel ill?'

'No, it shouldn't do. Some people do find they have a degree of fatigue, but that's all. You may find that you have slight sunburn over the area, but we can give you something for that.

So, we will see you on Monday for your first treatment. Just book in at the desk, and then take a seat in waiting area 'A'. You will be in the same room for every treatment, barring accidents.'

'Thanks for that. I will see you then. Bye.'

The next five weeks were tough, as it took such a large chunk out of the day. The children began to get fed up with being farmed out to friends, but at least Vikki was able to take them to school in the mornings. She was finding her energy levels were very low, and couldn't wait to finish treatment and start the process of recovery. They had hoped to book a holiday, but the new curate was due to join them, and Josh felt that it was imperative he was around. There were times that she resented the restraints that her husband's job had on them both, and now was one of them. Although the congregation made allowances for Vikki's illness, they still expected Josh to have prepared a sermon, and to lead services every week. And they still expected him to answer their queries at any time of day! It seemed as if their private life had less value than his professional role. But they had agreed to have a break away from the village after the Easter services. Easter, although not as big a deal in the secular world, was a major celebration in the Christian calendar, and had more services than Christmas. So that would be a perfect time to have a break, and hopefully to recover some strength and health. Vikki was already poring over the holiday brochures, and surfing the web, trying to find the ideal destination. Irene had offered to come and babysit, so that Josh and Vikki could completely relax, and have a holiday as a couple. Kate would also help her with the child-care. They had a family holiday booked in August, so the children didn't mind too much. They were very accommodating children, a handy attribute given the difficult circumstances over the last few months.

Sam and Kate had settled into a routine of one weekend in Bristol, the other in Ashton Kirby, although this was sometimes disrupted if Kate had church business to attend to. This didn't matter too much, as Sam liked to spend time visiting Vikki as well. Now that her treatment had finally finished, she was beginning to feel more human, although she still found that her energy levels were depleted, and had constant back pain. This was put down to the gruelling chemotherapy regime she had undergone, but it was a struggle with three energetic youngsters to look after, and a husband at the beck and call of three hundred plus parishioners. Kate was enjoying the fruits of her labours, as the church rotas were now working like clockwork, and so she had more time to spend on one-to-one visits, and helping Josh to manage his time better. Her reasons for doing this were mainly to help Vikki, as the less time Josh spent on parish work, the more time he could spend with his family.

The curate's house was now decorated throughout, and ready to receive Daniel Davies. His presence would be a huge help, and the congregation were all looking forward to welcoming him to the village. The church members had been collecting foodstuff as a welcome gift, and the fridge and cupboards were loaded with groceries.

Kate had a rare weekend to herself, as Sam was attending a conference in Paris. He had suggested that she went along with him, but she was keen to spend the time searching in the attic. She had not got much further with her quest to find out about her aunt's child, and was hoping that she could uncover more papers to do with the birth.

She treated herself to a lazy Saturday morning, loafing around in her track suit bottoms and pyjama top, and hoped that she would not have any visitors. Anyway, she would be in the loft, and could not hear the doorbell from up there, so that was that. She took her MP3 player up with her, and climbed up the newly installed loft ladder Robbie had put in for her. Looking around the dusty interior, her mind drifted off to the last time she had seen Valerie. She had looked so well! It was strange to think she had no idea it would be the last time, as there had been no hint of illness. Perhaps an aneurism was a good way to go? She had probably not suffered at all, for which Kate was glad. Her aunt was a fiercely independent woman, and would have hated to be a burden to anyone. Still, it was sad that she was not around to see Kate happily engaged. And she would have loved Sam! She heaved a sigh as she recollected her lovely aunt. What a shame there had been no reconciliation with her sister. Life was too short to hold grudges and resentments. Kate was determined to try and bring her mother round to the idea of meeting Sam, and visiting her at the cottage. If she could piece together the story of what had driven Val away from her home town, then she felt she might be able to persuade her mum to do the right thing. She had appeared so upset the last time she mentioned Val. Surely she should be able to forgive her, after all this time?

Pushing her way past all the boxes and bags, Kate found herself back at the place where she had made the last big discovery. There must be more here somewhere! She trod carefully on the wooden rafters, and jumped back when she thought she heard a rustling noise. *Please don't let there be mice or rats*, she prayed quickly. Her heart was beating as she looked in the direction of the noise, but thankfully it was just a disturbed bag tipping over. She peered into the dusty, discoloured boxes, their tape having long lost the stickiness that once held them together. In one box, she found a lot of old bank statements and electric bills, dating back to the eighties. They can go in the dump, she thought to herself as she threw them over to the exit. More paperwork was discovered, but it was just ancient filing. Then she came across a more interesting box. Inside was a collection of old diaries. She looked through a few, but these were obviously written when Valerie had been a child. It would make for fascinating reading, so she placed these beside her, ready to take down and glance through at a later date. Casting her eyes carefully round in case there was anything she had missed, she moved over to the loft hatch, and threw down the bags to be disposed of, and carried down the box of diaries.

She stepped down onto the landing, shaking her head clear of cobwebs, and sneezing away the dust. Coffee first, she thought. Her throat felt prickly from the fibre-glass wadding insulating the loft, and from the years of dust and dirt. *At least I didn't actually meet any rodents, even if they are up there,* she thought to herself. Robbie was going to come back and fit shelves to one side of the attic, so that she could access her papers and belongings more easily. He had been very busy helping to decorate and repair Daniel's house, so the shelves had been shelved, so to speak. She was just grateful to have a proper ladder up there. It had been quite precarious getting up without one, especially given her diminutive stature. Her aunt had not probably needed one, as her partner had been a giant of a man, and could probably just reach up and chuck the boxes in. Given the state of the loft, that was clearly the way things had been done!

She carried the bags of old bills and papers into the kitchen and placed them on the table. A quick peruse through and she could see that none of it was worth keeping. But the diaries were far more interesting. Some of them were just old, grey school books, and the handwriting was obviously childish. But some were fabulous oriental notebooks, from her aunt's travels around the world. What a find! She put the school books to one side, and started to read through Valerie's adventures.

Chapter 27

An hour and a half passed, and so absorbed had Kate become in the diaries, she had quite forgotten her coffee, which was now grey and cold, with a stale skin on the top. She lifted her neck, and stretched it from side to side, stiff with concentration. The places Val and Ray had travelled to, and the sights they had seen! She couldn't wait to show them to her mother. Surely she would be interested in these? They had spent months working in an orphanage in Kathmandu, and also in Albania. They had been good people. She had to persuade her mum to make peace with Valerie. It was too late to be reconciled to her in person, but at least she could be reconciled to the memory of her sister.

Putting the earlier diaries to one side, she got up to have a stretch. She did not think that these would be as interesting as the later ones. They would probably be full of the usual school girl stuff; who fancied who, what clothes were in fashion and which girl was the class bitch. She had kept diaries herself as a child, so she knew the kind of thing that would be in them. No, the really interesting stuff was sure to be in the adult diaries.

Kate decided to have a quick cycle to the shops and get something for lunch. It would enable her to get some fresh air, and a bit of exercise. Looking down at her outfit, she sniggered to herself. Perhaps she had better put something a bit neater on. Glancing in the mirror, she looked at the state of her hair; tousled and untidy after her forage through the loft. And perhaps a brush might be in order too?

When she returned, she flicked through the weekend newspapers, building up the anticipation of discovery. It was almost as if delaying the moment was adding to the enjoyment. Feeling a little guilty that she wasn't missing Sam more, she texted him, and told him that she was! He quickly replied, and said that he would love to bring her to Paris one day. *It is beautiful*, he texted; *like you.*

She told him briefly of her discoveries, and of her aunt's travels. Perhaps she and Sam would be able to travel together, and visit some of the places Val had gone to? But she knew that Sam did not share her enthusiasm for the past. He was a man of the present, and could not understand her constant need to dig around.

'It will only end in tears,' he told her. 'You've got me, now. We've got our future to look forward to.'

'But you've got a happy, normal family, who aren't afraid to talk about their background. It's what makes you, you,' she tried to explain, 'there are so many skeletons in my family's cupboards, and no one will talk. I don't feel whole, not knowing what went on.'

'So I'm not enough for you, is that it?'

'Don't be unreasonable. You know I love you. I love your family. They make me so welcome, and I feel like a sister to Vikki. But I still have to face the fact that I have my own family too. And I just want to, I don't know, clear up a few things.'

'Well, don't expect to drag me through your sordid past with you,' he said huffily. 'I'm just not interested.'

'Thanks a bunch, Sam. It's nice to know I have your full support.'

It was just one of the times that they had argued about Kate's family. He felt that if they couldn't be bothered to get to know him, he couldn't be bothered to know them. And Kate felt like a piggy in the middle. Her family made it too easy to walk away from them, but she felt a strange loyalty to them. It was their allegiance to the wretched cult church that made them so hard to love. It was so wrong. When Kate was a child, it had been a terrifying place to be. Whatever she did, she was punished for, but thankfully she had been a strong, wilful character, and had not been broken by them. But Kate still had roots, and it kept her coming back, trying to make peace. It was the Brethren that had made her sister such a rebel. Thankfully, Mel seemed to be finally growing up, and getting her life back on track. This new chap on the scene was a positive influence on her, and Kate thanked God for answering her prayers as far as Mel was concerned. But she still felt futile when she thought about her parents. They seemed so afraid and unhappy. It wasn't right.

Kate had just finished a light lunch, and was preparing to sit down and get on with reading the diaries, when her phone went. It was Robbie.

'Sophie's in hospital,' he told her. 'She started having contractions last night, and we've been here since. Poor kid, I don't like to see her in pain.'

'Don't worry,' soothed Kate. 'I've heard that once a woman has the baby, she forgets all about the pain. Is there anything I can do?'

'Well, that's why I rang, see. She asked me if you could pray.' He sounded embarrassed saying this.

'Sure I will, Robbie. That's what her friends at the church are for, you know. I'll even pray for you,' she teased him.

'You will?' he asked seriously. 'Oh, thank you, thank you so much!'

She felt guilty now for making fun of him, and promised him that she would pray for the pair of them, and could she tell Vikki and Josh?

'Yes, of course. I'm so worried, Kate. What sort of dad am I going to be? I just don't want to disappoint my Sophie; she's got such high expectations of me.'

'You'll be great. I've seen you around kids, and you're brilliant. I can't think of anyone else who would make such a great dad,' she promised him. 'Let me know how things progress, and I'll be in to see her and the baby as soon as it's born.'

She rang off feeling strangely excited. She had become so much a part of their life, and felt exactly like a surrogate aunt. Her mind was now preoccupied, so she placed the diaries back in the box, and popped over to Vikki's, to tell her what was happening.

She hadn't been there for more than an hour, when a text popped up in her inbox.

Baby Jacqueline born at 2.20 p.m., weighing 7lb 6oz. Mother and baby doing well.

'Fantastic news!' shouted Vikki, as she and Kate both had tears of joy glistening in their eyes.

'I can't believe she had it so quickly,' said Kate. 'When I spoke to Robbie, it sounded as if she had ages to go.'

'You can never tell with babies, especially first ones,' said Vikki. 'She must be so excited to finally be a mum. Jacqueline's a nice name, even if it is a bit old fashioned, isn't it?'

'She had the name from the moment she was first pregnant,' explained Kate. 'It was the name of her carer at the children's home. She was the first person who ever showed Sophie any real love, bless her. So I can understand why she chose the name.'

'I will get the children to make a card for them all, and you can take it in with you when you visit. I take it you will be going in?'

'Just try and stop me,' grinned Kate. 'I can't wait! I've had her card for weeks!'

'Don't get broody, now.'

'Too late! I'm always thinking of babies at the moment. Just don't tell Sam, will you?'

'Do you know what? I think Sam would love to have a baby. Have you talked about it with him?'

'Well, we have discussed having kids, but I think he would like to do the big white wedding first. It's strange, isn't it? It's normally the woman who wants all the trimmings, but with us, it's the other way round. I hate the thought of all the happy relatives on your side of the family, and my miserable lot on the other. That's if they turn up at all.'

'It will be alright,' said Vikki, holding both Kate's hands, and rubbing them affectionately. But Kate wasn't so sure. Sam really seemed to resent her desperate need to involve her family. As far as he was concerned, they weren't worth the effort. The trouble was, life had been so simple for Sam, growing up with loving parents and a normal childhood. He felt that her constant need to discover the past was an intrusion into his and Kate's life. It was almost as if he were jealous of the time she spent trying to sort them all out.

Kate felt that it was selfish on his part. Why couldn't he see her need for a family connection? He had never had to fight for affection, and it upset her to think he could be so mean about it. It was difficult having Vikki as her best friend and confidante, as she couldn't moan about him too much, what with Sam being her twin!

So Kate kept it all to herself. She did love Sam, and she wanted to get married and have her own family. She was thirty-five, for goodness sake! It was about time she settled down. She knew that it was her disjointed past that had prevented her becoming too close to anyone, until now. Sam had broken through her tough exterior, probably because he was so like Vikki. Having been involved in Vikki and Josh's family life, she had seen how happy a family could be, and it had given her a hope that she too could have that same happiness. But somehow, she had to reconcile her past with her future.

Chapter 28

Sophie was a natural and passionate mother. The baby was simply beautiful. She fed well, slept well, and they made a perfect picture. Robbie was fiercely protective of them both, and policed their visitors. If you had so much as a sniffle, you were kept away from mother and baby. But otherwise, guests were made welcome, with tea and cakes. It felt as if this baby were the most special child ever to be born; there was an air of Madonna and child surrounding them. As her breasts filled with nurturing milk, Sophie felt powerful, life giving, and content. This was what she had been born to do. Jacqueline was her life's purpose, and she was thrilled.

Kate became a regular visitor to the house, and always came bearing gifts. She couldn't stop thinking of the baby; how perfectly formed she was, her little head, and Cupid lips, seeking out her mother's milk, her hands clenching and unclenching, and her eyes, trying to focus on the new world she had arrived in. She was truly a gift from God, and Kate knew that she was hooked. She was desperate to start a family, but knew that it would be unthinkable to get pregnant before she was married if she was to try and get closer to her family. It was proving hard enough to get them to accept the idea of her marrying Sam here in the village, and not in Carshalton.

Kate walked from the Weekes' home to the new curate's house. Daniel had arrived just two days ago, and she wanted to see how he had settled in. She rang the bell, and stood back, combing her fringe away from her eyes with her fingers. From inside she heard a mad barking. Then the front door banged towards her, with a loud scratching noise. She leapt away, startled.

'Oh, hi,' said Daniel, opening the door wide, and holding back two hounds. 'Sorry about that. They're both rather enthusiastic guard dogs.' He held the door open wide, and Kate hesitantly slid past. The dogs pulled at the leashes, panting with their long tongues hanging out, eager to greet the new visitor.

'Jack and Max, meet Kate,' he grinned. 'Kate, meet Jack and Max.'

'Oh, er, hello dogs.' She stood stock still, with her arms raised high, looking down at the dogs.

'Don't worry, they're quite friendly.'

'They are?'

'Oh yes, their bark is far worse than their bite.'

'Well, I don't really want to put that to the test.'

'Come on, boys, back to your basket,' he clapped, and the two dogs slunk away under the table, looking quite sorry for themselves.

'Now I feel guilty,' she grinned ruefully. 'They look so disappointed that they don't get to tear me to shreds.'

He laughed at her, as she gradually relaxed her arms down, and followed him through to the lounge.

'I'm not used to dogs, as you can tell.'

'My parents ran kennels, so I grew up around them. I wouldn't be without them now,' he explained. 'I was going to come round to the office and say thanks for such a warm welcome. It will take me months to get through all that grub!'

'Yes, well, the congregation like to welcome people here. Have you er, had many visitors yet?' she asked hesitantly.

'Oh yes. From nine in the morning, all the way through till six in the evening,' he laughed.

'Mmm, I tried to tell them to give you a bit of breathing space. I'm afraid it's the old village network, you see. They all want to be the first to tell the rest all your guilty secrets.'

'You know about them already?' He laughed, in mock terror. 'Never mind, it's just lovely to be away from London, to be honest.' He breathed in deeply. 'Fresh air, you see, I'm not used to it.'

'Of course, you came from that inner-city church, didn't you? This must be quite a culture shock for you. I did much the same; gave up a job in the city. I love it here, it's so peaceful.'

'Not too peaceful I hope,' he joked, 'or I will get my coat and head on back to the smoke.'

'No, it's just a different kind of busy, if you get my drift. You'll soon see. I'm sure you won't get a quiet five minutes to yourself, and you'll be begging to go back to your inner-city sanctuary.'

'I can see you and I are going to get along just fine,' he laughed. 'What's Josh like as a boss?'

'He's a pussycat,' she said. 'Oh, you probably don't like cats, do you, being a dog man?'

'I think I can cope with the metaphor,' he replied. 'So, are *you* really the boss in this set up?'

'No, no. I really am just the administrator. I like to think I take the burden of paperwork and officialdom away from Josh.

It is a busy little parish, despite the rural appearance. He has done wonders in the village, and we have people joining the church in their droves. It's quite miraculous.'

'Yes, that's what appealed to me when I considered the post. He really is bucking the national trend, then. How does he do it?'

'He's passionate. And friendly. And a workaholic.'

'So, I haven't got much to live up to, then?'

'You'll be a great asset, I'm sure,' she said. 'There is so much more we could do here, if we had the right resources. Of course, you know about Vikki's illness?'

'Yes, I heard. Breast cancer isn't it?'

'Yes, she's been through a hell of a lot. And of course, it has been a terrible strain on Josh, what with three little ones at home, too.'

'Well, I'm looking forward to getting stuck in, and hopefully I'll have you to show me the ropes? That will make life a little easier on Josh from the start. Great house, by the way. Did you have a say in it?'

'I did, as a matter of fact,' she blushed. 'And of course, Bill Holmes, the church treasurer, who I think you met at the interview?'

'Yes, I think I did. The trouble is, I was so nervous I can't remember half the people I met. And I'm normally so good with names and faces.'

'So when do you want the grand tour? I'm free tomorrow afternoon?'

'I will schedule that into my empty diary, then. It's a date!'

'It won't be empty for long,' she warned.

Sam came down to the village the following weekend, and they all met at the vicarage. Josh had also invited Daniel, as a way of getting to know him, before he was plunged into work on Monday.

Kate was shocked to realise that Sam was behaving quite rudely towards the young curate. It reminded her of how he used to behave towards her when she first came to the village. Then, it was because he was jealous of her friendship with Vikki. Surely he couldn't be jealous again, only this time because of her?

She decided that it may be best if they spent some time away from everybody, so she said that she wanted to go back to the cottage after lunch.

Vikki was visibly disappointed. This was the only downside of Sam and Kate's relationship. She now had to share her brother, but she really didn't mind. She loved Kate so much, and was glad that they would soon be related by marriage.

Sam and Kate walked hand in hand back to the cottage, and slumped down on the sofa.

'I swear I've put on a stone since I moved here,' said Kate, pulling at her waistband. 'How do they eat so much, yet stay so thin?'

'Look at you, you're a virtual beanpole,' he joked, putting his arms round her trim waist. 'I can't see you ever getting fat. Not like me.' He stared down at his own belly, pulling at the non-existent fat with two fingers.

'Get away! You're a keep fit junkie and you know it. If you eat too much, you just exercise more. I wish I could be more disciplined.'

'You could always join the gym here.'

'When would I find the time?' she sighed. 'I'm Josh's slave, in case you haven't noticed.'

'Soon you'll be my slave, and I will lash you to the treadmill, forever to keep fit.'

'I love it when you talk dirty,' she laughed, and closed her eyes. She loved being in Sam's company.

'So Miss Hartwood. When are we going to make it legal? Have you thought of a date yet?'

'Oh, Sam, it's been manic, you know that. I haven't really had time to think about it.'

'Well, think now. Come on, get your diary out. I want to make you Mrs Cornell.'

'I might keep my own name,' she chided. 'I'm a modern woman, you know.'

'How about Hartwood-Cornell then?'

'No way! I would always think about Mrs Brown-hyphen-Smith, and want to call myself Mrs Hartwood-hyphen-Cornell. That would be a right giggle!'

'No, you're right, I don't like hyphenated names. Would you really keep your maiden name?'

'No! I'm kidding. I can't wait to be your slave and mistress. I want to put out your slippers, and bring you your tea. I can just imagine the two of us, can't you?'

'Will you move to Bristol?'

A long pause hung in the air. This was one of those subjects that Kate had not allowed herself to think about. She took a deep breath.

'Gosh, I'm not sure. It's so complicated, this marriage lark, isn't it?'

'Well, I have the option of moving nearer here, you know. We have a main office in Basingstoke that I could assign myself to.'

'I hadn't thought of that.' Kate felt quite excited. 'Would you really be able to do that?'

'I can certainly look into it. I mainly work for myself, and obviously my customers come from all over the country, so geography is not as important for me. It also means that I would be nearer Vikki.'

'You're right, and she would love that. The children would love it, too!'

'Is she going to be alright, do you think?' he asked pensively.

'I think so. I mean, she still has aches and pains, and she gets breathless quite easily, but they put that down to the chemotherapy. Her hair's growing back. Don't you think she looks cool?'

'Quite the little rock chick,' he said. 'I do worry about her, though. And yes, I would love to be nearer her. It would mean that you get to keep your friends here, even if you pack up work.'

'And why would I pack up work?'

'To have babies, wench!' he laughed, and grabbed at her. They fell back against the sofa, kissing deeply. 'I do love you, Kate,' he murmured.

'I love you too,' she whispered, and kissed him again.

They pulled apart, and he brushed his fingers through her hair, smoothing it away from her face, and then etched her features with his finger.

'So?'

'So what?'

'When?'

'Soon, Sam. As soon as I've persuaded my parents to come and visit Ashton Kirby.'

He leant back, aggressively. 'Not that again. Why don't you accept that they're never going to come round to visiting you in the village? Just get over it, Kate!'

'Hey, this is my parents you're talking about! How would you feel if it was your mum?'

'But it's not! She's not that stupid.'

'Hang on, there's no need to be rude.'

He slumped back in the sofa, belligerently.

'For Pete's sake, Kate, we can't wait forever.'

She was angry at his attitude towards her parents. 'I'll go up next weekend and talk to them, and then we can discuss dates. If they won't come round to a visit, we will just go ahead. But let me try, just one more time. It matters to me,' she pleaded.

'I know. I'm sorry, darling. It's just, well everything is perfect, apart from your family. We have no real reason to delay the wedding. We are both in a good financial position, you have a house; there's no problem booking a church, that's for sure!'

'Would you consider living here at Wisteria cottage? Or would it be a bit small?'

'Well, you've got a great garden. I could build a workspace at the back; the lighting is perfect, and with the proceeds of selling the flat, cost wouldn't be a problem.'

'That sounds great. I would like to stay here, I have to admit. This village has really ingrained itself into my soul. I have made so many friends here, and I feel happy for the first time in my entire life. Happiness was in short supply when I was growing up.'

'That's why I find it hard to go along with your desperate need to reconnect with your family. It's just wrong that you had such a miserable childhood. Don't you feel bitter towards them?'

'No, I feel sorry for them,' she mused. 'Even more so when I know what belonging to a church like St John's is like. It's so warm and welcoming; almost like an extended family. I love you, of course I do; but in a different way, I love these people, this community.'

'As long as you don't love that ginger creep,' he muttered darkly.

'Sam! Take that back! I won't have you being racist.'

'What's racist about saying I hate ginger creeps?' He laughed, but she was not amused by his cruel humour. It was something that would continually come between them. She knew firsthand what it felt like to be on the wrong end of Sam Cornell's sharp tongue. It was something she would have to work on.

'Come on upstairs and see what I've found,' she said, pulling him by the hand, and breaking the tension. She showed him the diaries that she had read so far, pointing out passages of interest.

'They had such a marvellous life together,' she mused, 'and there is so much more to find out. I still don't know what happened to her little baby. She must have been just a young woman when it happened, and without the support of her family. So, so sad.'

Once more, Sam looked disinterested as soon as she mentioned her family; but it was part of her, so he would have to get over it. She put the books away reluctantly, and went downstairs to prepare supper for the children, who were coming round later, to give Vikki and Josh some much-needed time alone with each other.

As the weeks went by, baby Jacqueline grew ever more beautiful. The child smiled constantly, and Sophie was the perfect mother. She took her to all the services, including the aptly named 'Pram Service', which never failed to make Robbie laugh. He imagined it as a kind of garage repair service for baby-mobiles! But it was a great meeting place for the young women; a service where it didn't matter a jot if the babies cried, with noisy worship and jangly instruments for the older toddlers. She also attended the morning service still, but never put the baby in the crèche. She would feed her discreetly in a chair at the back of the church, and murmur softly in the baby's ear if she became restless. After the service, all the old ladies would coo over the downy-haired infant, and Sophie would smile beatifically throughout. It seemed as if she were never troubled by the usual lack of sleep or distress that young new mothers usually went through. Nothing was too much trouble, as far as Jacqueline was concerned.

Chapter 29

Kate had a rare Saturday morning to herself. Josh and Vikki had gone to visit relatives, and Sam had a deadline to meet, so was working overtime. She treated herself to a lie-in, and then ambled down-stairs for a croissant and coffee. The postman knocked at the door, and handed her a bundle of letters, while exchanging pleasantries. Kate stretched her arms and gave her body a shake. *Maybe I can go for a long, lazy cycle?* she thought to herself.

She wandered over to the sofa, and aimlessly picked up one of her aunt's diaries. This looked like an early one, judging by the handwriting. Kate thought about how our writing changed as we grew older, and how you could age a writer by the script.

She sat down and started to read through the diaries and curled up on the sofa, snuggling down inside her dressing gown, sipping coffee.

If you had looked through the cottage window, you would see Kate, still stationary on the sofa, although now turned to stone, a diary lying by her side. What you wouldn't be able to see was her expression. It was one of deep shock and pain.

She turned over the birth certificate, unable to believe what she was seeing. It was baby Paul's birth certificate, and had the same address as his death certificate. There was no father's name on it, but the mother's name was not Valerie. It was Gillian. And her age was just fourteen. She kept shaking her head, as if to remove the evidence before her. How could this be? It couldn't be her mother! Kate finally found the ability to move, and paced up and down the room. Her hands were shaking as she tried to fill the kettle. She put it down and banged the surface repeatedly. As the kettle boiled, Kate picked up the phone, and then put it back down again. She felt crazy, manic, confused, bewildered, cheated and betrayed.

Without making a coffee, she tipped the boiling water down the sink. Her actions seemed to have no order or sense to them. She wanted coffee. Her mind was fugged and maybe caffeine would help her think. She walked over to the window, then back to the kitchen and tried again, filling the kettle and watching the steam rise from the spout. With shaking hands she tried to unscrew the lid of the coffee jar, but nearly threw it across the room. Violence was not a natural emotion for Kate, yet she felt like wrecking something, anything, everything. She took a deep breath, and held her hands out in front of her, fingers splayed wide, wider, until the digits ached. Then she gradually curled her fingers back into the palm of her hand and found she was able to calm the shaking down. She managed this time to open the jar, and made herself a hot, sweet mug of strong coffee. She knew that she was in shock, and she didn't know what to do about it. Looking at the abandoned diary on the floor, she lifted her face upwards, seeking some sort of guidance.

Finally, she picked up the phone again, and dialled a number.

'Hi, it's Kate. Are you free for a minute? I need a friend.'

Minutes later, Daniel opened the cottage door, and found Kate crumpled in a heap on the floor.

'Hey, hey, hey? What's up, Kate?'

'My mother has lied to me! My whole life has been a complete and utter lie!'

He wrapped his arms around her, and held her while she sobbed.

'Tell me what's happened.'

She managed, in between dry, heaving sobs, to explain what she had unearthed in the diaries.

'All this time, I thought my aunt had been the one who had done a bad thing. And now, it turns out to be my mother. I don't understand?'

'Have you had a chance to read on any further?'

'No, I just fell upon the certificate and freaked out. Oh, Daniel, I simply can't get my head around it all.' As she found comfort from her friend, the door was pushed open.

'Sam! What are you doing here? I thought you were working?' She wiped her nose with her hands, and broke away.

'Yes, I can see you weren't expecting me,' he replied sarcastically. 'You have other things to keep you busy.'

'Hello, Sam.'

Sam nodded curtly to Daniel. 'Thanks, I can take it from here.'

'Sam, it's not like that!' cried Kate. 'I've just had some terrible news about my mother.'

'Oh, not that old chestnut again. Get over it, Kate! The past is the past.'

'Get out!' She shoved him hard in the chest.

'Hang on! It's me that's the hurt party here. I come and catch my *fiancé* in another man's arms, and you tell me to get out.'

'Listen, old man, I was just here to help.'

'Yeah, that's what it looked like,' he snarled. 'Don't worry. I'm off.'

He stalked out of the front door, and Kate rushed after him.

'Bastard!' she yelled at him. Then taking off her ring, she threw it at him. It caught him on the side of his face, but he just continued walking.

Kate slammed the front door, and flopped down on the sofa.

'That's the end of that, then,' she cried.

'Oh, Kate, he's just angry. He'll be back.'

'I don't want him back! He's a selfish, jealous pig! Just because everything is rosy perfect with his family. He can't see how difficult my life is, never knowing the truth. He doesn't even try to understand why it matters to me. Oh, what am I going to do? My whole life is falling to pieces.'

'There, there,' he soothed, taking her hand. 'Do you want me to stay? Go through the diaries with you?'

'Would you?'

'I have a clear morning, so why not? Things are always easier with a friend to share the confusion and pain with.'

'You are such an understanding man, Daniel.'

'Come on, drink up your coffee, and let's dig through this mystery. Then you can go and make it up with Sam. He's probably gone over to the vicarage to lick his wounds, knowing him.'

'You're right.' She sniffed and heaved a huge sigh. 'Right. Let's find the truth.'

Thursday

I can't understand why Gillian hasn't come home. Mum and Dad won't discuss it with me. They just said she's okay, and I should get on with my work. Gillian has been acting really strangely lately. We used to be so close. I'm so upset. This house is weird. No one I know is normal. I wish we had a normal family. Normal, normal, normal! I love that word. It's the same at school. We're freaks. We're not allowed to have friends home, nice clothes, make up. I know how difficult Gillian is finding it. She's not as tough as me. At least I can go out to work, and escape this strange house. I hate the fellowship and the stupid brethren!

Tuesday

Mum and Dad still insist that I should go to church and 'repent'. As if! I'm never going back to that place again. It gives me the creeps. Just wish I knew Gillian was alright.

Friday

Spoke to Richard the postie. He reckons he's seen Gillian at the pastor's house. What's she doing there? I bet he's got her working as some sort of slave. It's illegal, that's what it is. She should still be at school. I'm going over there tomorrow, and having it out with him. Bring her home. The evil old weasel, he can't keep her there. It's not right. Why have Mum and Dad let her stay there? Mind you, they're as thick as thieves with him. I can remember the last time they forced me to church. Had me up on the altar in front of all those morons, and told me to get on my knees and confess. Yeah, right. I just upped and walked. It's because I won't go through their baptism rites, like Gillian did. Poor kid looked scared out of her mind. It's since she started all that lark, that her and me have drifted apart. It's like she's been scared to talk to me. What on earth have they done to her mind? Brainwashed her, I reckon, just like Mum and Dad have been brainwashed. I'm going over there in the morning, you'll see.

Here, there was a large gap in diary entries, and then a long entry, written in a different pen.

Tuesday

Can't get my head around what's happened. It's too awful for words. What am I supposed to do about it? I've got no choice but to keep quiet. I've had to give in my notice at work. Shame, I loved that job. Now I am stuck in this dump of a flat in London, with no friends, and no family. Crackpot family anyway. So where do I start, dear diary?

I went over to the manse, creepy old place it is. Crept round to the back door and I could see that prat Brother John, and his miserable bitch of a wife sitting in the kitchen. I waited in the garden, until I saw them walk through to the study. That was my chance, so I shot through the back door, and into the hall. Gosh, my heart was pounding! I was sure that they must be able to hear it, it was so loud! I stood still, listening, and once I could hear them talking, I tore up the stairs. I felt like a criminal. Guess I was, especially after what happened subsequently.

I whispered at each door I came to. 'Gillian, where are you?' I couldn't hear a thing, so I just kept opening each door I came to in turn.

My hand is shaking, just writing this out, but I must get it down on paper, or else it will keep haunting me. Well, I think it always will, anyway, so who am I kidding?

The last door I tried, the very last one! I nearly didn't bother, thinking Richard the postie must have been mistaken. Shoot! I wish he had been. Pushed it open, and nearly fainted. There was blood everywhere. Lying on that filthy bed was my poor little sister. I thought she was dead, I really did. She was so pale, like porcelain. Her hair was matted to her head, and lying in a cardboard box next to her, was a baby. I nearly threw up. Bile rose up in my throat, and I choked it back. The baby looked like a doll, it was so tiny. But it was well dead, that was obvious. What on earth had happened? How could Gillian have had a baby? She never went anywhere. I can't believe I hadn't known she was pregnant. I stroked her cold, clammy forehead, and whispered in her ear.

'It's okay, poppet, I'm here now, your big sister will look after you.' I looked around for a phone, but there wasn't one. Gillian opened her eyes, and stared at me.

'Baby,' she whispered hoarsely. 'Where's my baby?'

'Hush now, Gillian. We need to get you a doctor. It will all be alright.' I hugged her frail little body. Suddenly, there was a commotion at the door. It was that nutter and his crony wife.

'What the hell has been going on here, you stupid, stupid git!' I shouted at him.

He lunged forward at me, but I turned round and grabbed the nearest thing I could find. I hit him with the heavy bedside light, and caught him on his shoulder. He staggered away from me, and swore. Yes, the saint swore at me!

'Phone for an ambulance, you stupid woman!' I shouted at the wife.

She ran from the room, and I just hoped she would do as I asked.

The wretched man stood up and glared at me.

'Call the police as well,' he shouted down the stairs. 'Tell them I've been attacked.'

I stared at him in disbelief.

'What have you done to my sister?'

'We've been caring for a poor sinner, that's what we've been doing.'

'That baby is dead!'

'It is God's will.'

'You evil idiot.' I lunged for him again, and flew at him with my fists, but he held me at a distance.

'You are going away for a long, long time,' he said evilly. 'You will be charged with breaking and entering, and grievous bodily harm.'

'Huh! That's nothing compared to what you're going down for,' I spat at him.

I heard the ambulance arriving, and ran to the window. There was a police car on the drive, and I recognised with dismay that the policeman was one of the brethren.

I looked at my poor, damaged sister, and the dead child, then sunk down on the carpet and wept.

The medics came in, and visibly blanched at the scene before them.

'Please look after my sister,' I cried, as the policeman took me away.

Gillian lay soundless in the bed. I didn't know if she would live or die, and my heart was breaking.

I was taken to the station, and charged with GBH, but later the pastor came and told me he was dropping the charges, as long as I left the area, and never tried to contact my sister again. I told him to get lost. But then he warned me that my sister would be charged with the death of her baby, if I didn't do as he said. I couldn't believe what he was saying. I didn't know if he could do this, but he was a powerful character, and had so many people under his sway. He then handed me a brown envelope, and told me it contained enough money to set myself up somewhere. I knew then he was serious. It was a cover up. What could I do?

'I can't believe it. It's all such a horror story,' said Kate, as she laid the diary to one side.

'I need to speak to my mother.'

'Is that wise? Do you think she will tell you anything?'

Kate got up from the sofa. 'I have to. I need to hear her side of the story. I can't live with just half the picture.'

'Well, I'm driving you. You're in no fit state to drive yourself.'

'No, it's too far. I can't let you do that.'

'And I can't let you drive. End of.'

Reluctantly Kate agreed with Daniel. After the row with Sam, and this awful revelation, she knew that she would be too preoccupied to do the long drive on the motorway.

She packed an overnight bag, and they set out. On the way to the car, Kate scoured the ground for her ring. They both searched the area, but could not find it. Kate thought to herself that it was an omen. She and Sam were history. With her heart shattered, she lowered herself into Daniel's car.

The journey to Carshalton was driven in silence. Daniel realised no words could bring comfort, so he put on a Bach CD and they soon covered the distance to her parent's house. She silently got out of the car, and walked round to the driver's window.

'Thank you so much, Daniel. I owe you big time.'

He shrugged it off.

'I'm sure you would do the same for me. Take care, Kate. Stay in touch.'

She walked up the path with a heavy heart.

Melanie saw Kate arriving and rushed down the stairs.

'Katie! I didn't know you were coming?'

'Neither did I,' she replied grimly.

'Does Mum know you're here?'

'No, and I would like to see her on her own. Do you think you could take Dad out for a bit?'

'Well, I'll try. You know what he's like. Are you ill? Are you in some sort of trouble?'

'I'm fine. I just need to talk with Mum.'

Her mother appeared from the back garden.

'Oh, hello, Kate. Why didn't you ring and tell me you were coming? I'll just pop to the shops and get something for lunch.'

'No, sit down, Mum. Mel can go to the shops, can't you?' She glared at Mel.

'Sure thing. I'll go and ask Dad to drive me.'

'Oh, don't disturb your father. He's so busy.'

'He's not too bloody busy! He's just sitting pretending to be,' roared Kate.

This shocked her mother and sister into silence, and so they did as she told them.

Once Kate was sure that they were on their own, she took out the two certificates.

Her mother blanched. Her hand flew to her heart, and she started to slowly shake her head, denying what she was seeing.

'Talk, Mum. I want to know what happened.'

'Oh, my dear God!' her mother wailed. 'Where did you get these?'

'You know damn well where I got them from. What I want to know is why Valerie had them, and why she had to go away?

Why didn't you tell me, Mum? It was *you* who had the baby. Why didn't you tell me, when I thought it was Val?'

Kate sat there with huge tears rolling down her face. Nothing she could hear now could make things worse.

She looked at her mother, now a broken woman. But she felt no sympathy. Not until she knew the whole story.

'I'm so sorry, Kate, my love.' She stretched her hand out to her daughter. 'I'll tell you the whole story. But let's have a drink first. I can see you need one, and I know I do.'

Her mother went through to her father's study, and brought out a bottle of sherry. Her parents never drank alcohol, unless it was a special occasion, such a Christmas or New Year. But she poured them both a large glass and took a long swig, before launching into her story.

Chapter 30

'That man had such a hold on me. It started when I was just thirteen, but all the time, he made me feel that I was the sinner. I was the bad one. I knew it wasn't right, but he was too powerful. Once I knew I was pregnant, I wanted to kill myself. I couldn't tell anyone. To begin with, I tried to get rid of it. I mutilated myself, stabbing my stomach, falling downstairs, hot baths...you name it, I tried it. Of course, there was no alcohol in the house, so I couldn't get drunk. As I got bigger, I hid it under large baggy jumpers. Valerie was my best friend, Kate. It was so hard not being able to confide in her. We shared a room, you know. So you can imagine how difficult I found it.

Eventually, my mother guessed. She was livid. Called me a slut, a sinner, a harlot. I couldn't tell her who the father was. He had sworn he would kill me if I did. So of course, she confided in him! He said he would deal with the little problem. Little problem! When I was about seven months gone, I was sent to the manse to stay with them. He told my mum he would get someone in to help me when it was my time, but he didn't. I was just a kid, scared and frightened out of my mind. I had no idea what to do when the pain started. I started to scream, but they came in and put a gag on me, so that no one could hear. They sat in the room, reading the bible, and praying, asking God to forgive my sins. The pain got so bad, Kate. I thought I was dying. Suddenly, I remember thinking my body was going to split apart. The burning ripped through me, and suddenly I was pushing, pushing. There was blood everywhere, and then it stopped. I think I fainted. When I came to, his wife was holding the baby, and they had obviously cut the cord, and she had cleaned me up a bit. She shoved this baby at my breast and told me to feed it. I was fourteen. I had no idea how to breastfeed. The baby clamoured at my breast, and he seemed to know what to do, so I just let him get on with it.

They left me then.

They would leave food outside the door, and told me that the baby would be taken away and given to adoptive parents. In the meantime, I had to look after him. They gave me a pile of nappies and grotty old babygros that they must have got from a charity shop or something.

But I got sick. I started to bleed, but they wouldn't get help. I think I must have got an infection. I don't remember much else. I have no idea how long I was sick for, but at some point the baby died. Obviously I was too ill to feed him, but they hadn't noticed until it was too late.

I just remember Valerie appearing. I thought I had died and gone to heaven. Then there was a lot of shouting and screaming, and then a load of uniforms. Police, I think, and the ambulance people came.

I came to in the hospital. He was sitting by my side, and I cried out for my mother. He grabbed my wrist and warned me that I would be arrested for the murder of my baby if I ever mentioned what had happened. Then he prayed for the forgiveness of my sins.

When I left hospital, Valerie had gone. I was told that she was a wicked girl, and that I was never to mention her name again. I never went back to school, but was taught at home for the next year. After that, I had to work as a cleaner for the fellowship. I was never allowed my own money, and then your father was introduced to me as my future husband.'

'You mean you had to have an arranged marriage? That's illegal, Mum!'

'I had no choice, love. I was young, terrible things had happened to me. I had brought shame on the whole family.'

'But you were just a kid, for God's sake! He raped you, and held you as a slave. The police should be told.'

'Don't be daft. Anyway, he's dead now. There's nothing to be done.'

'But why did you stay, Mum? What hold has he got over you now?'

'He told the elders of the church, you see. Said I would ruin my family, and that I had to spend my life repenting. Your dad had been a bit of a tearaway as a lad, and so they had a hold over both of us.'

'But, Mum, come on! It's not the dark ages now! Why on earth do you think they still can control you like this. It's... it's just inhumane! I cannot believe you've stayed in that crazy fellowship all this time.'

'I'm a sinner, Kate. A bad woman. I have no choice.' Her mother was sobbing now. Kate looked at this broken, crushed woman in disbelief. There were no words to describe the hatred she felt towards the brethren. Suddenly, she was hit by a huge wave of compassion.

If I don't reach out to her now, I'm as bad as they are, she thought to herself. I cannot let them poison me all these years later.

She fell at her mother's feet, and all the love she had withheld over the decades poured out with her tears, as she finally allowed her defences to fall by the wayside.

'I'm so sorry, Kate. I've been a terrible mother, a terrible person.'

'It's okay,' Kate soothed, 'It's all in the past. We can move on from this, and rebuild our family.'

'But it's too late. Valerie's dead now. I can never make amends. I miss her so much.'

'But it's not too late for us, is it? And Valerie had a wonderful life. Much better than the misery you've had to endure, Mum.'

'What do I do? What can I do to make it up to you and Melanie?'

'You can start by being honest with Melanie. Do you think Dad will be up to facing the truth?'

'He's so unhappy, Kate. He struggles so much with all the threats of hell and damnation. Why do you think he spends so much time reading the bible and praying? He finds it all so hard, but is frightened to own up to it. He's not like those other men, the brethren. It's all been such a lie. We've been living a lie, but couldn't see the way out.'

'Well, now's the time to move on, Mum. I love you and Dad, really I do.'

'You do?' Her mum started to cry again, but this time, the tears were cathartic.

The afternoon was spent explaining the whole sorry story to Mel, and allowing her dad to give his side of events. Kate felt shattered, and took herself away for a much needed doze.

For the first time ever, her family sat down to a meal together, and were able to be honest in their conversations. The past was now out in the open. Gillian was hungry to find out all about Valerie's wonderful life. She explained how Valerie had got hold of the certificates. Apparently, she must have crept into the manse after she had been expelled, to gather up any remnants of her sister's belongings, so that she could have something to remember her by. The pastor and his wife had obviously just got back from the registry office, and the certificates were lying on the kitchen table. She must have grabbed the certificates, and that was the last time she ever set foot in her home town.

The following morning Kate was overcome with a terrible wave of depression. Her mother and sister were at a loss to know what to do or say. They had never seen Kate anything other than in complete control, but they didn't know of her argument with Sam.

'Hey, Katie,' said Mel softly. 'Do you want to talk?'

'I've done enough talking thanks. I'm tired.'

'Okay, but I'm here if you want me. Shall I ring Sam for you?'

'No, I'm good.' She turned her back on her sister, and closed herself off.

This continued for a week. Gillian started to wonder if they had better get the doctor in to see her. She was eating very little, and didn't want to do anything, or go anywhere.

'I don't understand it,' Gillian said to Mel. 'I thought it was going to be fine now that everything is all out in the open.'

'I have a feeling it's not all to do with us, Mum. She hasn't mentioned Sam, and she's not wearing her ring. Didn't you notice?'

'Oh no. They were so happy. I wonder what that's all about?'

'She won't open up at all, Mum. I'm really worried about her.'

Josh and Vikki had been frantically texting Kate, as she refused to answer her phone. It was clear they were worried sick about her.

Eventually a very fragile Kate got up, and began to interact, on an extremely limited basis, with her family.

Josh was shocked to receive a letter of resignation in the post.

'What!' shouted Vikki! 'She can't just up and leave. I'm going to throttle that brother of mine. What the hell has he done to her?'

But Kate was unreachable. The weeks turned into a month, and still she refused to face up to any sort of future. It appeared that her heart had been well and truly broken.

And so, on Friday morning, the doorbell rang, and Mel opened the door to find Sam on the doorstep.

'Oh, thank goodness. I am so glad to see you!' She greeted her once future brother-in-law with a hug.

'Can I see her?' he asked grimly.

'Sure,' she said, but by the look on his face, it wasn't going to be the joyful reunion Mel had imagined.

He shuffled in to the sitting room, and took a seat on a dining chair, looking stiff and uncomfortable.

'Do you want a coffee?'

'Um, I just want to see Kate,' he replied tersely.

'Right. She's just coming, I think.' She stepped out of the room, feeling a chill air emanating from him.

Kate walked into the room. He was shocked to see the weight loss she had incurred. She looked gaunt and ill. He resisted a strong urge to rush over and wrap his arms around her. She had walked away from him. He had been a total idiot, and she was right to leave him. How he had behaved had been unforgivable, but he had underestimated how hard it would be on her.

'Sam.'

'Kate.'

'Oh, Kate, I don't know how I'm going to tell you this...' Suddenly, Sam broke down and started crying dry, heaving sobs.

Kate didn't know how to respond. She had frozen her emotions deep within her heart, and had forgotten how to react with love. She stood with her arms limply by her sides.

'Kate, it's Vikki. The cancer's back. It's terminal.'

Chapter 31

They drove back to Ashton Kirby in silence. Kate's head was spinning with the knowledge that her dear friend Vikki was ill once more. She was also finding it difficult being in such close proximity to Sam again. While there had been a distance between them, she could persuade herself that she did not love him. But that was patently untrue. The motorway was clear and they made good time. Sam drew up outside Kate's cottage, now a riot of colour as the warm summer sun encouraged both flowers and weeds alike. Lupins and freesias, asters and roses, all jumbled together and fought for pride of place among the dandelions and daisies. A tabby cat languished on the lawn, and stared up at the car with sleepy eyes.

Sam turned the engine off. Then both Sam and Kate spoke at exactly the same moment.

'I'm sorry.'

'I'm sorry.'

'No, really.'

'No, really.'

'Shut up for a second will you? Let me talk. I am one big, ignorant idiot.'

'Well, yes....'

'I should never have spoken to you the way I did. I am so selfish, greedy, jealous....'

'Please continue.'

'I spoke to Daniel after you left. He gave me a right telling off, I can tell you.'

'Only what you deserved.'

'Yeah, well, I realise that just because I have never known anything but a solid family life, I have no understanding what it must have been like for you, my darling. I promise that I will listen, and try to appreciate how tough life has been for you.'

'Really?'

'Well, yes, after they've let you out of prison for assaulting me.'

'What?'

'Look.' He turned his face to show her the side of his face. There was a tiny gash by his ear, healed over now.

'I did that?'

'Yes, when you threw a dangerous weapon at me. But I forgive you. If you forgive me, that is?'

'I have a small confession,' said Kate. 'Well, it's quite a big one actually.' She winced as the memory hit her.

'Go on.'

'Well, after I threw the ring at you, I went to look for it. Sam, I couldn't find it. I'm so sorry. I know it must have cost a small fortune.'

'It did,' he replied ruefully, with a forlorn look on his face.

'Well, *if* we are getting back together...are we?'

'Mmmm, I think so.'

'Then, I guess I had better contribute towards the price of a new ring.'

'Does that mean you would still consider marrying me?'

'Yes please, Sam,' she said in a small voice, her heart beating rapidly.

'Oh, that's grand! Because I just happened to go back to your house that night, and found said weapon.' He then produced the ring with a flourish.

'Sam! You had it all this time! Why didn't you tell me?'

'You sort of disappeared, remember? I didn't think you wanted to see me. If I were you, I wouldn't have wanted to see me. I was a total prat. I'm so sorry, hon. From now on, I will try to be a lot more tolerant, and a lot less jealous.'

'I love you, you idiot. I have never loved anyone like I love you. How you could even doubt that? I just don't understand.'

'Let's put all this behind us, and be a united front for Vikki. She will be so pleased we're back together. You should have witnessed the grief my sister gave me!'

'You deserved it!' There was a long pause, as they held hands and stared at each other, remembering the details of each other's faces, the features they had come to love and had sorely missed these past few weeks.

'I've missed you, Sam. So very much.' She reached out and stroked his cheek.

'Let's go in,' he said. 'I want to show you how much I've missed you.'

Later that day, they walked over to the vicarage, where Josh let them in. He looked terrible, his face grey and haggard.

'Oh, Josh, I'm so sorry to hear about Vikki,' Kate said as she reached out to hold him.

'Yes, well, I know she will be made up to see you again, Kate. We've both missed you more than you can imagine.'

'I've missed you too. I'm really sorry for leaving you the way I did.'

'You had your reasons, love. Crikey, you've been through your own hell by the sound of things.'

Kate had been writing letters to Vikki, telling her of all the terrible things she had discovered. It had been a cathartic act, writing it all down in longhand, and not just pounding it out on the computer. She had also heard that Josh hadn't replaced her position in the church office.

Hesitantly, she enquired, 'Will you take me back, Josh?'

'Oh, I can't tell you how pleased I am to hear you ask!'

'Great! I'll be in first thing in the morning then, shall I?'

'It will all be there waiting for you. Bill has been helping me out with a few bits and pieces, but essentially it's all there, untouched. Sorry.'

'No, don't be. I will just plough my way through. I can't wait. My mind has slowed down and become so sluggish with nothing to do.'

'Come on then. Vikki can't wait to see you.'

They went through the house, and into the kitchen, where the usual chaos reigned. Kate was glad to see her friend didn't look any different. Hopefully, that meant that the cancer was still treatable.

Vikki screeched with joy when she saw Kate and Sam. They ran towards each other, and hugged tightly. The children copied their mother and started screaming, and cuddling Kate's legs.

'Group hug, group hug!' shouted Daisy, as they all bustled around together.

'You lot are so loud,' complained Sam. 'Come on, Josh, let's go for a beer, and leave this motley crew to get on with it.' The two men gratefully disappeared down to the Yew Tree Inn.

As the kettle boiled, the children drifted off to the garden, bored by the adult conversation.

'So how are you, really?'

'Oh, Kate. It's all such a nuisance.'

'That's putting it slightly mildly, then?'

'Yes, well, it is a bit of a worry, I have to admit. Where were you, Kate?' She reached out for her friend, and Kate was gutted to see tears in her eyes. 'I really needed you.'

'What can I say, darling? I'm so sorry, but I'm here now. What can I do? I'll never leave you again like that, I promise.'

'Yes, I've given my brother a final warning, I can tell you. He will never, ever treat my best friend in that abominable fashion, I've made sure of that. Are you two alright, do you think?'

'Oh yes! We're best friends again. Even had a *lurvve in* to cement it!'

'Not too much detail, please! Don't forget he's my baby brother.'

'By five minutes, you twit!'

'Well, I seemed to have learnt a lot more than he did in that five minutes, that's for sure.'

'I would love to have known you two when you were little.'

'Well, obviously I can't remember everything, but by all accounts, Sam didn't talk till he was five years old! I used to say everything for him. It was almost as if we were telepathic, because no one ever saw him utter a word, but I always knew what he wanted. How weird is that?'

'Not a lot changed there, then. You're still a gasbag, and he's still a man of few words.'

'Well, he's going to be a man of even fewer words from now on. He is going to have to think very carefully before he opens that big mouth of his, in future.'

'Did you hear I threw my ring at him? I thought I'd lost it!'

'Yes, he came over with blood running down the side of his head. Good work! I clocked him hard on the other side when I heard how he'd behaved. Honestly, what is it with men?'

'Come on, that's all in the past now. Tell me what's been happening with you? Oh, Vikki, I can't believe you've got to go through it all again! Why didn't the chemo kill all the cells? I just don't understand.'

'No, I don't, either. The daft thing is, I put all those symptoms down to the after-effects of chemo. You know, all that breathlessness, and aching back. Well, it turns out it has spread to my lungs and spine. They have done a CT, and thankfully it hasn't spread to my liver, which I suppose is something to be grateful for.'

'No! Oh, Vikki, that's so awful. I must admit, your breathing worried me, but you seemed so sure it was just side-effects.'

'I know. But last week, it got so bad, that I had to go to casualty. They admitted me for tests, and drained a load of fluid from my lungs. The relief was enormous. I thought that was that. They said I could have got an infection, what with my immune system going through so much. But the tests came back, and they found the cancer had spread to my lungs. So then they sent me for an MRI, and the damn thing has spread to my spine, as well.'

'So what happens now?'

'They are going to try me on a trial drug. It might get rid of it, or might just buy me some time.'

Kate's eyes filled with tears. The pain she felt for her lovely friend was overwhelming, and she could no longer hold it together.

'It's okay, Kate,' Vikki said soothingly.

'How can you say that? I don't think I can bear anything more happening to you.'

'You've got to. I need you to be strong now, more than ever before. Listen, I want you to help me organise some memory boxes for Josh and the children.'

'Don't talk like that! You're going to beat this thing.'

'I intend to. But, I have to make contingency plans in case I don't. So are you in?'

'Of course I am. I'll do anything and more that you want me to, but it's only a standby plan. The main plan is that you beat this. Promise me?'

'I can't do that, Kate, please try to understand.' She was crying now, and Kate rushed round to her side.

'I'm here for you, whatever happens. So, what can I do right now?'

'Stay with me. Make me laugh again. Make sure I keep my sense of humour, please. I can't survive without that.'

'How's Josh dealing with this new turn of events?'

'Terrible. It's weird; he's always been so good at supporting his parishioners through all sorts of horrid life experiences. But he seems to have fallen apart now it's in his own back yard. Strange, isn't it? But Daniel has been fantastic. He is such a support for us all. Now I can't imagine what life in the parish was like before he arrived.'

'Yes, Josh needs someone to fall back on. It must be tough having to support others, and to build up their faith, when his own faith is faltering. Heck, I know I'm struggling with my friendship with Him upstairs. We're not on speaking terms at present.'

'Don't blame God. Bad things happen. Get over it.'

'How can you talk like that? Don't you want to know why?'

'There is no why, honey. It's the whole order of natural life. Cancer happens. God never promised us a completely perfect life, just because we are his followers. Otherwise, the church would be full of old people, who simply pray away every kind of disease and illness. Can't you see that? But he gives us the strength to get through it. And good friends to help, like you, see?'

'You are a saint, do you know that?'

'I don't think so! Not with my dirty mind, and foul mouth! But I know God loves me, warts and all, and that's all that matters.'

'Do the children know?'

'Yes, we've told them that the cancer is back, and that's why Mummy has been poorly again, and that I've got to have some more nasty medicine to get better. That's all they need to know at their age.'

'Poor kids. And poor you. What does Ellie have to say?'

'Oh, she's gutted, obviously. But she has been so helpful in explaining what all the terms mean, and what all the different scans do. Honestly, Kate, I'm so ignorant. I didn't know anything about cancer, before all this.'

'You're not. No one needs to know about this stuff unless they're going through it. Unless of course they're in the medical profession. So, will you teach me what you know, please? I want to get my head around all the facts, so that I can really stand by you through it all.'

'Thanks Kate. Oh, I'm so glad you're back. I've missed you so much.'

Chapter 32

Kate was soon back into the swing of things in the office. She had a few strange looks from the Churchwardens, but everyone else was delighted to see her return. She looked through the wedding certificates, and was so glad she had kept up-to-date with her administrative duties, as there had not been one single wedding she had missed. She set to work with her calligraphy pen, and wrote out the next two weddings that were due later that month.

She also wrote out the godparent's cards for Jacqueline's baptism. Thank goodness she had got back in time for that! It was going to be a real celebration of life, and the service was going to take place in the main service, this Sunday. Kate herself was a godparent. She had brought an antique compass for the baby as a keepsake, and had it engraved with a verse from the Bible: 'Show me your path O Lord, and point out the right road for me to follow.' She hadn't wanted to get the usual silver money box, or picture frame; Sophie had come to mean so much to her, and Jacqueline was like a niece.

That morning, the flower arrangers were bustling around dressing the church with colour and life. It was going to be a wonderful celebration! She just hoped that Josh would be able to enjoy taking the service, as she knew he was struggling with the terrible knowledge of Vikki's illness.

The morning of the service was perfect. Kate awoke to a clear blue sky, and she showered and dressed with a huge sense of excitement. Sam was joining her at the church, having spent the night at the vicarage. The children wanted him to have a sleepover with them, as they were getting a little jealous of all the sleepovers he was enjoying at Kate's!

The church was heaving! Although Robbie and Sophie did not have many of their own family, her carer from the home had brought along many of Sophie's old friends. They were all so proud of her. She had made a good life with Robbie and the baby, especially given her broken background. All her new friends from the church attended, and the music was joyful, to match the day.

As the weather was so perfect, they arranged to have the buffet out on the green, with the church kitchen providing teas and coffees. It meant that the men could get their pints from the Yew Tree Inn, which was an added bonus to many. Baby Jacqueline slept peacefully throughout the service, and afterwards was passed from person to person, smiling and gurgling to order. Everything was perfect.

Kate and Vikki had returned from a visit to the hospital to arrange her new therapy regime. She had tablets to take at home, but had to go back for an injection every three weeks. In all probability, she was going to lose her hair all over again. It was now sitting in a lovely short bob, and it seemed terrible to think she was going to be wearing hats and wigs, yet again.

'Good job I didn't sell all my stuff on Ebay, isn't it?' she joked.

'Who would want your old wig?' ribbed Kate. 'It looks like a dead cat, especially after your kids trawled it all round the garden.'

'I think you're right,' she mused. 'Perhaps I had better take it to the hairdressers, and give it a makeover.'

'You never know, you might not lose it this time.'

'What, with my luck? The worst thing is that I've only just got all my toenails back. That's not something you hear much about, is it?'

'No, that was really gross! I can cope with you sharing your missing booby, your bald head, and your ulcers, but I could not cope with those nails. Ugh!'

'Some friend you've proved to be! Love me, love my toes, that's what I say.'

As they pulled up to the vicarage, they were aware of a commotion in the drive.

'What's going on here, then?' Kate wondered.

They drew up, and realised that it was Robbie and Josh.

Josh raced up to the car. 'Kate! Thank God you're here. Please come quickly.'

'What's happened, Josh?' she asked, with a racing heart. Clearly something terrible had occurred.

He shook his head, his eyes red with unshed tears. 'It's Jacqueline. The baby's dead.'

Kate buckled over, as if she had been kicked in the stomach. 'No, please no!'

'I'm afraid so,' he replied grimly. 'It looks like a cot death.' Robbie was almost unrecognisable, his face ravaged with grief.

She walked over and hugged him tightly, wordless and shocked beyond belief.

'It's my Sophie,' he cried. 'What's she gonna do without her babe? The police are there, Kate. What do they think they're doing there?'

Kate looked askance at Josh, who nodded.

'They think it was a cot death, so the police have to make an appearance.'

'As if my Sophie would do anything to hurt that babe!' he wailed.

'They don't think anything of the sort,' she assured him. 'Let's get over there.'

She waved briefly to Vikki, and promised her she would get word to her as soon as she knew more.

She loaded the shaken Robbie into her car and drove off, her mind all over the place. *How can this be happening?* she thought to herself. Only a week ago they had been celebrating the baby's life. It was too cruel.

They arrived at the house just as Ellie Smith was going in.

'Thank God you're here, Kate. By all accounts, no one can get a word out of her, or get her to put the baby down.'

'This is too awful for words, Ellie. What can have gone wrong?'

'Sudden Infant Death Syndrome, I suspect. That baby was perfectly fit last time I saw her. I don't know how Sophie and Rob are ever going to cope with this. I have serious doubts about her mental health right now.'

'Let me try and talk to her. She has come to trust me over the last year or so. I might be able to get through to her.'

Robbie looked on helplessly, emotionally way out of his depth. His own grief for the baby was outweighed by his desperate concern for Sophie. The policewoman who had been assigned to the case was waiting in the hall.

'I didn't want to confront her until she had a friendly face around,' she explained.

Thank God for a compassionate police officer, thought Kate. Out loud she asked, 'Where is she?'

'Upstairs in the nursery. She's still carrying Jacqueline.'

In the pretty pink room, surrounded by Disney princesses, and delicate floral curtains, sat a mother and baby. It was a picture-perfect scene, except for one cruel thing. The baby was dead. Alabaster white, yet still perfect, baby Jacqueline was being cradled and comforted by her loving mother, her face wet with tears that poured down upon the baby's feather-fine hair.

Kate found herself falling at Sophie's feet, and wrapped herself round her legs, the pain and anguish overcoming her. Sophie put her hand to Kate's head and began to stroke her, with the same rhythm that she was rocking her baby girl. It was a tragic cameo. Time stood still, absorbing the pain and giving precious moments for the two friends to meld together. The police officer wiped the tears from her own cheeks. This was the first-ever SIDS case she had been assigned to, and she was finding it harder than she could ever have imagined. A mother herself, she found herself empathising with Sophie's situation, and knew she would react in the very same way. How could you ever let go of your child?

Suddenly there was a low keening; like a cat had been hit by a car. They all looked round, and saw that the sound was seeping from Sophie, slowly building up in pitch and volume, until she was screaming, all the while hugging Jacqueline ever tighter. Kate stood up and enfolded her in her arms, until the screaming turned to dry, racking sobs. Slowly, she began to take big, heaving breaths and sat down on the bed.

'May I take the baby now?' asked Ellie gently.

'Is that alright with you, Sophie?' asked Kate, holding out her arms for the babe.

Sophie turned her face up to look at Kate, a look of drowning in her eyes. She offered up the bundle to her.

Kate almost started weeping all over again, as she stared down at her godchild. She bent to kiss the cold cheek of the little angel, and then handed her over to Ellie.

The police officer and Ellie then stepped out of the bedroom, leaving Kate, Robbie and Sophie.

What do I say? Kate wondered to herself. Words seemed completely pointless. Sophie sat on the bed rocking to and fro, like a Romanian orphan, whose only toy had been snatched away. Robbie had no idea how to comfort his wife. The big bear of a man was crushed beyond comprehension. So Kate just sat alongside Sophie, and rubbed her back, silently.

The post-mortem confirmed that Jacqueline had indeed died of a cot death, as if there had ever been any doubt. The funeral was arranged by Kate, for Robbie and Sophie were still in a deep state of shock. Sophie had not uttered a single word since the baby's death. The GP had prescribed Diazepam for both parents, although she could not gauge Sophie's levels of anxiety. She refused to leave the house, and was being forced to take small amounts of fluids. Getting her to eat was impossible.

Kate had dealt with the undertaker, with Robbie's say-so, and had seen to all the practical arrangements. It seemed terrible that just a week earlier they had been celebrating the little girl's life, and now were arranging her funeral. Life was too cruel, sometimes.

A few days had gone by since the death, and Kate was working in her office, her heart still broken with grief for the little family unit, when there was a frantic knock at her door.

'Come in!'

Robbie entered her office with a look of sheer panic on his face.

'Kate! It's Sophie. I don't know where she's gone.'

'Calm down, sweetheart. When did you last see her?'

'I was working in my shed, and went back in to make her lunch. Not that she's eating anything I make, mind. But when I went up to her room, there's no sign of her. She hasn't left the house for days, and now she's gone without a word. I'm beside myself. If anything happens to her, I'll top meself.'

'Where have you looked, besides the house?'

'Nowhere. I didn't know where to start, so I came straight here. I know you are the first person she'd run to, if anywhere.'

Kate racked her brains. 'Would she have gone to the shops for anything? Have you phoned any of her friends?'

Just then, Betty Coates came through from the main church.

'Excuse me,' she coughed. 'Sorry to interrupt you I'm sure, but there's a strange 'goings on' through there.' She indicated with her head and thumb.

'Can't it wait, please, Betty? This is pretty urgent.'

'I think you'll find this is 'pretty urgent' too.' She put her fingers in the air to emphasise.

'Wait here, Robbie. I'll be straight back.' She glared at Betty and walked through the double doors into the church.

'Oh no!' She headed to the front of the church, quickly snatched off the altar cloth, and wrapped it around Sophie's naked form.

'Come on, sweetie,' she soothed. 'Let's get you out of here.'

Sophie looked up at Kate in bewilderment, not speaking a word.

She walked the traumatised woman back through to her office, where Robbie practically fell upon her.

'Oh, my poor baby girl. There you are!' he cried. He took her in his big beefy arms and squashed her tight. 'What do you think you're doing, giving me a scare like that?'

He seemed to pay no attention to the matter of her nakedness. Maybe, thought Kate, she's done this before? Poor Sophie seemed quite unhinged. Kate was getting increasingly worried for her. The sooner the funeral was over the better it would be.

Josh appeared to be sinking into his own pit of despair, unable to rationalise God's goodness with the awful situations playing out in his parish. It had been decided to let Daniel lead the funeral service, as he was more able to stand back from things at the moment. He had also been spending time with Sophie, trying to get her to talk. Before becoming a curate, he had been a trained counsellor, and was wise beyond his years. Kate was so glad to have someone professional helping Sophie, as she felt out of her depth.

The morning of the funeral arrived, and there was a large crowd gathered outside the church. When Sophie and Robbie stepped from the car, there was not a dry eye to be seen, especially when the pallbearers carried in the tiny white coffin. Only Sophie sat stone-faced and seemingly untouched, so far out of it was the poor, wretched woman. It was almost as if the pain had transported her off the planet. Perhaps that was a good thing?

Daniel led the service with great compassion and dignity. The songs had all been chosen by Kate, in Sophie's mental absence, but she knew which ones were her favourite. When they played the hymn that had been played at the christening, Kate wondered if it would reach down and awaken Sophie's soul, but it had no effect whatsoever. She just stared towards the front.

They had decided to have a small gathering afterwards in the church hall, but Robbie took Sophie home. It was the right decision, as it would have been too much for her, and probably for him too.

In the coming weeks, Ellie Smith was called out on numerous occasions, as Sophie slipped further and further out of reach. It was eventually decided to admit her to Parsonfields, the mental health unit attached to the main hospital. It was a modern centre, with in-patients allocated private rooms, and the rooms and corridors were all painted a friendly peach or green. It resembled a motel in many respects, only the guests were not going anywhere soon.

The unit had been built in place of the old asylum, which had been knocked down in the nineties. Until Parsonfields had been built, the nearest mental health unit had been in Southampton, much too far away for many of the small villages in this sleepy corner of Hampshire. This new unit was far less threatening, and not nearly as scary as the old hospital had been. But it was still a terrifying place for someone in a deep depression, like Sophie.

Schizophrenics and drug addicts shared the corridors with the depressed and anxious. Some looked quite threatening, others pitiful. The nurse who clerked Sophie in was an anxious looking woman in her thirties, but she had kind eyes. Kate thought she looked like a little sparrow! She had gone with Robbie to settle Sophie in. He had not wanted to have her admitted, but it was becoming harder for him to cope with her erratic behaviour. She still had not uttered a word, but frequently just took off, and was found wandering down the middle of the main road on one occasion. They left her at the mental health unit with heavy hearts, hoping that the professionals would get to the bottom of her grief, and help her to move on a little.

Chapter 33

Kate continued to deal with the backlog of work that she herself had caused, as well as helping to ferry Vikki to her hospital appointments. She had found it very hard to be happy again since the baby's death, but one day she sat at Vikki's kitchen table after they had returned from the hospital, and grinned at her.

'You know I told you Sam and I made up, that day I came back from my parents?'

'Yes,' replied Vikki slowly, wondering what was coming.

'Well, you know I told you we had really, *really* made it up to each other?'

'Yes?'

'Well, your brother's been a touch naughty...'

'Yes?'

'And... Oh come on! Guess, you silly woman!'

'No! You're not! You can't be!'

'I am!' Kate fell about laughing. 'I'm pregnant!'

'Kate! That's totally fantastic! Oh, that's just the sort of news we need right now!' They danced about the room and giggled. 'I wonder what you'll have? Hey, you might have twins!'

'No way! I couldn't cope with two at the same time.'

'You won't have a choice, young lady. If it is twins, you just have to get on with it. How are you feeling?'

'Well, I've been a tiny bit nauseous, but I just put it down to the trauma of the last couple of weeks. Then I got to thinking. I stopped taking the pill when I was at my mum's. Then Sam came on the scene suddenly, and brought me back here, and the rest is pretty obvious.'

'You wait till I see that brother of mine! Getting you pregnant out of wedlock! And me a vicar's wife. Oh, the shame of it! I'll never live it down.'

She brought out a bottle of apple juice and two champagne glasses.

'Well, I can't drink, and now you can't drink, but we can still celebrate. Cheers!'

They toasted the good news, and Vikki started clucking around Kate like a mother hen. 'Good grief, you probably weren't taking folic acid! We must sort you out with some supplements. Have you seen Ellie? Get booked in, and see the midwife. When's it due? Oh, I can't wait to see what sort of offspring my brother produces!'

'Steady on, woman, I've only just done a test. There's plenty of time for all of that. You're first to know, you see?'

'What? Haven't you told Sam yet?'

'No,' she grinned sheepishly. 'I'm a bit worried. What if he doesn't want to start a family quite yet?'

'Idiot. He'll be over the moon, I tell you. You should have seen the state of him when you left him. He was broken-hearted. Kept going on and on about you being the only woman for him, and how he'd driven you away. How he'd spoiled his chances at happiness. How he'd never have the chance of a family like mine.'

'Really?'

'Sure! He loves you *so* much, you daft cow. Phone him now! I want to hear his reaction. Put it on loudspeaker.'

'Okay!' They giggled as Kate dialled Sam's number.

'Hi, my darling wifey.'

'How did you know it was me?'

'Technology, you ignorant woman! I've got caller identity.'

'Oh,' she said, nonplussed.

'Go on,' urged Vikki in a loud whisper.

'Who's that you've got with you?'

'Your silly sister. Sam, guess what? I'm pregnant.'

Silence.

'Say that again.'

'I'm pregnant,' she said, a little hesitantly this time.

'No way! You mean I'm going to be a dad?'

'Yup.'

There was a loud crash from the other end of the phone.

'Sam? Sam, are you still there?'

'Oops, yes,' he said, struggling upright. 'I just jumped for joy, and brought my work board tumbling down on top of me. Ouch! That's fantastic news. I'm coming over.'

'You can't. You've got work to do.'

'But you've got my baby! See you in two hours.' He banged down the phone.

'He was pleased, then?'

'He was pleased.'

Chapter 34

Kate was aware that she was not giving Sam as much attention as he deserved. But surprisingly, he was being okay with it. He had certainly undergone a transformation since she left him. But she definitely liked the new Sam, especially now they were expecting a child. They had decided to postpone their wedding until after the baby was born. She really didn't want to waddle up the aisle! So they set the date for the following June. Vikki and Kate sat in the hospital waiting room armed with Bride magazines, and Kate's iPad, jotting down ideas and shops to search for on the internet, when they were home.

'Don't you think it's strange that women have spent years trying to be equal to men? We work as hard as they do, we fight for equal pay, equal rights in the workplace, and try to prove how strong we are, and then, all of a sudden, it all goes out the window.'

'We are thrust into a pure white virginal meringue, marched up the aisle like a lamb to the slaughter *by a man,* to be presented *to a man!* Then, the speeches are all made by *the best man, the bridegroom and the father of the bride.* Women are effectively silenced on the greatest day of their lives. Where's the equality in that, then? I'm telling you, it's going to be different at my wedding. I'm doing a speech, and so are you, as my chief bridesmaid.'

'Wow! You are the militant feminist aren't you? High five, sister!'

They slapped hands, and continued to look at veils, favours, and cup-cake style wedding cakes.

Vikki's hair had fallen out completely again, and she was looking very tired, although her sense of humour continued to cheer up the other patients in the waiting room. Irene had moved in to the vicarage for the duration of the treatment, and Sam had now moved into Kate's cottage permanently. His workroom was wonderful; a wood and brick construction, with floor to ceiling windows, and a modern, long slanted roof. Kate liked having him close at hand. It also saved her hours of travelling back and forth to Bristol. Daisy, Finn and Amy loved having their uncle on tap, and were frequent callers to Wisteria Cottage.

Gillian and Jim had stood up to the Brethren, who were constantly bombarding them with visits and phone calls, urging them to return and repent. They had discovered the delights of worshipping in a different church, with a congregation that found joy in their Lord, not punishment. Kate found it amazing to discover her father could smile! They had formed a new friendship as father and daughter, and she was so glad that he would be walking her up the aisle, even if she did not accept the term *giving her away*. Gillian had even joined the choir, and had made a lot of new friends. The shackles that had held her fast for so long had been removed, and Gillian was finally able to admit that her parents had been cruel and uncaring, in their bid to please the brethren. She had taken a course of counselling to help her come to terms with what had happened to her as a child, and had even taken the two girls along for one of the sessions.

Melanie had settled down with her boyfriend, had a steady job and had even moved to her own flat, something Kate could never have envisaged.

Sophie was eventually allowed home after twelve weeks in the mental health unit. But she was never again the bright, bubbly Sophie that everyone knew and loved. She was on heavy medication, which had dulled her mind, and made her sluggish and disinterested in everyday life. Poor Robbie missed the former Sophie so much, but he continued to treat her like a princess. Kate and some of the young mums had gone round to clear the nursery while Sophie was away, so that it would not be too painful for her when she returned. Robbie could not face going in there. He said that he was haunted by the image of Sophie wailing over her dead baby. It was a sad situation. Kate had tried to encourage Sophie to return to some of her former activities in the church, but although she did try, she was like an empty shell, not relating to anyone around her.

Kate and Sam had invited Josh and Vikki round for supper. It was a little squashed around their kitchen table, but at least she no longer had the printer and computer on it. Kate had managed to find a little niche in Sam's workroom for them.

'So, I guess we're having pasta tonight, are we?' Sam joked. It was a standing joke between them that pasta was the only meal she was capable of making.

'No, we're having Indian, so there.' A delicious smell was emanating from the kitchen.

'Wow! I didn't know you could cook Indian,' he remarked, with obvious surprise.

'Oh, Sam! How can I lie to you? I can't, I've brought it in from Waitrose. Sorry! I promise that I will try and learn a few more dishes, when I'm the little wife and mother at home all day.'

'That will never be you,' he replied. 'And I never want you to change. You're perfect, just the way you are.'

Kate and Sam had decided that she would continue at the parish office after the birth of their child. It would work well, as she would only be round the corner, and would be able to pop home at lunchtimes. With Sam working from home, he was happy to help with childcare. In fact, he was looking forward to it. He had reached the stage in his business where he didn't have to work every day. He could dictate when he saw clients, and they were both happy working through the evenings, when necessary. Kate was going to work three days a week to start with, and they had a young girl who was willing to help out with childcare, as and when needed. Kate had started to show very early on, but with her slight frame, it wasn't really surprising. Vikki still taunted her that she was carrying twins, especially with her looking so big, so early. But they had been for their first scan, and there was just one, very healthy little babe. Kate found it a little hard to be too excited, having just experienced the loss of Jacqueline. It felt somewhat tactless to be too happy, but in the comfort of their home, they planned and looked forward to the big event with mounting happiness.

Although the baby wasn't planned, they were both delighted with the outcome. Neither of them were teenagers, and both had yearned to have children. Vikki and Josh couldn't believe their luck. Not only had her brother managed to bag a suitable partner, she happened to be their best friend. The children were constantly coming home with fanciful names that they and their friends had thought of in the playground.

Pixie and Trixie were high up the list, though the happy couple appeared less keen.

Vikki had invited Ellie to join them for supper, when she had seen her in the surgery earlier that day. She knew that Kate wouldn't mind. It just meant squashing up a bit around the table. Two of the young people were babysitting, much to Finn's delight. He had a crush on Alexis, a pretty eighteen year old student. The girls however, loved her for different reasons. She wore beautiful clothes, and stunning shoes. She also knew a lot about hair, and would try out different styles on Daisy and Amy. Before they went out, Alexis had fashioned a hair piece on to Vikki's wig. She looked fabulous and the children clustered round her, taking pictures of her with her mobile phone, and their own cameras.

The friends sat around the table laughing at the photographs the kids had taken. Amy always managed to get an odd view, taken mainly from floor height, making everyone look long legged and large headed. They had also doctored the pictures with the various photo apps they had downloaded onto their mum's phone. Vikki didn't have a clue how to use them, but somehow even four year old Amy knew all about apps.

Ellie laughed as Vikki told them how Amy would expertly skim across the various pages on her phone, using her fingers to enlarge and decrease pages. It seemed that the children of today possessed skills they would never have dreamt of, just ten years earlier.

As they sat laughing and sharing anecdotes, Vikki suddenly put her hands up to her head, and winced.

'You okay, Vikks?' asked Josh, looking concerned.

'Yeah, sure. I just suddenly had a horrid shooting pain.' She scrunched up her face. 'I think it's going now. Ouch! That was strange. All gone!' She smiled up at the worried party.

The chat continued, until Josh looked up at the kitchen clock.

'Good grief! It's gone midnight! I've got a sermon to prepare. Thanks so much for a lovely evening, Kate and Sam. The meal was delicious!'

'It was nothing,' said Kate, as Sam pinched her bottom.

'Get off, you perve!' she giggled.

'Fine, I own up, I didn't make it. It was all from a shop.'

'Who cares? It was totally delicious,' said Ellie. 'Indian is my favourite cuisine.'

'And mine,' replied Vikki, standing up. Suddenly, she swayed to the side, and Josh managed to catch her just in time.

'Oh, I feel a little faint. It must be the alcohol gone straight to my head,' she laughed self-consciously.

'You didn't drink any,' Kate said anxiously. 'You were on the apple juice all night.'

'Potent stuff, those apples,' she giggled.

They were all looking at her with concern.

Ellie took on her doctor mantle, and marched her over to the sofa.

'Seriously, how are you feeling?' she asked, holding her wrist and finding her pulse. She looked up at the clock as she did so. Then she put her hand to Vikki's forehead.

'Don't fuss. I'm just tired. It's late, so come on Josh, let's leave these good people to the clearing up and bugger off home.'

'Listen, will you ring me if she gets any worse, please?' Ellie asked Josh.

'Yes, of course I will. Are you really alright to walk home, Vikki?'

'No, she's not. I'm driving you both home,' said Kate. 'I haven't been drinking. And it gets me out of the washing up.'

'Don't worry. It will still be here when you come home,' joked Sam. 'Take care of her, Josh?'

The three of them left, and Ellie stayed to help Sam with the clearing up.

'What do you think that was about?' he asked her.

'I'm not sure,' she replied slowly.

Minutes later, the back door was flung open.

'That was quick, what speed did you drive at?' Sam joked.

'Ellie, come quickly, please. Vikki seems to be having some kind of fit. She's in the car.'

'Sam, dial 999,' she shouted as she flew out of the door.

Vikki was laid across the front seat of Kate's small Mini. She appeared to have passed out, and was as white as a sheet.

'Let's try and get her out of the car, and lying in the recovery position,' said Ellie, grimly.

Josh carried her back through to the cottage, and they waited for the ambulance to arrive.

Chapter 35

The news, when it came, was grim. Vikki's cancer had spread to her brain. She was moved to the intensive care ward, and Josh sat by her side, broken-hearted. She still hadn't recovered full consciousness yet, but he held on to her hand and told her how much he loved her. He wasn't ready to lose her. It was all too soon.

Sam and Vikki sat at home by the phone, anxiously waiting for further news. They were shell-shocked at the sudden turn of events. It was all happening too rapidly. How could it have spread to the brain, when she was still having treatment? But the sad truth of the matter was that she possibly only had days to live.

As soon as Vikki had regained consciousness, they made the decision to bring her home. Arrangements were made to have a hospital bed delivered, and other vital equipment installed. There were those who thought it a bad idea, what with having three young children at home, but the family had discussed this at length and felt it was the right thing to do. Daniel took over the work of the parish, along with the vicar from a neighbouring village, leaving Josh free to stay with his wife.

The children were taken to and from school by Irene, helped out by Sam and Kate, so that they didn't have to go home with friends. They wanted to spend as much time as they could now with their mummy.

Many tears were shed in the long evenings, as Vikki began to drift away from them. Some days she was more lucid than others, and she would bark out orders to them, about how she wanted the children looked after when she was gone. They even managed to crack a few jokes still, although the mood was bittersweet. Vikki had already chosen the songs she wanted at her funeral, and had requested that no one wore black. She didn't want to be remembered in gloom, but with bright, vibrant colours. It was better for the children, she believed, if she could go out in a blaze of neon pink, and balloons.

The end, when it came, was peaceful and gentle. She appeared to just fall asleep, and never reawaken. Kate sat by her side, with Josh and Sam on the other. The children were all in bed asleep, when at ten o'clock in the evening, Vikki passed away.

Josh was inconsolable. His faith had left him, and he was a wretched man. Sam and Kate tried to lift him out of the deep pit of despair, if only for the children's sake. The three little ones crept around the house with tear-streaked faces, unable to comprehend that their mother had gone. Irene had to face the fact that she would be burying her daughter, a thing no parent should have to do. Sam felt like half his soul had been ripped away. The siblings had been so close, and scarcely a bad word had ever been spoken between them. Losing Vikki was simply devastating. A tsunami of grief swept through the whole village. Kate felt like she didn't deserve to hurt as much as she did. She had lost her best friend and soul mate, but surely it couldn't be as bad as losing a sister, mother, wife and daughter?

But to her, it *did* feel as bad. Her world had fallen to pieces. Ashton Kirby had been such a happy place. It had been a place where she had found the space to heal the hurts of her past. She had also made lots of friends, and had a job where she had discovered a joy in serving Jesus. But that joy was not forthcoming at present. She didn't know what crumbs of comfort to offer Sam, or Josh. She just loved them as best as she was able, and helped with the practical arrangements in her own administrative fashion.

The children were being incredible in their belief that Mummy had gone to a better place. This was where their Christian faith played a major role. It would have been so much harder if they had not believed. As it was, they were trusting Jesus to take care of her, and to comfort them all in their loss. The children's simple faith offered crumbs of comfort to the adults, each in their turn.

Another death, another funeral. Practically the whole village turned out to support Josh and the family, as yet again a coffin was carried into the village church. The church was bathed in a mass of wondrous flower arrangements, lovingly prepared by the same women who had once poured scorn upon Vikki's parenting skills. The music lifted the roof, as hundreds of voices sang with a catch in their throat, and tears in their eyes.

The Yew Tree Inn once more provided sustenance to the grieving community, and the church as a whole felt comforted by their shared grief, and a hope in the eternal.

All, that is, except one. Josh was confounded by the devil, who chased him in his dreams, and haunted his waking moments with doubt and despair. Where was the hope he had offered to so many? How could any good possibly come out of the loss of his wonderful wife? As comfort and food abounded, he took himself off to the vicarage, alone. The darkness continued to push down on him, making him sink deeper and deeper into depression. In the weeks that followed, the congregation missed him, and began to wonder if he would ever return to shepherd them again.

Daniel did a sterling job of holding the parish together, leading services, and taking communion to the sick. The lay preachers stepped in to fill the gaps that were left, and on the outside, no one would have suspected that there was a large wound left by Josh's absence. But the main person damaged by his loss of faith was Josh himself. He raged and prayed, empty on reflection, and angry at the silence he felt. He put on a brave face to the children when they were around, but sat brooding evening after evening. Irene had returned home now, feeling that her son-in-law needed the house to himself, so that he could learn once more to parent his offspring.

As Kate and Sam continued to plan for the new arrival and their wedding, they helped each other to heal, sharing fond memories of Vikki. Each of them knew a side to her that the other didn't, and it helped to cement their relationship even further. They were truly united in their grief.

Kate continued to visit Sophie, who, although it was quite obvious by now that Kate was expecting, never mentioned the fact. Their conversations were very light and one-dimensional nowadays, and again, Kate missed the good friendship they had once shared. It was as if she had lost two good friends all in one year.

One Sunday morning, Kate had managed to persuade Sophie to come along to the morning service. She knew it would be hard, as this was the one she used to attend with baby Jacqueline. It was probably the reason why she came to the evening services, as they held no memories for her. But this service was important. Daniel had told Kate that it was to be a time of sharing and praying, with laying-on-of-hands for healing. The parish had so many wounds right now, and both he and Kate felt that it was time to move on. That did not mean forgetting, but recovering, with all the painful memories alongside. The newsletter of the previous week had encouraged as many people as could make it, to come along. They were both hoping that Josh would put in an appearance, too.

The day dawned bright and sunny, a rare, balmy November's day, and the church was once more packed with villagers. As the welcomers stood at the doors doing their job, Kate looked anxiously down the path for Josh. It didn't look like he was coming. The children had arrived earlier to attend their Sunday school classes, which was the routine of the past few weeks, but no Daddy with them.

She made her way back to her seat with a heavy heart. She had really hoped Josh would make it this morning, but it didn't look as if that would be the case. As the heavy front door closed, she put her head down to pray, but someone tried to move past her. She glanced up to smile and acknowledge whoever it was, and her heart filled with joy when she saw that it was Josh.

'Hi,' she whispered to him, and she reached down and squeezed his hand. He placed his hand over hers, and then stared stone-faced to the front.

This is difficult for him, to put it mildly, thought Kate. This dear man, who has been there for so many of his congregation, desperately needs God's comfort today. She uttered one of her quick arrow prayers, as the sweet notes of a flute started, joined by guitars. As the singing got underway, Josh remained resolutely silent and stiff beside her, but she didn't mind. He was here, and that was enough for now. Glancing across at the front pew, she could see Sophie and Robbie. Robbie had come! That was a first, and she sincerely hoped it heralded the start of a new thing for the couple. They were so young, and hopefully would go on to have more children, although none could replace Jacqueline. Sophie had also lost that beautiful innocence of youth, and barely trusted the world any more. After all she had gone through as a child, too. It was still heart-breaking to think back to that terrible time. Tears formed in Kate's eyes, and she rapidly brushed them away. *Not again, Kate!* she berated herself. She put it down to pregnancy hormones, but she knew that she would feel just as bad if she hadn't been with child. These were sad times.

Daniel stood up to talk. He appeared to take a deep breath, as if steeling himself for a difficult task.

'Why do bad things happen to good people?' he asked. And then was silent. People shuffled in the pews, startled to hear a question being asked of them. They had learnt to expect to have answers in sermons, not questions posed.

He looked around at the congregation.

'We've all asked that, I'm sure. We ask ourselves, did I do something to deserve this? Is it because I'm a sinner? Why didn't I have enough faith? Perhaps I prayed wrongly, or didn't pray hard enough.'

'As if the way we pray would make a difference to the way God bestows goodness! When we look at other people, do we think, that won't happen to me, I'm a much better Christian?

I would have far more faith, and God would answer *my* prayers.'

'Let's look at Jesus. Did he stand in the garden of Gethsemane, and say, "It's okay folks, I have total faith in my Father. No harm will come to me. He will get me out of this."'

'No! He cried out to God, in fear and pain. "If possible, take this cup away from me." As one Christian said, *God never promised the tornado would skip our house on the way to the pagan neighbours, or that microbes would flee from Christian bodies*. We are subject to the same laws of nature as our next door neighbour. It is natural and right that we die, as our neighbours die. It is natural and right that we succumb to illness and disease, for we live in a fallen world. BUT... We have the hope of the resurrection, and that is what stands us apart from our neighbours. Even when Jesus walked the earth, he never healed everyone. Why? Who knows the mind of God? Perhaps because it keeps us dependant on him, I don't know.'

'Those of you who have children, consider this. From the earliest age, you take them to the surgery, and hold them down while a nurse sticks a needle into them. What happens? The baby bawls.'

The congregation laughed a little, following Daniel's every word now.

'But afterwards you pick them up and cuddle them. Why did you let that happen? Because you care for them. Now a baby can have absolutely no understanding of the adult mind, no knowledge of disease and cure, but can only go along with what you allow them to suffer. But they know you love them still. A sick child undergoes so many cruel and painful procedures in the hope of a cure, and his parents allow that. The child does not know why, but trusts the adult. Only when they are older, and have been to medical school, or taken biology lessons, or become a parent themselves, do they begin to grasp why that parent made them suffer.'

'Now, I will never, ever understand the mind of God. It is just too huge a thing to even begin to imagine, but do you see where I am going with this?'

The congregation nodded their heads, beginning to grasp where Daniel was heading.

'We are not exempt from tragedy; we are not exempt from temptation. But God will use us, broken and fallen as we are. God took the worst thing that could happen to him – the death of his only beloved son – and turned it into victory. From the terrible evil that was done to Jesus, we are healed. Death no longer has a hold on us. Now we who are left on earth may not appreciate it yet, when we are still in deep sorrow, but we have a hope. It is this hope that separates us from every other creature on earth. Without hope we are nothing.'

'Now you may not be feeling very hopeful right at this minute. I am sure many of you have had your faith battered by recent events in this parish, and around the world. It's a frightening place to be, isn't it?'

There were once more nods of assent. Josh shuffled in the pew next to Kate. She didn't want to turn and look at him, but he seemed to be listening as intently as she was.

'By His wounds we are healed, and by His weaknesses we are made strong.'

'The one fact we all know, in the face of doubt, is this: we all die. Why is it, that although we know this, when it happens to someone we love and depend on, our whole world is shattered, seemingly destroyed? You would think we would be used to it by the time we reached adulthood, wouldn't you?

But God shows us his love. Firstly, in his son, who died that we might live, and secondly, in our love for each other. Now this love is not like that of a dog, or any other domestic animal. Don't get it confused with loyalty. Love is boundless, unfathomable, without expecting anything in return. That's why God gave us each other, so we could see His love at work in each of us. But to love is to hurt. So do we stop loving? No way! We reach out to God in our pain, and he provides us with comfort, support and encouragement. That is why we meet together as a church.'

'I hope that my words do not wound anyone, rather that they may act as a salve. Each one of us has suffered from the huge, unbearable pain of losing someone, at some point in our life. Today, I ask you all to reach out and pray for one another. If any of you want to come forward for prayer, we have a team of folk ready to pray with you.'

In the silence that followed, Daniel uttered a prayer, and then the music group played some quiet, reflective songs.

Then an amazing thing happened. One by one, the people came forward; a small and steady stream of people made their way to the front. Some wanted to pray on their own at the altar, others knelt in front of the prayer support team, and had hands laid on them. The folk that remained in their seats watched in awe. The atmosphere was electric, and certainly not forced in any way. It was a beautiful thing.

Kate had gone forward to help pray, and when she returned to her seat, she noticed that Josh was no longer there. Her heart sank, until she realised that he was up the front, being prayed for by Daniel.

Chapter 36

Amazing things happened that Sunday, and there was a real air of peace surrounding the parish. The pain was still present, but you could tell that it had been lessened, as each learnt to comfort the other. Josh went away for a weekend retreat to a little convent on the outskirts of Oxford and seemed to regain his faith and peace.

Christmas came and went in the parish; a more muted affair than this time last year, but joyous none the less. Kate was becoming quite cumbersome now. It was quite difficult being so small and so fat! The children laughed as her belly button protruded and stuck through her clothing. Amy thought that was where the baby was going to come out of.

'Don't be silly,' Daisy said, 'it comes out of your front bottom!'

Kate blushed as they discussed her anatomy. Children were so knowing these days!

They had fallen into a routine of spending the weekend round at the vicarage. It took the burden of parenting off Josh's shoulders a little, and anyway, Kate and Sam loved the children dearly. They knew that their little girl, for they had found out the sex of the baby, would be part of this big extended family. Thankfully, the decision about her name had been made, and Pixie and Trixie were happily out of the equation. In one of her last, lucid moments, Vikki had told them in no uncertain terms that the baby was not to be named after her. It would be too odd for Sam to have a daughter called Vikki! So they had conceded and were going to call her Eliza, as Elizabeth had been Vikki's middle name.

The New Year brought heavy snowfall, and kept many people away from the church. Robbie came every morning to shovel the snow away from the path, so that the parishioners could safely visit, if they wished. Sophie was still behaving strangely, appearing to be going into herself more than ever now. Kate wondered if she was still taking her medication. She had tried to get an honest answer out of her, but she just smiled at her, and said she was alright now. That was debatable, but she was an adult, and could not be forced to do anything against her will.

One cold Sunday evening in the middle of February, Kate opened up the church for the evening service. They weren't expecting many to the service tonight, and had decided to hold it in the small chapel, where it would be warmer and cosier. Kate watched as a few stragglers made their way into the chapel, keeping an eye out for Sophie. It was going to be a tough day for her tomorrow, as it would have been Jacqueline's first birthday. Now heavily pregnant, Kate had some idea of how the poor woman would be feeling. The love she felt for her unborn child was incredible, overwhelming and urgent. She would die, literally, for this child, if the need arose.

But Sophie didn't come. Daniel kept the service short and sweet, and then they locked up and went home. Tomorrow, Kate thought to herself, I shall take a bouquet of flowers round to Sophie, to show her she understood what the day meant to her.

Back at home, she shut the front door, and headed for the lounge. She prepared a roaring log fire and snuggled down on the sofa, wrapped in a thick quilt. Sam was away at a conference in Harrogate, and she missed having him around. It surprised her constantly how little she missed being a single woman any more. She loved being part of a couple, and couldn't wait to make it legal. They were both looking forward to their wedding in June.

Back in the church, Sophie stood shivering in the little annexe next to Kate's office. She had crept in through the rear entrance of the church, and hidden until the service was over. Watching Kate through a small gap in the doors, she saw her turn off the kitchen light, and then the lights in the corridor. She was now plunged in darkness. From a distance, she heard the heavy *thunk* of the large front door, as the bolt was slid over, and then silence.

As her eyes grew accustomed to the dark, Sophie carefully made her way along the corridor, as silent as a shadow. In her hand she carried a Tesco's carrier bag, weighed down with essentials for the task ahead.

She carefully opened the double doors leading into the main church, and propped them open with the wooden wedge provided for that very purpose.

Slowly and with almost religious reverence, she took out the petrol canister and matches. She flurried around like a sparrow gathering feathers for her nest, collecting up unused song sheets and newsletters, piling them all on the carpet. Carefully, so carefully, she stacked them up, almost as if she were creating something of artistic beauty. Standing back, she surveyed her handiwork. Then she poured the contents of the canister over the top, and lit the match. The old bibles and hymn books were also piled up in the centre of the church. As the match struck, the flame leapt from matchstick to paper, tinder dry and thirsty for the fire. 'Eat me!' they screamed, as an orange glow swept down the aisle, devouring worn carpets, and spreading to the old wooden pews.

'Feed me!' screeched the fire, whipping papers from the back of pews. The glowing papers fell onto the stuffed prayer cushions, which burst into flames, and exploded stuffing into the air, spreading the fire further and further. Up onto the dais the flames danced and swirled, onto the lectern, and up onto the cross of Jesus. The altar candles were now pools of wax, spilling down the altar cloths, as the fire rose up to meet the rivulets of wax, encouraging it to burn brighter and stronger. Crackles and spits resounded through the chapel, a choir of devastation, burning ever brighter. Even the crypt was not sacred ground, as the flames licked and spilt further and further.

In the bell tower, the fire climbed up the pull-ropes, dancing and swirling round the coloured ropes. One by one, the choir gowns, hung on hangers, succumbed to the monster's huge appetite, skeletons burning.

While the church burnt, the village slept.

Kate turned restlessly in bed, and pulled her duvet closer, against the cold of the February chill. She looked at her clock. Two thirty a.m. She shook her head in disbelief, and tried to slip back into the land of dreams. At four a.m., she was aware of the sound of sirens, but could they have been part of her dream? At five a.m., the phone rang, shaking her from her disturbed night. She reached out to stop the noise. It was Josh.

'Kate, the church is on fire!'

'What?! Bloody hell, Josh. Are you okay? Where are the kids?'

'They're safe. We're all okay. You might want to get here fast. But you won't be able to get through the church yard, so use your car.'

'I'll be there as soon as I can. Bye.'

She pressed the end call button, and pulled on her clothes, stunned by what she had just heard. Hopefully it was only a minor blaze, and would be put out quickly. She searched for her boots, her head still fuzzy from broken sleep. Stepping out of the cottage, she shivered as the frosty air hit her. The car door was difficult to open, as the frost had frozen over the lock. Cursing, she went round and tried the passenger seat. Thankfully this opened, so she slid over the seat, catching her coat on the gear stick.

Please start, she prayed, as she put her key in the lock, and turned the engine over. Thankfully the car obeyed her command, and she was off. She knew that the heat wouldn't come through before she reached her destination, so she shrunk her neck into her scarf, trying to keep warm, her breath turning to mist. As she pulled into the road circling the green, her heart stopped at the sight of the blaze. This was no minor fire, as she had hoped. The church glowed from its core, as flames licked and lashed at every corner of the ancient building. Silhouettes of villagers dotted around the church gate, as fireman tried to contain the fire, in vain. As she neared the devastation, she could hear the sobs and cries of horror from the bystanders.

'Kate!'

It was Josh, swaddled by the three children, whose faces looked up in awe, lit by the vicious flames.

'Oh my God! It's bad, Josh,' she said, with tears running down her face. 'Have you any idea yet how it started?'

'No, the fire crew are too busy at the moment, but the Chief said he would come and have a word with me as soon as he knows more,' he replied grimly.

'Thank the Lord it happened at night. At least no one's hurt. There wasn't anyone in there, was there?' she suddenly panicked.

'Well, there shouldn't have been. I presume it must have been an electrical fault. Why didn't we listen to you when you suggested the sprinkler system?'

'Don't think about that now,' she placated. 'Oh, Josh. I can't quite get my head around it. It's just too awful.'

The church now looked like a matchstick shell, lit from the centre by huge orange and red flames. Although the fire was raging and crackling, there was a strange aura of silence surrounding it, as villagers tried to take in the destruction of the epicentre of Ashton Kirby. It was going to be much worse once the morning came, and people went about their daily activities. The shock and horror were too bad for words.

They stood there for what could have been minutes, or hours. Kate looked down on the heads of the children, and realised that they were shivering violently, but hadn't said a word.

'Come on, you three. Time to go in and get some hot chocolate, I think,' said Kate. The three children looked at her with grateful eyes. Poor kids, she thought. First losing their mum, and now this. They must be in shock. How much more could this sweet little family unit take?

Josh smiled at her with gratitude.

'Do you mind if I stay out here for a bit?' he asked.

'Of course not. I will bring you out a mug of hot chocolate, and a hot water bottle to stick under your coat. You must be freezing.'

'Thanks, Kate.' He squeezed her arm, this action saying more than words could convey. She walked off, glancing back to look at the sad, hunched figure staring at his ruined church.

Back in the warm vicarage, she allowed the children to put on the Disney channel, and slump in front of the TV. Hopefully, they would doze off in front of the screen, as it was still early morning. The dawn was breaking over a cold, grey sky, and Kate pulled her cardigan tight around her heavily pregnant belly. Suddenly, there was a loud banging on the front door. She ran to open it and Robbie stood there, looking anxious and afraid.

'My Sophie's missing! What if she's in the church!? I didn't realise she hadn't come home last night. I must have dozed off on the sofa. I'd had a few beers, you know? Thought she'd slipped through to the bedroom, but when I peered in this morning, she's not there! Oh, Kate, what am I to do?'

'Hang on a minute, Robbie. As far as I recall, Sophie wasn't in church last night. No, I know she wasn't. I'd remember, because I'd been looking out for her.'

'But she went out at the correct time for the evening service! I was a bit worried about her, it being the eve of Jacqueline's birthday and all. She didn't say anything, but I thought it would be the place she'd want to be. I can't get through to her since, well, since she's been away.'

'Look, come on in and sit with the children, and I'll go and see if I can have a word with the fire officers.'

'Thanks Kate. My head's all over the place, and now this.' He shook his head sadly. 'What's happening?'

'Let me go and ask. Hopefully it will put your mind at ease, and then we can start to think about where she would have gone. Have you called the hospital?'

'No. I just panicked and flew out.'

'Okay. You get on the phone. I've got the number here. Try the emergency department and also the mental health unit. I'll be right back.'

She put her coat back on and headed over to the church. The flames had now been put out, and there was just a thick plume of grey smoke rising from the building. She looked around for the chief fire officer, who was standing talking to Josh.

Her heart was beating hard, as she walked up to the grim party.

'Have you found anyone in there?' she asked. 'Please say no, please!'

Josh grabbed her arms. 'It was started deliberately, Kate. Can you believe anyone would want to burn down the church?' His face was ashen.

'Listen, Josh. Sophie's missing.'

'What? You don't mean...'

'I don't know. Apparently, she left home last night for the service, but I don't remember seeing her there, so hopefully it's all a false alarm, but, well, it was the baby's birthday today.'

'Hell!' He rushed over to the fire officer.

'Are you sure you haven't found anyone in there? One of my parishioners has gone missing.'

'Well, I can't be definite at this stage, but we haven't found any evidence of, um, human life.' He looked down at his soot-stained boots, shuffling uncomfortably.

'Jones! Over here. There's a possibility a young woman could be involved. Can you tell the men to take extra care, and report back to me as soon as.'

He turned back to a tear-stained Kate.

'Look, I'm pretty certain we would know by now if there was any sign of human remains.'

Kate winced.

'Why do you think this young girl would be in church? At that time of night?'

'Her husband says she's gone missing. She has been very distressed, and ill. She lost her baby to a cot death a few months back, and has been, um, not herself for a while.'

'Do you think you ought to go to the police, given the circumstances?'

'I suppose so,' she replied reluctantly.

Just then, there was a shout from the bowels of the ruins.

'Over here, sir!'

Kate stood rooted to the spot. 'Please Lord, please, no.'

She walked slowly in the direction of the firemen. Heat still poured from the charred building. Fearfully, step by step, her heart in her mouth, she continued forward.

'Don't panic,' he reassured her. 'They've just found the site of the start of the fire.'

'Where was it?'

'I can't discuss it with you, I'm afraid. This is now a crime scene.'

Suddenly, Kate ran off.

'Where are you going? Don't go in the building!'

Kate ran past the firemen, past the waiting, watching crowd, and round to the back of the church. Weaving her way through the gravestones, she fell down at the tiny alabaster angel, where Sophie lay, frozen and unconscious.

'Over here!' she shouted. 'Call for an ambulance. Quick!'

Chapter 37

Robbie sat holding Sophie's hand, as she lay on the hospital trolley. A policeman stood alongside. She was still wrapped in the silver heat blanket, as they waited for her core temperature to rise. It had been touch-and-go for a short while, but she was out of danger now, physically. Her mental state was another matter entirely.

'You don't need to hang around here, you know. She ain't going anywhere in a hurry,' Robbie barked at the policeman.

'Only doing my duty, sir.'

'Yeah, well, I'm only doing mine. Can't I have some privacy? My wife's poorly here, in case you haven't noticed.'

'I'm sorry, sir. I don't mean to intrude.'

Robbie let out a deep sigh, and turned his back on the officer. He lay his head down beside his wife, and whispered softly to her.

'It doesn't matter what you've done, sweetheart. I love you. We're going to get through this. I promise you.'

That morning, as the full horror of the fire ricocheted around the village, people stood in small groups, crying and reminiscing. Even those who had not attended the church were sad to see such a beautiful old building totally destroyed. The old bell tower was now a blackened skeleton, towering above the gutted church. It was hard to believe that they had been worshipping in there less than thirteen hours ago. The fire had left not a corner of the church untouched. It was now just a blackened shell, ashes still smouldering silently. The smell permeated around the village for miles, held down by the winter mists.

Josh and Kate presided over a sombre breakfast party, as the children tried to persuade their daddy to let them have the day off school.

'We're tired!' moaned one.

'We're upset,' tried another.

'Sorry, kids, but I can't have you home today. I have too much to do, and I can't be looking after you as well.'

'Kate can look after us, then!'

'No,' he said firmly. 'Kate has to help me sort out all the paperwork. Please help me out here. I'm tired as well, but we have so much to do.'

They reluctantly cleared up their breakfast crockery, as they had been taught to do.

'I wish Mummy was alive. She would look after us, and not send us to school,' sighed Amy.

Tears pricked in Josh's eyes.

'I wish she was too. I really, really do.'

Kate had returned to her cottage to get showered and dressed. She made herself a coffee, then sat down and dialled Sam's mobile.

'Hi, babe. How's you?'

Just hearing his voice reduced Kate to tears.

'You won't believe what's happened,' she cried. 'It's gone, completely gone.'

'What has?' he asked mystified. What could have upset Kate so much?

'The church. It has been burnt down to the ground.'

'Bloody hell, Kate! When?'

'Oh, I'm not sure when it started. We'll know more once we've met with the fire chief later this morning. It was terrible. You can smell it for miles.'

'Do they know how it happened yet?'

'I think they have a good idea,' she replied sadly. 'And we think we know who, as well.'

'Well, who then? Who would set fire to a church?'

'It's not been confirmed, and no one's been arrested, yet. But Sophie went missing last night, and we didn't know where she was. I finally found her half-frozen to death on the baby's gravestone. It's too sad, Sam. I don't know if I can bear it.'

With that she started crying properly, and Sam had a job hearing what she was saying.

'Hang on, babe, I'm coming home.'

'You can't. You've got work to do.'

'And you're my fiancé, and this is a crisis. I'm coming back.'

'What are we going to do about the wedding?' she howled.

'Listen, it's just a building, not a person. We'll sort it, my darling. Look, I'm packing up now, so hopefully be with you in a few hours. Love you.'

'Love you, too,' she sniffed.

Kate had gone back round to the scene of the fire, and was mingling with the villagers as they talked amongst themselves, stunned by the damage the fire had caused.

Suddenly, she doubled up with pain, as she stood watching the embers of the church smoulder under thousands of gallons of water. The sound of simmering echoed through her mind, as she felt the first cold trickle run down her jogging bottoms.

Then a pain shot across her abdomen, tightening, tightening.

No! I've still got another month to go! she thought, as she reached forward to grip the back of the person in front of her. The fireman looked behind him.

'You alright, love?'

'No, I think I'm in labour,' she gasped.

He reached round for her, and took her hands. 'Okay, my darling, what's your name?'

'It's Kate,' she bent double as another contraction racked her body. Breathing quickly, she looked at him with fear in her eyes.

'I'm not due yet,' she exclaimed.

'Don't you worry,' he assured her, 'The size of you, I reckon the baby will be fine. Let's go find you somewhere to sit, and call for help. Have you got a partner?'

'Yes,' she puffed. 'I haven't got my phone on me. If you could just help me over to the vicarage, I can phone from there.'

'Right ho, let's be having you, then.'

He carefully walked her over to the vicarage. Kate was now shaking with fear and anticipation. What a time to make an appearance! But it had probably been brought on by the shock of the fire, and also the frantic attempt to find Sophie.

Josh was amazed to see Kate looking in such a sorry state.

'Hey, Kate, whatever's wrong?'

'I've started,' she huffed. 'Phone Sam for me, please. Ow!' She panted as another wave of pain almost knocked her off her feet. Should it be this painful this quick?

Twenty minutes later, she was safely in the maternity ward, and the pain had all but disappeared.

'It was bad, honestly,' she told the midwife sheepishly.

'I believe you, pet,' she laughed. 'Let's get you on the bed and have a look at you.'

'But I'm not due till next month,' she said anxiously. 'Do you think the baby's alright?'

'Judging by the size of you, I should say so.'

'Why does everyone say that!' she asked crossly. 'I can't help how big I am!'

'Hey, this is one time in your life you're allowed to be big,' she laughed. 'Have you been in a bar, or something?' she asked, sniffing the air.

'What? Oh, the smoke. No, the church at Ashton Kirby was destroyed in a fire a few hours ago. I've been outside. I work for the church, you see.'

'What? Are you one of those female vicars?'

'No,' she laughed. 'I do admin work.'

'Seriously, did it really burn down? Do they know what caused it? If I recall, it was a pretty little church. What a shame.'

'Ouch!' exclaimed Kate as another contraction flooded over her. Good timing little one, she thought. She had managed to avoid talking about how the fire started.

'Right, before your next contraction, I'm going to examine you; get an idea how far along you are, if that's okay?'

'Fine,' said Kate, through gritted teeth. 'It can't be any worse than this pain is.'

The midwife carried out the examination, and Kate waited with bated breath. Just as she finished, another pain came on. She hung on to the midwife's arm and swore.

The midwife waited until that contraction was nicely out of the way, and then informed her, 'Well, young lady, you are 7cms dilated already.'

'Crikey! I thought labour went on for hours!' Anxiety swept through her. Was she ready to be a mum yet? She had all the baby equipment and clothes ready, but she was not sure if she was mentally prepared, such was the suddenness of the onset of labour. Although she was thrilled to be pregnant, the last few months had been a roller coaster of emotions, and she hadn't really had time to think about the outcome of her pregnancy yet. She just hoped that Sam would make it back in time. She looked anxiously at the clock, and prayed that the traffic wouldn't hold him up too much.

Thankfully, he arrived at the hospital in time, and just two hours later, Sam and Kate were proudly gazing down at their little baby girl. She weighed just 5lbs 8oz, but was absolutely perfect.

'Baby Eliza, born on the night of the fire,' rhymed Sam. 'She is just perfect, Kate. Oh, I'm so proud of you.' He bent to kiss her, his eyes glistening with tears of joy. He sniffed loudly and said 'I wish my big sister could have seen this little one. She would have loved her so much.' Suddenly, the enormity of losing Vikki and gaining Eliza was overwhelming, and he fell on his knees and wept.

'Hey, Sam, I know how hard this is for you, darling.' She stroked his head gently. 'But I reckon Vikki knows this little one already. I think she was sent down to comfort us all. She is going to be a total joy, our gift from heaven. You'll see.'

She looked down at the baby contentedly suckling at her breast, and then across at Sam. Despite all the sadness of the past year, she was overcome with a deep happiness.

Once Sam had gone home to inform everyone of Eliza's safe arrival, Kate got on the phone to tell her mother and father. They promised to come straight down to visit her that afternoon.

'Hey baby, its Valentine's day today, and you are the best present I've ever had.' She bent down and kissed her velvety head, then leant back and closed her eyes. 'Thank you, Vikki,' she whispered. 'She's perfect.'

Josh stood at the door of the junior school saying goodbye to the congregation. Life had settled down since the fire. The local school had kindly offered the church use of the school buildings whenever they wanted, as long as the school wasn't using them. This meant that the youth club could carry on in the evenings, including the after-school clubs. It was also an ideal venue for the Sunday morning services. The beneficial effect of using the local school, was that more children and their parents attended Sunday services.

Sam was working with the PCC and Josh to design a new church, fit for the twenty-first century. Out of the ashes came a chance to erect a building fit for purpose, and that would allow for a growing congregation. Every brick had to be removed, as not a wall remained fit to build upon, such was the ferocity of the fire. Once the village had got over the shock, the fund-raising began in earnest, and there was not a single person in the village who did not help or contribute in some way; such was the love and esteem that St. John's was held in.

The churches in the neighbouring villages offered to dovetail their weddings and baptisms in with the needs of St John's, so that every couple, and every set of parents were able to celebrate their joyous occasion inside a sacred building. For Kate, this had the added advantage of not having to write out her own Banns of Marriage and wedding certificates.

Sophie was admitted back to the mental health unit, after being found guilty of arson, but with a charge of diminished responsibility, due to her mental illness. Daniel was working closely with the psychiatrists and nurses on the ward to help her come to terms with her loss, and understand why she had acted in such a violent way. The church had no problem in forgiving her, as they realised that the deed was borne out of such terrible grief. Indeed, they made sure that Sophie was never without a visitor, and they had drawn up a rota for that very purpose. With medication, counselling and the love of Robbie and the fellowship, she was making great progress.

Robbie was also being supported by the men, who invited him for drinks at the Yew Tree Inn, and generally offered their friendship. He had even crept in at the back of the school during the odd service. He found it easier to attend church now that it was not in an official church building.

Josh and the children were gradually building their lives back together, and learning to live without Vikki. They loved the fact that their favourite uncle was now living in the village, with their favourite auntie. Daisy and Finn were even able to walk round to the cottage on their own in the summer months.

Kate and Sam were married on 2nd June, in the glorious sunshine of an early summer, and Amy and Daisy looked beautiful in their lilac bridesmaids' dresses. Finn looked dapper in a matching shirt and bow tie, a mini version of Sam's outfit.

The service was taken by Josh, who smiled and cried his way through the whole service! Kate informed him afterwards that it was supposed to be the bride who cried on her wedding day, not the vicar!

The wedding was attended by her parents, and Melanie was her Maid of Honour. Eliza was cared for during the service by Gillian. Kate's mum and dad were now happily worshipping at their local Baptist church. It was wonderful to finally have no barriers between them. Even Melanie had started going along to the church with them, which had amazed and delighted Kate.

The village of Ashton Kirby had been through so many changes, suffered so many tragedies, and yet the community had survived.